The End Of A Long Summer

The End Of A Long Summer

Rose Boucheron

PIATKUS

First published in Great Britain in 1994 by
Judy Piatkus (Publishers) Ltd of
5 Windmill Street, London W1

*A catalogue record for this book is available
from the British Library*

ISBN 0-7499-0225-6

Set in 11/12 pt Times by
Datix International Ltd, Bungay, Suffolk
Printed and bound in Great Britain by
Butler & Tanner Ltd, Frome and London

Chapter Two

On this lovely May morning all the blossom trees were flowering in Ainswick, one of the prettiest villages in the Cotswolds. Hanging baskets, tubs and containers had already been filled with summer plants and the proud owners hoped all danger of frost was past, for you could never be sure. Still, it had been an unusually mild spring, and it was worth taking a chance.

Peggy Mansfield stood in the hallway and adjusted her felt hat securely, brushed down her suit with the clothes brush, and secured the scarf to her shoulder with a pin.

She picked up a pile of books and several letters to post, a roll of yellow notices to be placed in shop windows and an envelope full of broadsheets to be taken to the Scout Hut and distributed among the boys that evening, the boys being the members of the Youth Club.

She was known throughout the village, not only for her good works, for being an active member of the council, a member of the school board of governors, chairman of the dramatic society, the horticultural club, the magistrates' bench, the boys' club, but also for her trim and neat appearance.

"Oh, she's a one off, is Peggy Mansfield," the villagers said, which was true. Almost sixty now, she had lived in Ainswick all her life; had been, in fact the vicar's daughter until she married young Dennis Mansfield. Nowadays, Dennis had his own solicitor's practice in the village at the end of the High Street, for it was called High Street although it was small and straggled around a corner.

It had the usual assortment of shops, a newsagent, an ironmonger's, and a greengrocer whose customers, having stayed with him out of loyalty, wondered how long he could keep going now that the Patels had started to sell greengrocery from their refurbished village store. Nowadays they stocked everything: American products, French cheeses, Italian bread, and carried a great freezer cabinet of pre-cooked meals. It bore no resemblance at all to old Mrs Butler's shop in days gone by, and now they were trying for a liquor licence.

The village had a small haberdasher's, a chemist, and a coal merchant who sold brass bits and pieces, several rather pricey antique shops, and a small dress shop which usually had just one outfit in the window and perhaps a pearl necklace placed carelessly alongside, with matching stockings or tights, and plenty of shops for tourists who kept all manner of pretty and useless things.

Peggy walked briskly and purposefully, for that was the way she did everything. "Good morning – good morning," all the way along the High Street where she posted the letters and strode on until she came to the wine shop.

"Good morning, Mr Phelps. Will you put two of these up? One in each window. It's for the Spring Flower Show."

"Certainly, Mrs Mansfield – with pleasure."

She never asked if they would, she knew they would. No one ever queried her requests. At the Scout Hut she unlocked the door and pinned up some notices on the green baize board, then put the envelope of news sheets on the rickety table, locked the door after her, and went on her way.

And then an unusual sight met her eyes: a bright yellow bulldozer rollicking and dancing along the High Street, like something escaped from a fairground. She began to smile. Fairly obvious where *he* was going – along to Little Field. Oh, well done, she said to herself for if it had not been for her efforts, Little Field might even now still be in the throes of planning enquiries and arguments among the council. But through sheer willpower and determination she had finally got the other council members to agree to a development of homes for the elderly.

As the yellow bulldozer drew alongside she felt like waving, but stood for a moment as he passed, seeing the young man in the driver's seat, looking like a gladiator. Well, she thought, they didn't waste much time. And yah boo to Louise Framlingham and others like her who argued that the village did not want such a development. In other words, let the old people go and jump in the lake.

Well, she'd seen to that, and could not help feeling that old Tom Bird would be pleased. When he had died two years ago, he had left the house and field to the people of Ainswick, to be used to their advantage for perpetuity, and had added a rider to the effect that he hoped it would be put to good use.

And the arguments that followed! Well, it was over now, and she walked on with the feeling of a job well done.

This morning she was going to call on Beth Pennington with a list of plays she had received from French's, suggestions for the forthcoming production of the Ainswick Players one act festival play. Beth, although a newcomer of only three years' standing, had taken on the task of secretary to the amateur dramatic society and was very keen. Peggy liked that. Keenness and enthusiasm were the two things she admired most.

As she neared the church and cut through the narrow path to Beth's house, old Granny Dorrington edged her lace curtain slightly aside to see the better who it was.

Ah, Peggy Durrant – for that's how Granny Dorrington remembered her. The vicar's daughter, small and plump and rosy as a ripe peach. From the time she had left college she had thrown herself into the life of Ainswick, a real little do-gooder. A born organizer. That's what came of being a vicar's daughter. When she had married handsome young Dennis Mansfield no one could believe it. The best-looking boy in the village, all the girls were after him, and he had chosen young Peggy. And she wasn't even pretty! A little nut brown face, like a russet apple, Granny Dorrington thought. Then they had a son – and she sniffed. He was no better than he should be, considering his parents and every advantage under the sun. Divorced not once but twice, according to her daughter Shirley who worked for Peggy Mansfield, so got all the news from her.

She let the curtain fall. Divorce, divorce, it was all you heard today. What had come over everyone that they couldn't stay married? She and Albert had been married for fifty-four years until he had died three years ago. Even her own granddaughter, Kylie, was living with a chap out Cirencester way, without the blessing of marriage lines or the church.

'Course, they said they was going to build places for old folk on Little Field, but she'd believe that when she see it. She bent down and poked the fire in its black iron grate. It might look nice outside, but she'd bet there was a cold wind blowing. She settled herself down in her chair to watch the television game, shook her head in wonderment. Some of the prizes! They was out of all proportion to what was asked – silly questions, things to which even she knew the answer, and she'd only been to the village school. She clicked her tongue in disbelief.

Across the small lawn Peggy strode, and pushed open the white gate to St Luke's Vicarage, a large Victorian house which she herself had lived in until her marriage. Now, it had had a facelift, painted inside and out, the garden restored to its former glory, for the girl, Beth – or so Peggy saw her from her advanced age – was mad on gardening and spent every moment of her time at it, and she couldn't have had much of that as a vicar's wife with two small children. Peggy saw that the lawns were closely cut, and the orchard had had the trees pruned, and now there were tulips and irises and wallflowers where in the summer there would be geraniums and fuchsias. The scent, even now, was quite strong.

Beth opened the door, a wide smile on her face when she saw her visitor.

"Peggy, how nice. Come in – I'm just making coffee."

"Very welcome," Peggy said, planting her feet firmly on the polished wooden floor which was covered with pretty rugs. "I've brought some plays from French's – I thought we might look them over."

"Sit down," Beth said. "It's almost ready."

Peggy looked around the kitchen which hadn't changed that much since her day, although now there was a new wooden floor and an Aga where there had once been a kitchen range. The huge cupboards were still there, and a vast pine table sat in the centre of the room. She opened her package of plays. "These are for the festival, one acts – I thought if you'd time you might look through these before the next meeting?"

"Surely," Beth said. Sometimes she still couldn't believe that she was here in the house of her dreams with two children and an adoring husband, living just where she wanted to be. After London, it was sheer heaven, and she didn't miss city life at all. Well, perhaps she missed her best friend, Camilla. And now she was secretary of the local dramatic society – although Marcus wasn't too pleased about that. Taking on too much, he said, what with her duties as a vicar's wife.

"Here we are." Beth placed two mugs on the table in front of them.

Peggy stirred her coffee then extracted another yellow poster. "On the gate?" she suggested. "Can you do with another – perhaps on the tree?"

"Of course," Beth said, anxious to oblige, and opened it out to read.

Peggy eyed her. She had always admired beauty in others and appraised the deep blue eyes and fair hair of this young mother, looking like a young girl to her eyes, her figure still trim, the ankle-length flowery skirt, her loose cotton blouse. Peggy was a good judge and saw Beth with a part in the one act festival of plays at the end of June, but of course it would have to go before the committee. She knew which play she would like to do, and if she had her way that was the one they would stage. Ambitious it might be, but they were a good little crowd, and who better than Arthur Lang as producer? He always got the best out of people.

"How is Dennis?" Beth asked politely, holding out a biscuit tin.

Peggy had a sudden recollection of cucumber teas on the lawn in the old days. The idea of sitting in the kitchen drinking coffee and eating biscuits was simply unknown then. For one thing the daily maid would have been there, and the cook. They'd have thought she'd gone mad.

"He's fine – as far as I know," she added. "We're always busy with something or other."

They were a strange couple, Beth thought, eating her biscuit. Handsome Dennis – even at his age – and this brisk little woman. Beth had never met anyone like her before.

"I think we may have a new member," Peggy said, nibbling her biscuit with very small bites.

"That's good."

"I had a call yesterday from a Mrs Hetherington – she lives in Milney Hatch."

Beth knew the village, two miles from Ainswick.

"She has just come to live there, and wants to join a dramatic society and there is none in Milney. She sounds quite young."

Peggy smiled. "To me, my dear," she added. "Someone of your own age, I expect. She's coming to audition tomorrow – so you may see her at the next meeting. Apparently, she had had quite a lot of experience one way and another."

"Oh," Beth said. "You mean – professionally?"

Peggy nodded. "Well, from what I can make out."

Finishing her coffee, she stood up and brushed the crumbs from her skirt. "Well, I must fly – I've a lot to do. Thanks for the coffee. Will you be there on Monday?"

"Wouldn't miss it for the world," Beth laughed.

"See what you think of those – we can't please everybody," Peggy said. "Don't come to the door. I'll see myself out." And she was gone before Beth had a chance to follow her.

Two or three more calls, and Peggy had finished distributing her posters. The flower show was in two weeks' time, and she must make sure they were all doing their bit to get the hall ready. You had to keep rallying everyone around or else they tended to slack.

Seeing a boy standing alone outside the grocer's shop, she halted and looked down at him. He was no more than six years old, and looked lost.

"Hello," she said, her clear sharp voice making him jump. He looked up at her, terrified. "Why aren't you at school?"

"I gotta cold," he said.

"Where is your mother?"

"In there," he nodded, looking anxiously inside for her to come and rescue him from this terrible old woman.

She took his hand and led him through the swing doors.

"Where is she?"

Speechless, he nodded. "Over there."

Peggy dragged him behind her until she came face to face with the woman.

"I should keep a tight hold on this little chap if I were you," she said. "You wouldn't want to lose him, would you?"

The woman recognized the "funny old woman" as they called her.

"'E keeps running orf," she said.

"Well, keep him on a chain," Peggy said sternly, her small eyes twinkling, and marched out of the shop.

As a magistrate, she knew too well what could happen these days to small children left alone. If it were up to her, she was quite sure what she would do about this new generation of violent children and teenagers. Discipline, that's what they needed, like they'd had in schools when she was young, and a short sharp spell in the army to follow. Nothing like it.

She could see a plump figure coming towards her, pushing a trolley, and recognized the American, Marty Forsdyke, married to the old Etonian Colonel Alistair Forsdyke, late of the Coldstream Guards. They were both members of the dramatic society, although Marty just came along to sit in and make the tea, while Alistair was in great demand with his wonderful voice and military bearing.

"Hi, there!"

"Hello, Marty, my dear," Peggy said. "Just the person I want to see."

"You too," Marty said. "We're having a breakfast party on Sunday – will you come? Around nine?"

Peggy smiled at her. "Is this something new?"

"Oh, we do it all the time back home. Please come, and Dennis too. Don't bring anything, I'll cater for all tastes . . ."

Peggy could believe it. Marty was an excellent cook and loved to play hostess. The social life of Ainswick had improved enormously since they had arrived.

"Thank you, dear," she said. "Now I wonder if you'll remind Alistair that there is a committee meeting of the dramatic society tomorrow evening? I'd like him to be there, as we are to discuss the festival play, and we shall be auditioning a new member."

"Oh!" Marty's eyes sparkled. "Anyone we know?"
"She's a Mrs Hetherington – from Milney Hatch."
"Oh, not a local?"
"No, but never mind. She sounded very keen and that's what we want. Well, my dear, I mustn't hold you up," for she knew Marty would have talked all day.
"See you on Sunday," Marty called after her. What a wonderful woman Peggy was, the sort of person Marty most admired.
Peggy walked on through the village, past the mellow stone houses, some of them sixteenth-century, some even earlier. Past The Stag and The Lamb, both old coaching inns, then to the True Lover's Knot, all of them popular with tourists from all over the world. Once upon a time the residents could call the village their own in winter, but nowadays sightseers came all the year round. Now, they were getting off coaches and car drivers were trying to park to no avail, passengers standing in little clusters, their pleasure at being in this pretty little village evident. They were mostly middle-aged and retired people, all out for the day.
Standing out from the usual tourists were two figures coming towards her that she recognized and wished she could have avoided, but there was nothing to be done now: Edith and Lydia Pargeter, the General's daughters.
"Good morning, ladies," she said brightly. "A lovely spring day."
"Good morning, Peggy," they chorused, Edith's eyes apprehensive, Lydia's cold and accusing. "We called on you, but you were out."
"Oh, I'm sorry." Peggy was kindness itself.
"About Little Field. We cannot believe our own eyes – there are demolition men at work."
"Yes, indeed. Did you not know? Did no one notify you?" Peggy looked most concerned.
"No. We saw this huge – thing – making for the house –"
"Bulldozer," Lydia interposed.
"Well, I know we sent you the result of the council's decision . . ." Peggy said.
Through both their minds was going the thought that their

father always tore up letters addressed to him that in his opinion did not concern him.

"Well," Lydia said, "it's a bit late now – but we certainly heard nothing."

"Father was dreadfully upset," Edith confided.

"Yes, well, your father is a very old man, and old people don't like change." Peggy smiled gently. "But, believe me, it will all be for the best. Instead of an empty house that might attract vandals, that sort of thing – and we don't want that, do we? – there will be a nice quiet development for elderly people, and I am sure as good citizens you will be pleased that Tom Bird's wishes are being respected." She didn't add that there was not much chance of their seeing the development behind all those trees.

They both realized at the same time that there was nothing they could do now. What was more important, there was nothing their father could do – and that took a bit of swallowing.

"Well, we thought we'd have a word," Lydia said loftily.

"Of course, and I am glad you did," Peggy said. "Well, I must fly. I hope to see you soon – at the Horty evening?"

"Yes, of course."

"Regards to your father."

That was not too bad, she decided, somewhat relieved.

In front of her a young man tossed away a cigarette packet, and she hurried after him and picked it up.

He turned as she spoke and handed it to him. "You dropped this," she said.

He looked down at the empty pack. "I don' wannit," he said.

"Neither does Ainswick," Peggy replied, and walked on, reminding herself that at the next council meeting she would insist on more waste paper bins.

Arriving home, she pushed open the gate and went in.

Hunter's Lodge, where she lived, was tucked away off the High Street in a narrow lane, while it's gardens were surrounded by farmlands whose wide white gates formed a barrier across the top of the lane.

Inside, it was almost exactly as it had been when they took it over almost forty years before. With most of the contents coming from the vicarage, and some nice old pieces from Dennis's family, it never changed, for Peggy had no time for fiddle-faddle, and would have deemed fussing over a house frivolous when there was so much needed outside the home.

Her daily help, Mrs Dinsdale, was used to it, for apart from tidying and dusting there was nothing much to do. Cooking was kept to a minimum, and since the son had married two spare bedrooms were empty, which left just his and hers – although it was a funny thing that ever since she had worked for them they had had separate rooms.

Sometimes she wished she could go to work in one of the old houses which had been "done over", bought by townies and having had a fortune spent on them. Kitchens like a dream, her neighbours said, fitted carpets, and bathrooms such as you couldn't imagine. Still, she had worked for the Mansfields too long to move on now. Besides, in her own way, she was fond of Peggy Mansfield.

Once indoors, Peggy removed her scarf and looked under the saucepan lids to see what vegetables Mrs Dinsdale had prepared. In the fridge was a pie, made by her, with a note on the side that it was to be cooked for forty minutes at gas mark 5. Peggy almost rubbed her hands. She loved Mrs Dinsdale's home made pies, and she liked to eat. She had never been much of a cook herself and certainly didn't intend to start now. Fortunately Dennis went to The Lamb for his lunch.

She cut herself some bread and cheese and propped up a copy of J. M. Barrie's *Twelve Pound Look*, the play she had chosen for the festival of one act plays. Dated, the others said, but she wouldn't listen to that. She usually got her own way.

As she read it through it came to life before her. An excellent choice. She saw Beth as Lady Sims, and of course Geoffrey Lattimer as Sir Harry – highly suitable, he was as pompous and cocksure in real life as Sir Harry in the play, but there was no part in it for Monica Latimer unfortunately. Poor Monica was so restricted with her type of looks. Tall, gangly, a nice voice if a bit plummy, but no stage presence at all. The only success she had ever had was the Joyce Grenfell part of Miss Gossage in *The Happiest Days of Your Life*.

The tricky bit was the best part of Kate – and she would have to give a lot of thought to that. Peggy closed the book, and cleared away the dishes before setting out for the hospital.

It was half-past five before she reached home, just as Dennis was closing his office for the day.

Philip Sanderson, his junior partner, waited at his desk for the post to be signed, as he did every day at this time, deep in his own thoughts. The old man was sixty-five now, even though he didn't look it, a tall, good-looking man with a luxuriant head of hair that many a younger man might envy. You'd think he'd give some thought of retiring – after all, what did he want to keep working for? – and Philip wondered what the chances were of his acquiring the whole practice someday? It wasn't as if the old man's son could take over. He was in a different line of business anyway.

When Dennis came in, Philip looked up and smiled.

"I'd like you to come with me to Brampton Hall tomorrow morning – things might be a little difficult."

"Of course," said Philip.

Later that evening Dennis and Peggy sat on either side of the brick fireplace, Peggy wearing a cream blouse with a bow at the neck, and Dennis, having bathed and changed, wearing his carpet slippers and an old tweed jacket.

"Did Malcolm phone? I thought he was coming down this weekend."

"Was he?" She looked across at him, and saw the frown. "What's wrong?"

She could see by his expression that something was troubling him.

"Nothing much. Just that I have to go and see Ariadne Gilbert tomorrow and give her the bad news."

"Oh." Her mouth set in a straight line.

"Yes, I know how you feel – I feel the same myself, but it has to be done, and I don't relish the telling of it."

"It won't be the first time you've had that to do."

"No. But with someone like Ariadne, spoiled as she is, I'm expecting hysterics."

"Have a bucket of water handy."

He smiled in spite of himself. "Peggy! It was a bit of a shock, Alec going like that."

"Well, people like her bring out the worst in me."

"It's the daughter I feel sorry for."

"Lucy? Yes, she's a nice little thing – I can't think how she is with a mother like Ariadne."

"I expect she takes after the father."

"She'll have taken his death badly," Peggy observed. "After all, he was only forty-eight, wasn't he?"

"Mmm. It's a nasty business."

"What will she do? Will she have to sell up?"

"Can't see anything else for it. I will be glad when it's over with, I can tell you."

"Poor you," Peggy said.

"And how did your day go?"

She looked across at him, then eased herself out of the chair as the timer went.

"So so," she said. "Much as usual. That pie should be ready. Let's eat."

Chapter Three

Lucy Gilbert went straight upstairs to change after the funeral of her father.

"Mother, do I really have to wear that ghastly hat?" she had wailed.

Her mother had insisted that she wore the long black skirt and jacket and the ridiculous stylish black hat, which she knew her father would have hated. With her black shoes and stockings she looked like a crow, she thought rebelliously. Now dry-eyed, for she had been unable to shed a tear, she changed into a pair of blue jeans and a shirt, tying her thick brown hair back from her face, and peering at herself closely in the mirror.

It had been her father she adored from the very first. A gentle, kindly man, he had loved her dearly. Spent all his spare time with her, taught her about nature and wild things, read to her from her favourite books, and always listened when she was troubled. She would never have dreamed of going to her mother with a problem. Ariadne just wasn't that sort of person. And now, coping with the shock of his early death, the future seemed unknown and terrifying to Lucy. The only good thing to emerge from it all was that she was no longer a child. At nineteen she had her own life to lead, but still she had a duty to see that her mother was all right. Her father would have wished that. And now Mr Mansfield, her father's solicitor, was coming later this morning to tell them about the will.

Lucy sighed. It was common knowledge that her father had gone bankrupt – ugly word. The family business inherited from his father, going on forever as they had thought, was finished, and everyone, they said, was in the same boat. Well, that didn't make it any easier.

Putting a cardigan round her shoulders, she went down the back stairs, avoiding the kitchen and the front of the house where she could see all the parked cars. Soon they would be leaving, surely, and she had done her bit, shaking hands and receiving condolences while her mother stood at her side, a lacy handerchief held delicately to her nose, looking strikingly beautiful as she always did, even in the midst of grief.

Lucy was a small girl, not in the least like her tall and elegant mother. Petite and dark-haired, with greeny-grey eyes, and a sprinkling of freckles over the creamy skin of her short straight nose.

Now she went round to the stables to see her mare, Daisy, who nuzzled up at the sight of her. Lucy laid her face against the mare's golden head, saw the great dark eyes look into hers as if she really knew what was going on. Lucy swallowed hard and went on to find Henry, her Golden Labrador. She would walk round the lake and get some fresh air. It was one of her favourite walks.

"Come on, boy!" she called, and Henry followed slowly in a laboured fashion rather than a run, not surprisingly since he was almost nine years old.

By the side of the lake, beneath the great willow tree, she sat with Henry beside her, looking back at the house. She had been born there, had never known any other home unless you could call the flat in London a home. Her mother loved the city, but Lucy was a country girl, born and bred.

She loved everything about country life: horses, the land, the wonderful trees that grew on the estate. She wondered, not for the first time since her father's death, what would happen now. He had loved it too, had inherited it when his father died. Her great-grandfather had been part of the industrial revolution and had established engineering factories in Birmingham. No wonder her father had had a sense of failure, and although the coroner had brought in a verdict of accidental death by drowning, would they ever know the truth about that night? It seemed that, taking his evening stroll, he had stumbled across a fallen tree and into the river, experiencing a slight heart attack from immersion in the cold water, and drowning before anyone could reach him.

Earlier that day he had come home at the usual time and after dinner, as they sat in the drawing room having coffee, had dropped his bombshell. He was bankrupt. At first they couldn't take it in, especially her mother who had given a little cry and fallen back against the cushions, but at the sight of her father's ashen face, Lucy had felt a sense of despair for the first time in her life. This sort of thing happened to other people, not to them. Not to a firm like Gilbert's, who had been established in 1884. It was the recession, her father had said. Even the largest firms had been affected and they were no different from anyone else.

"But what will it mean?" her mother had asked. She looked horrified.

"That all this must go – The Hall, everything, to pay my debts."

"What debts?"

"Oh, Ariadne!" he said sadly, and at that point Lucy decided to leave them alone together.

Now, at the thought of what he must have experienced in those last dreadful moments, the tears came and fell unheeded. Henry put out a paw and looked at her with his great soulful eyes, which made her feel worse than ever, and she cried as if her heart would break. Her slight body was racked by sobs until she felt she could weep no more. She was left with a great sense of relief that her emotions were no longer bottled up, and although exhaused, felt better and ready to face whatever lay in store.

Henry waited, watching her, until she put an arm round his neck and hugged him.

"Come on, boy," she sniffed. "Let's get it over with."

The last of the guests were leaving and Lucy joined her mother in saying farewell, seeing her look of disapproval at what she was wearing. She supposed she was a disappointment as a daughter but there was nothing she could do about it now.

She stood at the top of the steps watching her mother stand outside, looking exactly what she was: a beautiful, wealthy widow. But was she – now? Presently they would know what the immediate future held for them, and Lucy had an idea that she was going to need all her strength to support her mother, for if there was no money forthcoming, how would they live?

In the large flagstoned hall, with its Persian and Oriental rugs, lovely bowls of flowers everywhere, a few people were gathered. Among them she recognized Mr Mansfield, her father's solicitor, who was with a young man she didn't know, and her Grandmother Aston, her maternal grandmother, who was every bit as lovely as her daughter even at sixty. There were two aunts, sisters of her father, both dark and small and petite, her mother's younger brother and his new wife, all looking unfamiliar in their black mourning clothes.

Dennis Mansfield came forward and held out his hand.

"Lucy, my dear." He took her hand in his. "This is a sad day."

She felt like crying again – he was such a nice, kind man.

She nodded and he drew back to meet the young man. "This is my junior partner – Philip Sanderson – Lucy Gilbert."

Lucy felt her hand gripped firmly, and looked up to see two dark eyes surveying her seriously. She couldn't have explained why, but a tremor went through her as their eyes met.

"How do you do?"

Their words were lost as Ariadne Gilbert came through the open doorway and everyone turned to her, seeing a lone figure, tall and slim. There seemed nothing of her. In a long black flowing gown, a large black cartwheel of a hat almost hiding her face, she looked strangely beautiful, almost ethereal, and Lucy felt her heart contract.

"Mother . . ." she began.

"Lucy dear, would you go upstairs and change? We will see you in the library in ten minutes," Ariadne said coolly.

Biting her lip, Lucy hurried upstairs. She wished her mother wouldn't treat her like a child, especially in front of – well, in front of people.

Most of her relatives were in the library when she returned, while Mr Mansfield sat at her father's desk, beside him Philip Sanderson. He glanced up as she entered, having changed into a white blouse and dark suit. She took her place beside her mother who raised tear-drenched eyes in her direction.

Dennis Mansfield looked at them.

"By now, of course, you know the contents of the will, and apart from bequests made to various charities and relatives the bulk of the estate is held in trust for you, Mrs Gilbert, and your daughter, Lucy. None of this means very much, however, for there is no money – and, harsh though it sounds, we have to deal with facts. Which means that there are only debts."

A tiny sound escaped from Ariadne's lips while inside Lucy rose a spiral of anger that her father's business, his life, should be laid so bare in front of everyone. She glanced up at Philip Sanderson who sat with an impassive face, looking in front of him.

"There is no need to detain any of you except Mrs Mansfield and Lucy. I'm afraid there are many things to discuss, things which must be made clear."

Her grandmother and aunts and uncle left the room, after a cursory word to her mother, and then they were alone, the two of them, having to face up to the worst.

"This is a very sad day in every sense," Dennis said, looking at them both. "I'm afraid that you are in for a tough time, Ariadne. Alec did his best but – well, like many other men today . . ."

Her mother would never forgive him, Lucy thought. She didn't really care about Daddy, only in as much as it affected herself. Poor Daddy.

"No need to beat around the bush," Dennis said gently but firmly. "Brampton Hall will have to go and the life-style that you have enjoyed up to now, Ariadne – thanks to Alec – will come to an end, I'm afraid. Everything that you own personally will be safe – that is, things that belong to you, and of course to Lucy, personal things – other than that, the Receivers will need to come in and take an inventory of everything that must be sold. The house, for instance." He didn't say that he had advised Alec some time ago to put the house in their joint names, but he had either forgotten or hadn't bothered to do so. Like most people, Dennis realized, thinking they had plenty of time to get around to it.

Ariadne was sobbing gently into her handkerchief, and Dennis cleared his throat.

Since her mother said nothing, Lucy took a deep breath.

"So what happens now?" she asked.

"We have been going through your father's papers and also the accounts, and to put it bluntly there are many creditors."

"Yes, I understand that, but what do we have to do?"

"The Receivers will take over, and from then on everything will be in their hands. I am sorry to put it so bluntly but that's how it is in the case of bankruptcy. I believe you own the lease of the flat in town in your own right, Ariadne?"

She nodded.

"It might be a good idea if you both went up there to live. The house will have to go on to the market, and everything will be sold to defray the debts."

"Not everything, surely!" Ariadne cried in horror. "The cars, the land – the house in France?"

"I'm afraid so, Ariadne."

"It's monstrous – wicked!" And Ariadne wept.

Lucy found it hard to take in. She couldn't imagine any life-style other than the one she had always had. As for her mother – what would she do?

"Do you understand what bankruptcy means?" Dennis asked Lucy.

With the young man's eyes upon her, Lucy flushed.

"Of course I do!" she said hotly.

"Well, then, you will understand what all this is about, lamentable though it is. I hope you will not blame your father too much. He was a good man, and I expect it broke his heart that he couldn't keep up the life-style to which you were accustomed." He gathered his papers together. "After all, Ariadne, there are thousands in the same boat. Your husband's employees, for instance. The factories will have to close down, men will lose their jobs . . ."

Ariadne flashed blue eyes at him. "I don't need a lecture, Dennis. I understand the situation perfectly well. I'm not a fool."

"I'm sorry. I –"

"How can I help?" Lucy stood up and went over to the desk.

Dennis took off his glasses and polished them. Like her father, he thought, a chip off the old block.

"Well, my dear," he said, "you could make a start by going through all your father's personal papers and trying to sort them out. The Receivers have made a date for Wednesday next – they will take the inventory then and I suggest Philip should be here to give you a hand."

Lucy heard her mother's intake of breath and knew she was about to argue the necessity of such a thing, but she quickly decided to take advantage of the situation. They were going to need some help, her mother would be quite useless if Lucy knew anything about her, and she would be glad of young company about the place.

"Thank you, Mr Mansfield. Yes, that will suit us very well."

After they had gone, Ariadne blazed at her.

"What on earth do you think you were doing? Allowing that young man to come here and put his nose into everything! What do you hope to achieve? You know no more about such matters than I do."

"Then it's time I learned," Lucy said, and stormed out.

She flung herself on her bed, feeling guilty, and lost – and alone. She couldn't believe even now that her father had gone – left them forever. How much they had depended on him. How her mother would miss him, though they had never really got on. Whose fault it was Lucy didn't know, but they were poles apart in temperament. Now she realized that her mother must be feeling almost desperate at the thought of losing everything she had ever had and, remorse overtaking her, she hurried along to her room.

Ariadne sat at the dressing table in the window, staring into space. Lucy bit her lip and went swiftly over to her.

"Mother, I'm sorry if I . . ."

"Oh, what do you know about anything! How can you possibly understand what all this is about? You've always had everything you ever wanted: education, money, a lifestyle to be envied."

"But I do know that it will have to change."

"But what about me? What sort of provision did your father make for me, tell me that? Everyone will know. I'll have to leave here – my home."

And now she wept, and Lucy put an arm round her shoulders. "At least you can go to the flat."

Ariadne sniffed. "And where do you think you're going? You can't stay here. You'll have to get a job."

"I don't mind that."

"And what can you do, pray?"

"Lots of things, I daresay," Lucy said belligerently.

"Oh, what a mess!" Ariadne wailed. "I shall never be able to hold my head up again."

"Nothing's that bad," Lucy said, with an attempt at a smile.

"It's all right for you, you're young."

"Mother, so are you. Barely forty." She didn't add. "And you'll probably get married again." There were surely lots of men who would be delighted to marry the beautiful and glamorous Mrs Ariadne Gilbert?

She looked around the bedroom with its canopied bed and expensive silk drapes, at the hundreds of yards there must be in the curtains which dropped and lay in folds on the floor. The carpet was Aubusson, she knew, her mother had been so excited when it arrived, while the elegant French furniture had been bought in Paris on one of her mother's shopping sprees. The dressing table held crystal and cut glass bottles of French perfumes, and silver-backed brushes polished by the two maids who kept everything in pristine order under the guidance of Mrs Clayton the housekeeper. Now they too would lose their jobs.

The next few days saw a flurry of excitement as Ariadne began moving most of her things to town. Suitcase after suitcase was packed with small belongings: first all her jewellery, then her silver dressing table set, silver from the dining room, small pictures, and objets d'art.

Lucy spent some time going through her father's desk and was horrified at what she found. Bills, bills and more bills. Water rates, electricity accounts, gas bills, cleaning bills, final demands, and horrendous bills from exclusive stores where her mother had accounts, to say nothing of an enormous bill for designer clothes from the small shop in Ainswick.

Lucy's face flamed. All this money owing! It must add up to thousands and thousands of pounds. How long had it been going on? How could they have allowed her father so much credit?

By Sunday evening Brampton was looking quite bare, shorn of the small treasures that made a house a home.

"There!" Ariadne said triumphantly. "I think that's scotched their little game."

"Were all those things yours, Mother? I mean, would they ask you to prove it?"

"I couldn't care less," Ariadne said. "Just let them try to get them back – and we'll see! If you think that all those things rightfully belong to the Receivers then you're no daughter of mine!"

"I didn't mean that. I was just wondering if they had any way of knowing – how you could prove that they belonged to you?"

"Just let them try to get them back," Ariadne said, her lovely eyes glinting. "Over my dead body!"

The Receivers arrived early, two nice, harmless-looking men with businesslike papers who greeted the two women politely.

"We'll try not to get in your way," they promised.

Swift on their heels came Philip Sanderson, and away from Dennis Mansfield, he seemed very much in charge.

"Let's go to the library, shall we?" he asked. "Did you make any headway with your father's papers?"

"I sorted them as best as I could," Lucy said, very much on her mettle, knowing what he would find.

"Good, let's have a look through them."

"Would you like coffee?" she asked.

"That would be nice. No sugar."

Lucy went down to the kitchen, seething. Pompous young man, who did he think he was?

Mrs Clayton had already got the coffee under way. She was due to leave the following weekend after being with the Gilberts for ten years.

Lucy sat down heavily on the stool. "I'm really sorry

you're going, Mrs C," she said. Her world seemed to have toppled around her.

"So am I, my dear. Still, it's an ill wind. My sister Alice has wanted me to go down to Wales with her for a long time, and now, well, I've had my mind made up for me. But what will you do?"

Lucy was such a nice girl, she thought. Nothing like that selfish bitch of a mother. Still, she was young. She would get married and have a home of her own one day. She had her future in front of her. As for this lovely house, it was difficult to imagine anyone else in it. The Gilberts had lived in it for such a long time.

Lucy took the tray of coffee into the library and, putting it on the desk, sat herself opposite in a huge leather armchair and watched Philip coolly until, slightly disconcerted, he looked up. "Oh, thanks."

"How is it going?" she asked politely.

"Well . . ." He poured milk into his coffee. "Your father was very methodical – it makes my task so much easier."

"He was a very methodical man," Lucy said quietly. "Which makes it all the more sad that we are in this position now." She couldn't bear for this pompous young man to know so much about their private lives.

"Yes," he agreed. "Still, one has to say that up to now you have probably always had everything you wanted – lots of people never get that."

So that's it, Lucy thought. He has a chip on his shoulder.

She took a deep breath and smiled sweetly. "Yes, that's true," she said. "So I must be brave. A stiff upper lip, and all that."

He seemed puzzled.

"What will you do?" he asked curiously, and when she didn't answer, looked slightly embarrassed. "I mean, you presumably have had no training for anything?"

Lucy sighed. "No. I'm hopelessly spoiled, I'm afraid. I've never had to do anything." And realized that it was true. She really had never had to do anything – nothing that mattered. Except school, and tennis, and horse riding.

He finished his coffee. "Shall we go upstairs and see how they're getting on? I expect they could do with some assistance."

"Of course," Lucy said, following him.

He obviously wished to look around for he walked into the dining room with its long refectory table and twelve Jacobean dining chairs, saw the paintings that lined the oak-panelled walls, but said nothing. Lucy followed him, hands behind her back, trying to see it through his eyes. Into the drawing room, then through to the conservatory which was ablaze with colour. The sun was shining and it looked luxurious. Glancing at him she was an unfathomable expression in his eyes. He has probably never seen anything like this before, she thought, and it was followed by a deep sense of guilt which she could not shake off. Swiftly he turned and walked up the wide oak staircase with its beautiful balustrade and Lucy followed him. At the top of the stairs, he looked down into the grand hall below, at the rugs and paintings, the antique furniture, the mirrors, and she saw his nostrils dilate as he turned to look at her, his eyes almost hostile. She returned his look calmly.

"You don't need me, do you?" she asked coldly.

"No, thank you," he said. "If you're busy . . ."

"I'll be downstairs," Lucy said, and running into her bedroom, flung herself on the bed, and wept.

Half an hour later, and changed into her jeans and shirt, she made her way to the stables. If he wanted her he would have to find her, and there wasn't much likelihood of that.

"Come on, Daisy m'dear," she said in a Cotswold accent. "Let you'm me go for a ride, eh?"

Daisy was delighted.

Once up, Lucy rode slowly across the field then down into the lane and into the High Street, making a picture that many visitors eyed with envy. A slim young thing, her hair tied back under her riding hat, a lovely young face – one of the lucky ones. Not for her the problems of today, no job, wondering where the next penny was coming from. Just the freedom to ride where the will took her.

Slowly along the High Street, and left into The Avenue, where it seemed to her something seemed to be going on. The old house was down and everything flattened. There wasn't a tree in sight. On the dry earth a few bright machines were working, back and forth, back and forth. So, she thought, the development has started. I don't suppose Ainswick will ever be the same again.

She hadn't gone by unnoticed, however. The wolf whistles started almost at once.

"Cooee, my love!"

"Hallo there, darling!"

She smiled and rode on as the lane narrowed and she came to the sign: Ainswick Riding School.

She tethered Daisy and made her way to the office in the barn.

A fair young man with suntanned face and arms, sat at the desk his face lighting up at the sight of her.

"Lucy!"

"Hello, Jack."

"What are you doing here?"

"Have you got a job for me? I'll do anything: mucking out, teaching, stable girl, head cook and bottlewasher –"

He sat back and looked at her, blue eyes smiling.

"Well, I'm blowed," he said.

Chapter Four

To the purist, St Luke's Vicarage stood out like a sore thumb in Ainswick since it was an unmistakably Victorian house in what was otherwise a Georgian village of some distinction, although since it stood down a narrow side street next to the church, it was not immediately apparent to the eye.

Connoisseurs of Cotswold villages, however, ignored it, while tourists often missed it unless they were interested in the church. Most visitors came to see the High Street and the little inns, the antique shops and the purveyors of quaint items not seen at home.

Beth Pennington was not at all interested in what people thought of her house, she loved it passionately. It was the sort of house she had always wanted to live in with its turrets and long windows and Gothic porch, the huge dining-room bay window with the velvet-covered window seat. It had seven bedrooms, three on the top floor, and a bathroom on each floor, one at the end of the downstairs tiled hall having been put in for an elderly vicar. She loved it all. Since coming here three years ago with her family, she had tried to furnish it as far as possible with the kind of Victorian furniture found at auction sales, the sort held for people who wanted classic pieces but could not afford them.

Collecting Freddie, four, from his nursery school at midday, she bundled him into the back of the car and watched as he did up his safety belt, grinning at her, his red-gold hair a mass of tight curls, his baby teeth just very slightly prominent.

He picked up a piece of paper from the seat where he had put it, and gave it to Beth. "This is for you. Miss Reynolds said you could have it."

"Oh, thank you, darling," She was about to ask what it was, but refrained.

"It's a beetle," he said, forestalling her, and waited breathlessly for her reply.

The thing crouched in one corner of the thick maroon paper, in brilliant colours, and truth to tell, there were two small legs, or antlers – a little of Picasso there, Beth thought.

"Freddie, it is ab-so-lutely beautiful! I can't wait for Daddy to see it."

She switched on the engine, leaving him to beam to himself in the back of the car.

Once back home, he sat himself on the seat in the porch as he always did while she unlocked the door. It was one of his favourite bits of the day. He jumped down when the door opened.

The hall was cool with its black and white tiled floor and red rugs, the enormous mirror bought at auction for fifteen pounds reflecting every bit of light from every corner.

"Better go to the bathroom," Beth said automatically, going straight through to the kitchen with her shopping.

"I don't want to go," he said.

"Yes, you do," she said, and he walked down the step to the cloakroom, and presently she heard the seat go up, then the tap running, as he came out with his hands soaking wet. He never stayed long enough to wipe his hands.

"Now play with your toys while I get the lunch."

He stood with hands on hips surveying her as she busied herself at the sink.

"Do you like Russell?" he asked presently. Russell was his best friend.

"Yes, I do," Beth said. "He's a nice little . . ."

"Well, I don't," he said, and walked off.

Beth smiled as she lit the gas under the potatoes and carrots, putting on the grill for fish fingers which were his favourite.

When it was all underway, she unpacked the shopping, stacking the packets and tins in the vast cupboards which were all in the house when they bought it. "You are not to remove one – not one," she had ordered when they moved in. "I like them that way. You can't have too many."

She put on Classic FM softly, then turned down the potatoes and got the fish fingers out of the freezer. When Clarrie had been born eight years ago, Beth would never have given her frozen food. Sieved fresh vegetables and home made bone broth – those were the days, she thought. There had seemed all the time in the world then. Things were different now. With help just once a week and two young children and a garden which took up most of her spare time, every moment was precious, but it was her own fault for wanting such a large, spacious, old-fashioned house. Still, she wouldn't have exchanged it for anything new and labour-saving.

"Ready!" she called. "Wash your hands."

He came into the kitchen. "I did. I –"

"Do it again." She smiled, and he did. He was such an obedient child, she never ceased to marvel after her experience with Clarrie – and people said girls were easier! Well, she hadn't found it so. From day one, Clarrie had stood her ground and fought the battle for superiority, usually winning the day owing to Beth's inexperience. Now that she was eight she was a nice little girl, but she knew how to dig in her heels when ruffled.

Freddie sat up at the table, eyes shining as he contemplated his lunch. "Shall I cut it up for you?" Beth suggested, knowing what the answer would be.

"I can do it," as he manfully struggled with the small knife and fork. Then she would bend over and do it for him without words and he would carry on, satisfied.

"After lunch, I thought we'd go and see the ducks by the pond – would you like that?"

"Yes, please!" he cried, his eyes shining. She smiled across at him, never ceasing to wonder at this small scrap of humanity with hair just like her father's but eyes unlike anyone she could think of. A sort of dark wine colour, with incredible lashes, tipped with gold, that Clarrie would have given her eye teeth for. "It isn't fair," she cried, already at eight conscious of her looks.

Beth opened the back door and Charlie waddled in, a black and white spaniel who moved slowly, just about Freddie's mark.

He leaned down and patted him. "Good boy," he said in a very grown up way.

"There was a little field mouse in the garden this morning," Beth said, "and Charlie found it, and sat there watching it for ages. The little mouse was scared stiff – I don't know who was more frightened, the little mouse or Charlie." She laughed.

"Oh, my God!" Freddie said. It was his usual reply in the last two weeks, and Beth knew if she said nothing it would disappear like all the other things he had come home with.

"Finished?" she asked as he cleaned his plate. He nodded.

"Yoghurt or an apple?"

"No, thank you. May I get down?" He was not a puddy person, Beth decided. She wiped his hands on a damp cloth and dried them. "Yes, go into the garden and play while I clear away."

Finishing in the kitchen, she dried her hands and went into the garden, snipping off the dead heads of tulips and Bellis daisies, smelling deeply the perfume of the wallflowers – it was a lovely time of year, the month of May. Soon be time to put everything outside now that the threat of frost had gone. She remembered the geraniums and begonias she had kept in the spare room on the top floor, and hoped that they hadn't died for want of water.

She could see Freddie in his toy car, his small feet pedalling underneath as he rode down the path towards her, eyes alight with sheer glee. He pinched the hooter over and over to urge her out of the way.

"Goodness," she cried, "what a speed!" And he laughed up at her. It seemed to her that from a very early stage children betrayed the difference between girls and boys. Boys might like a doll and girls a car but fundamentally the basic difference was there. The sense of challenge for a boy, competition – it was all there from birth.

"Come on, poppet," she said. "Let's go. I've put the bread in a bag for the ducks. Will you hold it for me?" She closed the heavy door behind her and walked up the gravel drive.

Freddie trudged next to her, clutching the bread bag, along the narrow path until they reached the High Street.

There were lots of tourists on this lovely day, all ambling happily along or standing in little groups and peering in windows, menfolk behind them, hands behind their backs. Nothing, she thought, was lovelier on a spring day than an English village. Several people stopped to admire the small boy with the red curls who looked so friendly, clutching his mother's hand, a pretty girl in blue. They looked as though they might live here. How lucky they were. Many glances were envious.

Beth was well aware of their thoughts. She had felt like that before she came to live in Ainswick.

Now they had reached the pond. They walked round it, ducks swimming swiftly to the edge when they saw someone coming with what looked like food.

Freddie pulled out an enormous crust and threw it in, and Beth laughed.

"Let's break it up, darling."

She broke it into small pieces and gave some to him. He was delighted as the ducks and moorhens fought over the pieces, quacking away, and then came the swans, two of them, majestic as they glided up.

Soon the bread was gone and Freddie ran to put the empty bag in the litter bin.

"Now," Beth said, "how would you like to go along to Little Field and see a tractor?"

His eyes shone like stars. "Yes, please." And he ran ahead so fast she could hardly keep up with him.

When they turned into the avenue, they passed a young girl on a horse who gave them a wave, and then they could see the empty field, bereft of lawns and house and trees, and Beth felt a pang of sorrow. How bare it looked – so derelict.

"There!" she said, pointing to the great yellow beast.

"That's a bulldozer," Freddie said. "That's a tractor over there." You could see he felt nothing but scorn for someone who didn't know that. Then as something came rumbling towards them, "It's an excavator. An excavator!"

They stayed for some time, and it made Freddie's day. Thoughtfully, Beth retraced her steps along the High Street, just in time to see Maggie Frobisher going into her double-fronted cottage with the huge tubs outside full of pink tulips. It was such a pretty house, The Old Bakery. With her was her young son Simon, six years old, and, like Beth, she had a daughter aged eight who was in Clarrie's class at school.

"Hallo, Beth! Are you on your way home or can you spare time for a cup of tea?"

"That would be nice," Beth said, always pleased to see Maggie, who had moved into Ainswick eighteen months ago. Apart from seeing each other at the dramatic society they seldom met, for Maggie was a children's dancing teacher.

The two small boys stood eyeing each other, hoping that some playtime together would come out of this. When Beth ushered them in, they were both delighted.

"Outside you go," Maggie laughed. "There's plenty to keep them occupied in the garden."

Although Beth had been in the house once or twice before, she never failed to appreciate Maggie's taste. It had been exquisitely furnished, with pastel colours on the chairs and cushions which were offset by the dark oak beams and old fireplace. There were flowers on low tables, and plenty of books. She wondered, as she often did, what lay behind Maggie's equable expression since both the children bore another surname, though they were both like Maggie to look at.

"I'll put the kettle on – won't be a tick. Sit down and look at a magazine. They're my weakness, I'm afraid."

Only too glad to do so, Beth subsided into a comfortable chair and let the atmosphere wash over her. Looking through the French windows, a later addition to the old house, she saw that the small garden was a riot of colour, and that clematis cascaded over a pergola which went all the way up the path.

Getting up, she walked over to the window. "Maggie, the clematis – it's wonderful."

"Yes, it's Don's speciality. He'd grow nothing else if he had his way."

"Neither would I if I could grow them like that," Beth said, full of admiration.

"I've given the boys orange juice and an apple," Maggie

said. "They're playing in the sand pit. Can't come to any harm there."

"They get on well together, don't they, considering there's two years' difference in their ages?"

"Erica has gone to play with Emma James," Maggie said, pouring the tea. "Well, has it been decided – the one act play for the festival?"

"I'm almost certain it will be Barrie's *Twelve Pound Look*. Peggy is very keen on it."

"Oh, well," Maggie laughed. "Then that's what it will be. I remember doing that at drama school – oh, years and years ago."

She really was a very pretty woman, Beth thought. About thirty-five, with dark auburn hair and wide, very light blue eyes. When you looked at her, or spoke to her, she had a way of sliding her eyes away and concentrating on a distant spot – as if she were dreaming, which Beth suspected she often was. Sometimes she wondered how Maggie managed to concentrate on teaching dancing so well to small children. Clarrie adored her.

"I've just taken Freddie along to see the new building site at Little Field – they haven't wasted much time, have they?"

"No, Don walked along there last night. He's fed up with the whole thing, and feels we didn't make enough of a protest."

"I suppose it was bound to happen – sooner or later."

"The way I see it, there's not much we can do about it now. After all, the village did band together in a formal protest, got up petitions and so on."

"Well, Peggy was all for it, and I suppose if we had a social conscience and were as charitable as she is, we'd none of us mind."

Beth sat back in her chair and relaxed. "Do you like it here – in Ainswick?"

"Love it," Maggie said with some warmth. "We came from Chester – I was born there – and this is so different. I miss some things but – well, my life changed totally when I married Don, and all this was part of it. Yes," she decided, "I am very happy here."

She held out a plate of biscuits. "And you, Beth?"

"Yes – we came from London, and I wouldn't go back for anything. Of course, you do tend to miss some things. The shops, the parks, people. But, no, I wouldn't go back."

They were silent for a moment, then Maggie said, "Don is my second husband, of course."

"Oh," Beth said. She had wondered. He seemed much older than Maggie.

"Yes," she said slowly, eyes fixed on something in the distant past. "My first, the children's father, was a bastard. Handsome as all get out, and always broke. He walked out on me when Simon was a baby. My dear, went without a backward glance. I was standing in the window nursing the baby, six weeks old he was, and he left – just like that."

"Oh, Maggie!" Beth really was shocked. She had had no idea of the story behind Maggie's arrival in Ainswick.

"He'd always had an eye for women, but this one seemed rather special. He went to live with her in a flat on the sea front at Lytham St Anne's. I went to see her . . ."

"Maggie – you didn't!"

"I did. Why not? She'd taken my husband away from me. My mother made me go. 'Don't let them get away with it,' she said. I went and of course she was pregnant. No more than twenty. Poor little bitch. I didn't have a leg to stand on. Besides, he hadn't any money. I don't know how they managed. My mother supported us, the baby and Erica and me. After a time I went back to teaching, and my mother used to look after them while I went out in the evening. That's how I met Don."

She brought herself back to look at Beth.

"Bit sordid, isn't it?"

Beth felt sad, confronted with another woman's wretched experience. What, she wondered, would she herself do in similar circumstances?

"She was tough, my mother," Maggie reminisced. "I don't know what I'd have done without her. She's dead now, and so is he."

"Your husband?"

"Yes, he died a year later – cancer," she said. "So she didn't have him for long, did she? More tea?"

"Er – yes, please," Beth said, coming down to earth with a bang.

"And then my mother said, 'You must look out for a husband. Not every man wants to take on a woman with two children.' And when I met Don, she said: 'Secure him now.' Like a supermarket offer. I've often laughed at that. 'One door closes and another opens,' she said. I thought about it. I wasn't keen, he seemed quite old to me. Still," she added, "he was good in bed." And Beth found herself blushing.

"It's important, isn't it?"

"Oh. Yes. Yes, of course," Beth said, realizing not for the first time what a very sheltered life she had led, and was delighted when the boys came running in through the doors. "We saw a squirrel!" Simon cried breathlessly. "A squirrel with a long tail – he was digging on the lawn."

"I expect that's where he had hidden some nuts off the walnut tree," Maggie said, matter-of-factly. "We have a walnut tree, you know – donkey's years old, they say."

"He's a nice little chap," Beth said, looking after Simon's retreating figure.

"Yes, he is, although I say it. He adores Don, and a good thing too. It was harder for Erica. She missed her father for a long time. It wasn't easy . . . Oh, well, enough of that."

Beth glanced at her watch. "Is that the time? Goodness, I've been here for ages – but it has been nice, Maggie. I mean –"

"Water under the bridge, my dear," she said. She went to the door and called Freddie. "Come on, sweetie, Mummy is going now." They heard his wail at being interrupted.

Maggie bent down. "You can come another day and play in the sand pit," she promised. "You'd like that, wouldn't you?"

He nodded vigorously.

"You're going to the meeting tonight?" she asked Beth.

"Yes, see you at eight."

"I hear we have a new member."

"Yes, so Peggy said. Well, see you later – thanks for the tea."

Freddie kept up a continual stream of chatter all the way home, about frogs and sand, and squirrels and tractors, but Beth's thoughts were on Maggie and her story.

Who would have thought those wide ingenuous blue eyes and that dreamy expression hid such a background?

Life was full of surprises.

Chapter Five

The hall was full for the meeting of the dramatic society. The old barn, being used for everything that went on in Ainswick, was busy on most nights. Tonight the caretaker had arranged the chairs in rows as he did every Monday for the Ainswick Players.

Peggy Mansfield was there, and most of the members, and the producer of the play, Arthur Lang, who had come out of retirement in order to support them. Maggie was there, and Beth, distributing copies of the play, Marty could be heard in the kitchen busy with cups and plates ready for the mid-evening break, while Alistair's rich baritone voice rose above the noise of the crowd. He was limited inasmuch as his voice, while excellent for superior parts, was in no way suitable for the part of Sir Harry Sims, about to be knighted, a pompous little man who had come up the hard way as a self-made man. They were all sure that Geoffrey Latimer would get that part, while Alistair would be excellent as his stiff, deep-voiced butler. After the reading this evening, the auditions would be held on Friday. Beth and Maggie stood together at the committee table, having a word before proceedings began.

"Will you be putting in for Lady Sims or Kate?" Maggie asked Beth idly.

"I thought I would try for Lady Sims – I'm not quite sure if I'm up to Kate. It's a wonderful part but I think Lady Sims would be better for me – not so much to learn."

Maggie surveyed the group without seeing them. "I've played both those parts – but of course it depends on who puts in for Kate. Anyway, I'm going to have a try."

"Good luck. You know Molly Dean and Priscilla are going for it?"

Maggie made a face. "Yes, so I heard."

They were interrupted by the sharp banging of a gavel on the desk by Peggy who had made her way to the committee table.

"Hush – could we have hush, please?"

She was smiling but firm, her diminutive figure able to command despite her size.

Everyone made their way to the chairs and sat down.

"Well." Peggy smiled when they were seated. "Good evening, ladies and gentlemen." And they answered dutifully. She held up a copy of the play. "Has everyone got one of these? *The Twelve Pound Look*, by Sir James Barrie."

"Yes, Peggy."

"Well, this is your committee's final choice so I hope you are happy with it. Not many parts, just four, but the name of the game is to put forward an excellent production which will win the festival for Ainswick." Her little nut brown face beamed at them.

"Hear, hear." There was a faint cheer from the company as Peggy looked towards the door. She had thought the new member was to be here this evening and had a vague feeling of disappointment.

"So we'll start. I suggest Geoffrey reads Sir Harry . . ." and saw Geoffrey's self-satisfied smirk as a sudden rap on the door made them all look round. A girl entered and they all stared as she smiled at them, a warm, beautiful smile. Her hair was a dark cloud around her head, lovely eyes – which they could see from where they sat to be of a strange greeny colour – and sparkling white teeth, but above all her presence was mesmeric.

"Hallo, everybody, I'm sorry I'm late." And the voice was delightful. Low-pitched, warm, breathy.

"Bang goes Kate," Maggie whispered to Beth.

Peggy was relieved and delighted to see her. "My dear, don't worry." And she put an arm around the girl's shoulders. "Everyone, this is Jackie Hetherington – our newest member."

"Hallo – hi – hallo."

"Come and sit next to me," Beth said, moving along, and saw that the eyes of all the men were on Jackie with that particular avid or sheepish look, while the womenfolk looked somewhat apprehensive.

"Thanks – thanks awfully," Jackie whispered gratefully to Beth who was immediately enveloped in a faint wave of sensuous French perfume. She handed Jackie her copy as Peggy gave her another.

Peggy smiled at the new arrival warmly, and began to speak.

"As you are new to the district, I will explain that every year there is a festival of one act plays and most of the societies in our area of the Cotswolds compete. We have won it twice in the last eight years, and this year we are going to do Barrie's *Twelve Pound Look* – so, shall we begin? Maggie, will you read Lady Sims, Priscilla read Kate, the butler, Alistair – and Sir Harry, Geoffrey."

Halfway through the evening when they broke for coffee it was fairly obvious that they had a new member of some importance. That she was experienced professionally, no one was in any doubt. Her voice, its cadences and warmth, was far superior to anyone else's in the society, even Maggie who had had professional experience. That and her looks more or less decided that the main role in this play – and possibly future productions – would be given to the newcomer.

When she had gone over for a word with Peggy, Maggie joined Beth. "Bit of a comedown for her, isn't it? The local dramatic society. It stands out a mile she's a professional."

"Well, perhaps she gave up the stage when she married?"

"Did you see the engagement ring? That solitaire blinded me."

"Here she comes."

Jackie smiled at them both. "Oh, isn't this nice? Such a friendly crowd."

"Where do you live?" Maggie asked.

"In Milney Hatch."

"Been there long?"

"No, six weeks or so. My husband has been re-located to London."

"Oh – quite a way out."

"He travels a lot – mainly to the States. That's where we've been for the last three years."

"Oh, I see."

"Peggy said you've acted professionally?" Beth said.

Jackie gave a little laugh. Such a musical sound, Beth thought. She seemed to have everything.

"Yes, I have, in the States. I started out as a dancer in London, then I got acting parts in New York, then I married, and – well, here I am. I've done a lot of summer stock."

"What's that?" Beth was curious.

"Going out on the road, a bit like our travelling repertory companies."

"Come along, everyone, tea break is over – take your seats." It was Peggy's voice again.

"Isn't she nice?" Beth whispered, referring to Jackie.

"Mmmm," Maggie said.

At the end of the session they were all asked to put down the names of the parts for which they wished to be considered. Glancing at the list, Maggie saw that Jackie had put down both Lady Sims and Kate.

"She's not going to waste much time, is she?" she remarked to Beth who had added her name to the list for Lady Sims.

Beth smiled. "See you on Friday, then." And they all went their various ways.

Peggy was delighted. Such an addition to the society, and right out of the blue. She had come up to expectations too, a real little actress. Peggy could see her on stage now in those wonderful clothes worn in 1912. Jackie would look stunning. There was no doubt she would get the lead – it could not be avoided. She hoped everyone would not think it unfair, but for a festival play one simply had to have the best.

"Well, Arthur," she said, meeting the producer on the way out, his silver hair shining under the light from the overhead lamp. "What do you think of our new member?"

"Peggy, my dear," his voice was deep and carried across the car park, a voice that had moved many a matinee in the good old days, "what a find! The girl is a natural. Where is she from? A newcomer to the village?"

"No, she's a new resident from Milney Hatch."

"Oh, I hope she doesn't find that too boring – not much going on there."

"No, that's why she came to us."

"Our good fortune, then, my dear Peggy," he said, kissing her lightly which never failed to please her. "Can I give you a lift?"

"No, thanks all the same – I'm just minutes away and I like to walk."

"Very well. Goodnight, my dear. I'll see you on Friday."

"Goodnight, Arthur."

Peggy hurried home, anxious to tell Dennis how the evening had gone. He had not the faintest interest in the dramatic society, but always liked to hear the story of her day.

Once home, she took off her coat and gloves and went into the sitting room where Dennis sat, the daily paper on his knee. Unless she was mistaken, he had just woken from a nap. She didn't blame him. After ten o'clock was quite late for them these days.

"You should have gone to bed," she said. "I'm sorry I'm late."

"And you still out?" he said. "Never, my dear. Well, and how did it go?"

And she told him, especially about the new member.

"Imagine, Dennis," she said, "a real actress joining our little society – and she's a stunning-looking girl."

"What age is she?"

"I don't know. Twenty-eight . . . thirty . . ."

"That reminds me," he said.

"What's that?"

"I went up to the Hall this morning, only to find that Ariadne has already moved herself to her flat in London, leaving that little girl to do all the clearing up! But hopefully Lucy won't be short of money. She has some in her own right, and will obviously get a job, but what she's looking for are digs in the village. Any ideas?"

Peggy frowned. "What sort of digs?"

"Well, I don't think she minds for a start – she may end up buying a little cottage, something like that, but for now she needs somewhere to live – the house is on the market."

Peggy's face fell. "Already!"

"Well, that's the way it is. So Lucy needs to get settled. It won't be for a week or two, but if you should hear of anything –"

Peggy bit her lip. "Well, she could come here if it was only for –"

Dennis shook his head. "Not a good idea, Peggy."

They both looked at each other as they heard the sound of a key in the lock of the front door, and Dennis glanced up at the clock.

"It's gone ten-thirty," he said. "Who can that be?"

Then the sound of a door being closed, and a heavy thud on the floor. They both walked out into the hall and saw Malcolm, their son, standing there, a grin on his face, a packed holdall at his feet.

"Malcolm!" Peggy cried. "What on earth are you doing here?"

He came over and kissed her. "I've come home, Mother," he said. "Your wandering son returns. Is that all right with you?"

Peggy stared at him while Dennis looked shocked, finally finding his voice.

"Well, let's not stand out here talking . . ."

Malcolm was pale, Peggy could see under the light, and not half as sure of himself as he professed to be. Why was it, she wondered, she spent all her time doing things for other people, yet she had never had much success bringing up her only son?

Following his father into the sitting room, Malcolm flopped on to the sofa, legs outstretched, with an air of nonchalance he was far from feeling.

"What's wrong?" Dennis said. "You haven't driven up from London at this time of night just to see us."

"Janice has left me," he said, and for the first time, the smile left his face.

"Left you!" Peggy repeated. "What do you mean? She's gone? Where?"

"Damned if I know, and I couldn't care less!"

"I'll go and make us some tea," Peggy said. This, she thought, was all they needed at their age. What did he mean, come home? Surely not to stay?

When she came back with the tea things, the men were speaking in low tones. Malcolm got up and took the tray.

"I'm really sorry about this, Mother," he said. "It was an impulse, really. I just felt I wanted to come home." And he buried his head in his hands.

"Oh, Malcolm!" she said. It really wasn't his fault. Women were at the root of it all. They flocked around him – and why shouldn't they? With his looks, even though he was her son, he really was a handsome young devil. Thirty-four coming up to thirty-five, with two broken marriages behind him, and now what looked like a third, although fortunately he hadn't married this one. And she had seemed such a nice girl.

Dennis got up and poured himself a stiff whisky. He held the decanter out to Malcolm, who shook his head. At least drink was not one of his vices, Peggy thought. They had spoiled him, she knew that. That's what came of having all your eggs in one basket.

She handed him a strong cup of tea. "Have you eaten?"

"Yes, thanks. I'd had dinner out this evening with a client – and came home to find Jan's note."

He fished in his pocket and brought it out, handing it to Peggy.

She hesitated.

"Read it," he said. "She doesn't say much."

It was true. A small sheet of paper. "M. I'm leaving you – this time for good. J."

Peggy looked up. "She's done it before?"

"Oh, several times," he said wearily.

"And why was this?" Dennis asked acidly. He had long since lost patience with his only son.

"Who knows? I've come to the conclusion that I don't make a very good partner."

"Well, they certainly came to the same conclusion," Dennis said drily.

Peggy shot him a glance. "You're not helping, Dennis. You'd better tell us what all this is about," she said severely.

As Malcolm stirred his tea, she wondered why he hadn't stayed in his apartment in London. As a West End estate agent, he surely needed to be in work the next day.

"Well," he began, "The ridiculous thing is that I got a flat for this guy – he'd only been there for six weeks, I'd met him before, briefly, so I asked him round for a drink. He wasn't married – well, divorced – and one thing led to another, and it seems Jan has been seeing him."

"How do you know that?" Dennis asked.

"She told me when I questioned her."

"Why did you think there was something going on?"

"Well, she accused me of seeing an ex-girl friend, and we had a blazing row, and she went off, then she came back . . . oh, it's been going on for about six months."

Dennis was staring at the floor.

"How long do you intend staying?"

"To tell you the truth, I'd like to stay for a bit. I'm giving up the flat in town." And he gave a quick glance at his father. "And the business. I've had an offer from Roseley and Goff – they want to take it over – and I have to say, with the market being so dead in town . . ."

"What would you do?" Dennis was genuinely interested.

"Thought I might start something down here. Well, in the area." As he saw his father's frown: "I mean, business in these parts is a damn sight more energetic than the London scene, I can tell you."

"Is that so?"

"Look," Peggy interrupted, "I'll go up and see to your room – I am sure it's aired – and you and Dad can come up when you're ready. We'll talk about this in the morning."

She looked at him, six feet of manhood, as handsome as his father, but whereas Dennis had been fairish, Malcolm was dark. Broad-shouldered and upright, she had seen women look at him from the time he was a boy. He had her dark colouring , like her own father who had been Irish, and he had all the Irish blarney about him, too.

He got up swiftly and went over to kiss her. "Sorry, Mum," he said.

She reached up to return his kiss. "Malcolm, you are welcome any time – what are parents for?"

But later, as she waited for Dennis to come up, she lay there, worried. What would happen now? He couldn't go on like this. Or could he?

She thought of his first wedding. He had been twenty-two, and little Marie Louise eighteen. They were such a handsome couple, she so pretty and Malcolm so tall and good-looking. They were like wild creatures, flying here and there, having fun, never seeming to want to settle down, until the baby came. Fancy, she thought. I have two grandsons somewhere in this world, and I never see either of them and probably never will. It's a good thing I'm not that dedicated to grandchildren. Little Adam had been born in the second year of the marriage, and from that moment things seemed to go wrong. Who was to blame she had never known; it was six of one and half dozen of the other, she suspected. For Malcolm had always had an eye for the girls, and it was fairly obvious that Marie Louise liked the men, so between the two of them the marriage was fated from the first.

When they parted, a swift divorce followed and Marie Louise went with the two year old and the new man in her life to live in Holland. Occasionally they had news of her but after a time that dwindled out, and now Peggy never asked, and Malcolm never said.

Hot on Marie Louise's heels came Miranda, as different from Marie Louise as chalk from cheese. A real beauty, a girl with a high-powered job who didn't take kindly to settling down when she knew she was pregnant. Peggy supposed Malcolm got up to his usual tricks, and Miranda was certainly not the kind of girl to put up with that. When the baby was born, another boy, Bobby, the marriage seemed to disintegrate rapidly. It lingered on fitfully until the boy was three, and then, quite suddenly, Miranda too had gone. To Spain, if they'd heard correctly. From what Peggy had seen, Malcolm had accepted the loss of his second son quite philosophically. Sometimes she wondered if there were not one or two more children somewhere she knew nothing about.

And then came Janice. A nice, simple, home-loving girl, and Peggy had thought, This is the one. She'll keep him straight. There was a sincerity about her that touched Peggy. She was the only one of the three Peggy had really liked. She had made the flat so comfortable, was a good cook, it seemed on the face of it to work. but now . . .

Peggy sighed deeply and hoped he would not stay long. A week or two – that would be enough. She and Dennis had their own lives to live, and it wasn't on for a man of Malcolm's age to come back home to live. If she knew anything about him, he probably had another girl up his sleeve at this very moment. Anyway, and she felt somewhat irritated, it was difficult to explain his presence in the village. She would have to think of something.

When Dennis came up, she pretended to be asleep. She didn't want to talk about it any more tonight. She heard him go quietly into his own room and close the door softly.

Malcolm breathed a sigh of relief in his single bed. Well, that was over and done with, and it hadn't gone too badly. The old man had taken it quite well, considering he had put up the money for the business in the first place. And what was the point of telling his mother that Jan had found hotel bills in his jacket pocket, and not for the first time, bills for two that had not included her?

Well, life was for the living, Malcolm thought, and was soon asleep.

Chapter Six

Marcus Pennington, preparing his sermon, knew by the way Beth came in the front door and almost ran down the hall that she had got the part she wanted. She came in, eyes shining, coming straight over to him and giving him a hug.

"I've got the part of Lady Sims!" she cried, her excitement knowing no bounds.

Marcus kissed the top of her head, pleased for her. He positively disliked the idea of her belonging to the dramatic society, scared lest one day she had a part which entailed her acting intimate scenes with someone else, but he was too nice to say or do anything which would prevent her from doing what she wanted. Her joy was obvious, and besides he loved her.

"That's great, darling. How did the others get on?"

She put the script down on the table and flopped into a chair.

"Well! Our new girl, Jackie, got the part of Kate, that's the leading role – and she was absolutely wonderful! Of course it was a shame for Maggie, but she's been made prompt lady – I don't think she was overly pleased – but, well, that's the way it goes. She put in for my part, too, so you may be sure that to get neither wasn't very nice. I have to say, though, she may be a better actress than I am, but I think I'm more suited to the part as it were." And she grinned at him.

"Modesty not being one of your strong points." He smiled back at her.

"Exactly," she said. "Children all right? They didn't wake up?"

"They wouldn't dare."

"So what have you been doing?" she asked, getting up and plumping cushions and tidying the room.

"The Sermon," he said, and she made a face, and they smiled at their private joke.

He watched her moving about the room, her fair hair tied back, scarlet sweater over slim black pants – she had never looked her age. She still looked like the girl he had first met at eighteen. He was such a dull stick, he often wondered how she could have fallen in love with him.

"You won't find it too much – to learn your lines?" he asked. "I can't imagine how you'll fit it in with all you have to do."

"No, it isn't much of a part – Jackie has the longest and we will be able to rehearse together when we get a spare moment."

"What does her husband do?"

"I've no idea. She doesn't say much about her home life."

"No children?"

"No, I don't think so. At least she's never said."

It was the next morning, around ten, when Freddie was at nursery school, that the white Mercedes sports car drew up outside the front door, and out stepped Camilla Blakeney. Looking through the kitchen window, Beth's heart leapt. It couldn't be – yet it was. No one else could look quite like that. In skintight white pants and an enormous white sweater, a band round her head and masses of ethnic chains round her neck, the eternal cigarette smoking from her fingers, Beth's best friend from London and schooldays was walking up the garden path. Dark glasses, tanned by the sun – she hadn't changed a bit! Beth thought joyfully.

Running to the door, she flung it open and went to meet her, throwing her arms around Camilla, who hugged her tightly. They stood for several seconds until Camilla drew away and stood back, appraising her.

"I have to say, you look great. Country air seems to agree with you."

"Yes, even being out here in the sticks," Beth said. "Oh, what a lovely surprise. Come on in and I'll make you some coffee."

Camilla followed her in, looking around her with an expression of disbelief. "What a barn of a place! A bit different from Slaters Court." Which was where they had both had flats until they were married.

"You can say that again . . . Well, what are you doing down here?"

"I'll tell you." Camilla sat herself on the kitchen table and Beth could see she was bursting with suppressed excitement. "We didn't get back from France until Thursday, and –"

"Yes?"

"We've already bought a house!" She waited for it to sink in. Beth spooned coffee into the percolator.

"Camilla, that's wonderful! Where?"

"Here – in Ainswick."

Beth turned, her mouth open.

"Here?" The idea seemed too ridiculous to take in. "But where – why?" She just couldn't imagine anything so bizarre as Camilla living in a country village.

"Well, we've been looking for a while. Nick thought it was time we had a country place."

"Of course," Beth said stoutly.

"He's doing well – just made another film."

"Yes, I know. I read the reviews."

"Good, isn't it? Of course, it's temporary money in that sense, either we make a bomb or nothing at all, but Nick says he'd like to invest in this – for the future. So you see in our old age we're becoming sensible people – boring though it sounds. Like the Penningtons."

"Cheeky," Beth said, pouring out the coffee.

She sat herself down opposite Camilla. "Oh, this is exciting. So where is it? I can't think of anything offhand . . ."

Camilla walked over to the windowsill where she found a small bowl and stubbed out her cigarette in it.

"Not Brampton Hall?" she asked nonchalantly, returning to the table with a wicked smile.

"No!" Beth cried in disbelief. "Not Bram—"

"The very same," Camilla said. "It's just come on the market. The agent sent us the details on Friday. We came up yesterday and sorted the whole thing out, made an offer which was accepted, and a contract has gone out for yours truly, Mr and Mrs Nick Blakeney."

"But it was – I heard they were asking –"

"Yes, an awful lot of money, but they were quite keen to take an offer – not a lot of lolly around at the moment, sweetie, and Nick is a cash buyer. From what I've heard the family who lived there are in Queer Street."

"So I believe. Now forgive me, Camilla, but the last time I saw you, when was that, just before Christmas, you were broke. Not a bean in the world, you said. Am I right?"

"Perfectly correct. Well, you see, Nick had put his all into the movie – and since then it's paid off. You know the film world, it's all or nothing, and we might, just might, have to sell the flat to cover this – but Nick wants to keep it, while I say get rid of it. We can always rent something in town."

"I can't believe it," Beth said. "But I am delighted for you and Nick, and for me. It will be wonderful to have you nearby and you'll love it here, honestly."

"I fell in love with the house," Camilla said. "Beth, it's absolutely fantastic!"

"Georgian, isn't it?"

Camilla nodded.

"And someone has spent a fortune on it. Well, come on, don't just sit there."

Beth stared.

"I've asked if I can take you over it."

"What – now?"

"Of course now – what time does Freddie come out of school?"

"Twelve."

"Well, then, we've oodles of time."

Camilla drove through the High Street until she came to Turpin's Lane. Overhung with wild prunus and cherry trees on this spring morning, it made a wonderful approach to the house which stood slightly elevated and could be seen through high wrought iron gates.

Camilla got out and unlocked them, and drove through.

Brampton Hall sat in the sunshine, its old gold façade mellowed with time, the front hung with wistaria, two great urns filled with trailing ivies and pale mauve pansies.

The front door gleamed white against the old stone and Beth took a deep breath as Camilla rang the bell.

"Oh, Camilla – it's a dream!"

The door was opened by an elderly woman who recognized Camilla instantly.

"Good morning, Mrs Clayton."

"Hallo, Mrs Blakeney – do come in."

"Thank you. I did ask if I could bring my friend, Mrs Pennington . . ."

"Yes, of course, I was expecting you. Do carry on, I won't disturb you. Can you find your own way around?"

"Yes, thanks."

Camilla seemed quite carried away. Beth couldn't recall seeing her so enthusiastic about anything before. In the hall, the bare flagstones were cool at their feet, the great stone fireplace lacking a fire, but overhead hung the immense chandelier which sent myriads of colours over the floor and walls from the sun which came in from the large landing window.

"We're buying one or two things," Camilla said, almost whispering, she was so overcome.

How sad it must be to leave a place like this, Beth was thinking. She had been told about the people who lived here, a couple with a daughter – what had happened to her? She had heard the gossip in the village about the man going bankrupt. Apparently he and his family had lived in Brampton Hall for three generations. It was so sad.

But Camilla was in the drawing room, a huge room, square in dimension, with long sash windows overlooking the garden, then into a dining room, almost as large.

"This'll take a bit of furnishing," she said. "Can you imagine our modern dining-room furniture in here?" And they both laughed. They walked into the conservatory, where baskets still hung from the roof, the flowers wilting now, it was so warm.

They walked out of the conservatory and into the garden where there was a pool under its bright blue cover, the changing rooms discreetly hidden behind a shrubbery. Nearby was a large barbecue area.

They both looked at each other, and Beth sighed.

"What more could anyone want?"

"Not a thing," Camilla said. "I can hardly wait until it's all ours."

There was a small library, and a family room, an enormous kitchen which had been completely done over and refurbished with everything in it that money could buy.

"Are they leaving all this – the fitments? I can hardly believe what I'm looking at," Beth said.

"I think some things are to be sold at valuation, but you know me, I'm not missing out on a thing if I can help it. Wait until you get upstairs."

Six bedrooms, each with its own bathroom, each one superbly furnished with luxury fittings. But Beth could not escape the feeling that she was trespassing. One of the bedrooms was locked, and Camilla explained that this was the daughter's room. She was going to move out just as soon as she found somewhere to live.

"Oh, how awful," Beth wailed. "Imagine having to give all this up."

"That's life," Camilla said. 'The luck of the draw."

"Oh, spare a thought . . ." Beth said.

"Might be my turn next."

"Yes – I suppose you're right . . . Lucy," she recalled. "That's her name – Lucy Gilbert. I've seen her mother in the village, a gorgeous-looking woman, about forty-two or three. So elegant."

"Oh, quite young? I imagined someone older. Well, I'm glad I didn't meet her. It's much more satisfactory to take over an empty house."

"Do you think so?"

"Sure of it. Well, come on, I think we've seen enough. It gets better each time I come."

In the kitchen they found Mrs Clayton. "Thank you so much," said Camilla. "I must say, I wish you were staying on. Everything is so beautifully kept."

"Thank you." The housekeeper was obviously pleased.

"Can't be bad, can it, Beth?" asked Camilla as they went down the drive.

It could only happen to her, Beth decided.

They sat outside the nursery school in the car waiting for

Freddie, then at five minutes to twelve Beth got out and walked up to the door of the little school. The children came tumbling out, looking slightly dazed, clutching drawings and pieces of paper, hats were rammed on heads, and Freddie, holding Beth's hand tightly, looked towards Camilla's car.

"Do you know who that is?" she asked him.

"It's a Mercedes," he said, eyes lighting up. "Like mine."

"But this is a real one," Beth said, and through the window he could see his glamorous Aunt Camilla. He stuffed his fist in his mouth and turned away, cheeks flushed with embarrassment.

"Oh, don't tell me you're shy!" Beth laughed. "You remember Auntie Camilla."

"Hi there, young Freddie," Camilla said as he got into the back seat and fixed on the safety belt. "Well, what a clever chap. And what have you been doing today?"

His shyness forgotten at being called a clever chap, he proceeded to tell them in non-stop conversation which lasted until they reached home.

"I've got a Porsche" he said. "I'll show you."

"Yes, please," Camilla said, taking his hand.

"Make yourself at home," Beth said, "I'll get his lunch first, then we'll have something to eat."

She could hear Camilla and Freddie talking away nineteen to the dozen, and smiled to herself. It was a pity Camilla had no children of her own, though it was something that had never been mentioned between them. Yet children liked her, which was surprising since she had a very direct manner and showed very little warmth towards children or grown ups, outwardly at least, though deep down she was a warm person and loved animals.

After Freddie's lunch, when Beth had sent him outside to play in the garden, she and Camilla sat over cold roast beef, new bread, and cheese and tomatoes.

Camilla ate her meal with gusto. Slim as a reed, she loved to eat and was quite a good cook, although she never hid her dislike of housework and anything domestic.

"Super bread," she said. "Tastes home-made – you didn't bake it, did you?"

"No, sadly," Beth laughed. "It's something I'd like to do,

but there's never any time. Which is something you won't have in the next few weeks if the sale of Brampton Hall goes through."

Camilla pushed her plate away, and brought out her cigarettes.

"I can't believe it myself," she said. "Nick is over the moon – and I've been thinking about the furnishings. I think we'll keep all the curtains – they are for sale. And let's face it, Beth, they're magnificent, even if they're not what I'd have chosen, I'll have to force myself to accept them. I mean, can you imagine the sheer yardage – all those drapes!" And they both laughed.

"Oh, yes," she said. "I think it will all be rather nice. And don't forget the pool. We shall have swimming parties, lunches and barbecues. I intend to use it, Beth, to its fullest advantage. As long as Nick doesn't start bringing down that film crowd – you know how I hate them."

It always rather surprised Beth that Camilla so disliked the movie world, and all that went with it. She was a sophisticate, yet at the same time very basic and down to earth. She didn't like pretence of any kind.

"Let's sit outside," Beth said. "I'll bring the coffee out."

Camilla lay stretched out on a chaise in full sun, eyes closed behind her huge dark glasses, her sweater off to reveal a tiny lacy bra, snow white against the tan of her skin. She was lucky enough to tan a rich golden colour.

"Don't mind my stripping off, do you?" she asked, nodding towards Freddie.

"Of course not." Beth laughed. "He's got to start sometime."

"Hmm," Camilla said, lighting another cigarette. "Some of 'em start way too soon."

"So tell me about France. Where did you go? Same old place?"

"Well, it may be the same old place to you, duckie, but to me that French village is home. I didn't want to come back – it was sheer heaven. Nothing to do all day but lie in the sun, no clothes to worry about, no dressing up. I never take any luggage, just a change of bikinis, and I buy the espadrilles when I'm there. We live on peaches and salads . . . you must come out there with Marc and the children."

She was the only person who called him that, and he never seemed to mind.

"You're a bit of a gypsy, really," Beth said. "You were always the same, even at school."

"The trouble is, Nick hates it. Doesn't like the sun, or the beach, or even the swimming pool – a few days and he's anxious to get back home."

"But it's his work that entices him home, isn't it? He lives for his work, and now that he's a successful writer producer, surely he can't look back."

"I hope so. We've had some grim times. Almost starved when we were first married."

"I know. It's odd how you're so different, but I suppose that's what keeps you together?"

"Well, at least we think alike over Brampton Hall. I want it as much as he does."

"What will you do about France when you move up here? I mean, you'll have a pool and a lovely home. Surely you won't want to go traipsing off?"

"But I won't have the sun – and the warmth," Camilla said, lighting another cigarette. "I know the weather this year has been super up to now, but you know how ghastly some of our summers are and I just can't bear it. I have to get away to the sun."

She had always been the same, Beth thought. They had been at boarding school together, she because her parents travelled all over the world in search of botanical specimens and Camilla because she had no parents, both having been killed in a plane crash. When Beth's parents were home, Camilla spent her holidays with them, but if they were abroad, then both the girls were sent to an aunt of Camilla's who lived in Scotland and was Camilla's guardian.

Throughout schooldays and into adulthood they had stayed together, as different as chalk from cheese. Camilla was always the leader, daring to do things which the more cautious Beth would not. She had been a model, then a photographer, then she had married Nick when she was only eighteen and he twenty-one. Beth's parents had held the wedding at Beth's home, and then Camilla and Nick had flown to Canada where he hoped to make a start as a film cameraman. They had lost touch for a while when Beth got married, but picked up the threads again when Camilla and Nick returned from Canada.

By then Beth had her daughter and Nick was making a name for himself in the film world. It had been touch and go for a start, but now he seemed well established as a talented writer.

"Believe it or not, it was the garden that fascinated me. I've always wanted a garden like that."

"Perhaps you'll turn out to be the new Gertrude Jekyll." Beth said.

"Stranger things have happened."

"There's always something going on in a village. I've joined the local dramatic society."

"Oh, my God!" Camilla moaned. She hated anything to do with acting.

"And, what's more, I have just landed my first part in a one act play for the festival in June."

"You were always good at acting in school. Do you remember when you did *Midsummer Night's Dream*, you were Titania and that awful cow Marcia Lindstrom was Oberon?" And they both fell about laughing.

Beth re-surfaced as she heard the front door bell, and getting up, hurried to open it.

At the door stood an apologetic Jackie Hetherington.

"Oh, Beth, have I called at an awkward time?" Her lovely breathy voice was wistful, and she looked like a dream. Beth could no more have sent her away than fly.

"Of course not!" she said staunchly. "Come on in. I have a friend here I'd like you to meet."

"Oh, you are a dear," Jackie breathed.

"Camilla," Beth said with Jackie close on her heels. "This is Jackie – Jackie Hetherington – she's new here to. Jackie – Camilla."

"Hello, Jackie."

It was difficult to know whether Camilla was looking at her from behind those dark glasses.

"Here, take this chair. I'll get another one."

Freddie chose this moment to want to go in and use the bathroom. He stared at Jackie without saying a word.

"Hello, little boy," she said warmly as Beth dragged him off by the hand to the house. "What a lovely garden. Do you live round here, Camilla?"

"No, I'm from London, but I am about to move here, hopefully."

"Oh, how nice. To Ainswick?"

"Uh huh," Camilla said.

"We've just moved to Milney Hatch – do you know it?"

"No, don't know the area at all," Camilla said. "Do you smoke?"

"No, I don't," Jackie said politely, easing herself on to the chair as Beth returned with Freddie who made to run off to the sand pit again.

"Here – say hallo to Mrs Hetherington, Freddie."

"Hello," he said.

"Hello, Freddie," Jackie whispered, and when he had gone, looked after him longingly.

"Oh, what a little darling," she said as Beth smiled.

Jackie took out her dark glasses, but not before the two girls had seen her wonderful green eyes, the incredible black lashes which fringed them, and noted the soft peach down skin and the cloud of black hair which framed her face.

"I've got an awful cheek barging in on you like this, Beth, but I really wanted to know whether you could spend an hour or two on my lines – well, our lines – tomorrow morning? Could you possibly?"

Her smile was lovely and exposed beautiful teeth. She was wearing blue jeans and an emerald green silk shirt which exactly matched her eyes. On her left hand was a wedding ring and a single large emerald in a diamond setting. Beth saw Camilla's eyes go down to the ring and then look at her as though to say: Get that!

"I think so," she said slowly. "Well, an hour perhaps."

"I'm usually not too bad on lines, but it's quite a long part, very wordy." She laughed. "And I suppose, what with one thing and another –"

"What are you doing?" Camilla asked through a puff of smoke.

"*Twelve Pound Look.* Barrie," Beth said. "I don't suppose . . ."

"I do know it, as a matter of fact," Camilla said. "I don't know why she thinks I'm such an ignoramus," she said to no one in particular.

"You, Camilla?" Beth laughed. "You're anything but that."

"Where are you moving to?" Jackie asked, suddenly but pointedly.

"Me? Oh, to Brampton Hall – do you know it?"

"Oh, that lovely old place? The Georgian house – up the lane, what's it called . . ."

"Turpin's Lane," Camilla said succintly.

"Yes, that's it. Oh, how lovely. How lucky you are to be moving there."

"Well, let's say I hope to move there," Camilla said. "If all goes well." She stubbed out her cigarette and made to move.

"Well, I must make tracks," she said, stretching herself.

"Oh, but I was just going to make tea," Beth said. "You'd like a cup before you go, wouldn't you?"

And Jackie took the hint.

"Look, I must be going too – it's nice to have met you, Camilla," she said, holding out her hand, which Camilla didn't appear to see. "I hope we meet again. And thanks, Beth, I'll see you tomorrow then – around ten-thirty?"

"Yes, that's fine – I'll come and see you out."

When Beth returned, Camilla had made herself comfortable again on the chaise.

"You're not going yet, are you?" asked Beth.

"No fear. I'm waiting until Marc comes in – besides, I hoped you'd ask me to stay to dinner."

"Of course you can stay!" Beth laughed. "Well, what did you think of her – Jackie?

"I thought she'd never go."

Beth laughed. "She's lovely, isn't she?"

"If you like the type," Camilla said. "Ugh – all that smarm!"

"What smarm? I thought she was rather nice. A bit – sort of – lost."

Camilla sat up straight.

"Lost? Jackie? Oh, come on, Beth!"

Freddie came running down to them, his hands dirty and sandy and wet, pulling a face.
"Yuck," he said.
"Exactly my sentiments," Camilla agreed.

Chapter Seven

Lucy Gilbert, driving home from town where she had stayed overnight with her mother, saw the white Mercedes parked outside the front door of Brampton Hall. She had no desire to meet the people viewing the house – it was more than she could bear. Surely they wouldn't be long?

She drove down the lane and back through the village until she came to the new development she had seen earlier in the month, curious to know what they were doing. Parking the car, she walked along the lane alongside Tom Bird's Little Field, reading the huge notice board. So these were the new retirement homes for the elderly. Well, they were nicely tucked away and would do no one any harm. She wondered what the people in the large house next door thought of it all. What a difference it would make to their lives.

Already, the narrow lane was churned up and it only needed heavy rainfall to make the place a quagmire. Still it was harmless enough. The foundations were going down, and the development would be quite small and on two floors. You could hardly give old people lots of stairs to climb. Yet they did in high rise flats in London. She shivered at the thought. There should be a law aganst things like that. Peering through the laurel hedges she decided that the house next door was hardly visible through the trees, and wondered idly who lived there.

Men were working on site, stripped to the waist, with long hair and bracelets that glinted in the sun. She got the usual catcalls before she decided that she had seen enough to satisfy her curiosity and, getting back in the car, drove towards Brampton Hall, hoping that the people had gone.

She saw the car, a noticeable white Mercedes sports, driving away in front of her. Well, they would need plenty of money to keep the Hall going, as her father had found to his cost.

She let herself in as Mrs Clayton came to greet her.

"I waited until they'd left," she said with a smile.

"Mrs Blakeney brought a friend with her – the vicar's wife from St Luke's in the village."

"Oh, so she's not a complete stranger to Ainswick?"

A faint perfume lingered in the hall, and Lucy wrinkled her nose trying to think what it was. Oh, well, it didn't matter. They were strangers from London, no one she would know, according to the name given by the estate agents dealing with the property. Not that Lucy knew anything about house prices, but she was sure they were getting a bargain.

But she had come back to do a job, and that was to sort out her own finances after talking things over with her mother the previous evening. She unlocked the door to her room, and thought how unfamiliar it looked with the small pieces of furniture that were hers bundled together against the bed, her packing cases alongside. On the bed she laid out the things she would deal with first. Bills. Local bills. She had money of her own, thanks to her grandfather, and more to come when she was twenty-one, so she could perfectly well afford to settle the bills that were worrying her. If she was to stay in Ainswick, and she wanted to, it was only fair to pay outstanding accounts herself. The dress shop, for instance, the wine merchant, and Mr Patel, the grocer. Other outstanding bills for the upkeep of Brampton Hall must be left to the people dealing with her father's estate. Mr Mansfield said she didn't have to deal with accounts, it was up to her.

Well, she had decided she would. It would be a great relief, and help to restore her self-confidence. She would be able to hold up her head again. Especially, she thought, in front of that nasty partner of his, Philip Sanderson. Superior clot.

Having sorted out whom she would pay, she made out the cheques, feeling very businesslike and important, and heaved a sigh of relief when it was done.

She was more than grateful to Mrs Clayton for agreeing to

stay on to look after her until the house was finally sold, postponing her own plans. She would have hated to stay in the big house alone, and Mrs Clayton had been quite firm in her offer to stay on for a while. It was the least she could do, she'd said.

This weekend Lucy would be returning to London to stay with her mother again. Hardly a flat, Ariadnes was an apartment on two floors in Cadogan Square, a gift from her father to her mother when they celebrated their twentieth wedding anniversary.

Well, at least her mother was as happy as a sandboy up there. Some of the furniture had gone with her, and some been sent to auction, which would come up sometime in June. There was nothing left that Lucy herself wanted. She had kept only the things that belonged to her.

She looked around the room and across the gardens, at the well-kept lawns and flower beds. Dear old Charlton. She hoped the new people would keep him on. He had worked at Brampton Hall for longer than she could remember. He had always been there.

Well, it was no good crying over spilt milk. She had to start her life anew, and even without what she was used to, she was still fortunate. What had that young man said? "Some people never get what they want." That was true, but it didn't give him the right to judge her.

She had been lucky that Jack Dulverton had given her a job of sorts, helping out with the riding school, for he was always short handed at the weekend and she quite enjoyed seeing to the young riders. He had also allowed Daisy to bed down with the other mares, so that was a great help.

She had thought of suggesting to him that she put the little money she had into enlarging the riding school, and was still thinking about it. She had no desire to act too hastily, and at the moment everything was ticking over. One of the first things was to see Mrs Mansfield, at her husband's suggestion, for it seemed Mrs Mansfield knew what was going on in the whole village, and would know first hand of a small property that might be available to buy. But if she did that, then there would be no money to offer Jack for the riding school, and she would have to find another job.

You would be quite surprised, Mr Sanderson, she thought, how very careful and enterprising I can be.

She decided to walk on this lovely morning, and made her way down the lane and through the village towards Manor Lane where the Mansfields lived, hoping to find someone in.

The door was opened by a middle-aged woman wearing a flowered overall.

"Good morning. I'm looking for Mrs Mansfield. Is she in?"

Shirley Dinsdale saw a pretty young girl standing there whom she recognized by sight as the Gilbert girl. She was even prettier close to than seen from a distance.

"I'll see if she can see you." Shirley Dinsdale was used to people coming to the door of Hunter's Lodge. There was always somebody wanting something.

She poked her head round the door of the study, where Peggy was knee deep in pamphlets and council papers.

She looked up with a frown.

"Excuse me, Mrs Mansfield – a young lady to see you. I think it's Miss Gilbert.'

The frown disappeared. "Oh, show her in, Mrs Dinsdale. Take her into the drawing room, and tell her I'll be with her in a moment."

"Will you come in, Miss?"

"Thank you."

"Mrs Mansfield won't be long."

Lucy followed her into the drawing room, which looked as if it was seldom used. On this bright and sunny day it was cool. There was no feeling of warmth or welcome, and Lucy, who was sensitive to atmosphere, was surprised since the Mansfields were known to be the good samaritans of the village.

Peggy, her little nut brown face beaming, showing strong excellent teeth, went towards Lucy, hands outstretched.

"My dear, I am so pleased to meet you! I feel I know you so well, and yet we have never met. Do sit down.'

Lucy was struck by her appearance, so unexpected. Strange how when you knew only the husband, you felt you knew what his wife would be like. She couldn't have been more wrong. For Peggy Mansfield was small and vivacious, with a little pug-nosed face and bright dark eyes, and a clear forceful voice, a voice with authority.

"How do you do, Mrs Mansfield? Your husband said you may be able to help me."

Peggy sat down opposite her. What a pretty thing!

"Yes, well I hope so. Dennis told me about you, and I've been scouting around. If I don't know what's available in the area, then no one does! I've lived here all my life, so you see . . ."

"Have you? Well, so have I," Lucy said, and at that Peggy laughed, a loud, joyous sound that immediately put Lucy at her ease.

"Could I get you some coffee?"

"No, really, thank you. I shall be going back to lunch soon."

"You're still living up at the Hall, I think Dennis said, and you're working at the riding school?"

"Yes, Jack Dulverton has given me a job, temporarily, and housed my mare. It's just for the time being until I decide what to do."

Peggy had no intention of discussing private business with the girl. It was more than she dared do, which pleased Lucy.

"Now, what exactly are you looking for?"

"Accommodation, mainly. A little flat or tiny cottage – I'd rather that, if possible – somewhere of my own, in or outside Ainswick. It doesn't matter about it being in the village, and I like the country."

She'd got some pluck, considering her background, Peggy decided. Not in the least like her mother, thank goodness.

"Well, believe it or not, I've been looking around and I've found three. Perhaps not at all what you are looking for, two in Ainswick and one on the road to Milney Hatch. That's a farmworker's cottage – not much in the way of mod cons, I'm afraid, but if you were stuck . . ."

Lucy already had the feeling she was in safe hands. This was someone ready to help her.

"There's one in Shoe Lane, a tiny place, two up, two down. It belonged to old Mrs Bagshot who has arthritis very badly and has gone to live with her daughter. When the retirement homes are built she will move in there, but at the moment her place is empty. Normally, of course, you wouldn't find anything in Ainswick for love nor money, but there you are, this recession does some people some good. The other one is part of Smethwick Grange, at the other end of the village. Some years ago it was divided into three, and one apartment is available on the first floor. You do get a little garden. Not much, but I don't suppose you are bothered about that."

"Oh, but I am," Lucy interposed. "Does the cottage have a garden?"

"Tiny," Peggy smiled. "There's not much difference in the price, it's a question of personal choice. The one advantage to The Grange is that you have a garage, whereas at the cottage you would have to leave your car outside."

All these things to be taken into consideration, Lucy thought, when all her life she had taken things like space and garages and central heating for granted.

"Oh." And as if reading her thoughts, Peggy added, "There's no heating in the cottage, only a coal fire. All right in the summer, my dear, but in the winter – brrrr!"

"When could I see them?" Lucy asked. Already she felt a glimmer of excitement.

"Whenever you like. They're all three empty and I have the keys to two of them. What about the farm cottage out on the Milney road? I have to say it is rather isolated, and not somewhere I would like a daughter of mine to live."

"Well, I have a dog," Lucy said doubtfully.

"Look at the others first." Peggy beamed. "See what you think. I'll just go and get the particulars. Are you sure you won't –"

"Yes, really, thank you."

Through the window she saw a bright red sports car pull up, and a man stepped out, tall and dark-haired. He made his way to the front door, let himself in, and Lucy heard him call: "Mother?"

"In here, dear," she replied, and came out to meet him.

Then she was in the room with Lucy, smiling and handing her the particulars.

"Now, my dear." And almost immediately she was followed by her son, a tall man who stood close behind her, smiling warmly at Lucy. She saw Peggy's frown quickly replaced by a swift smile of politeness. Lucy saw a man of around thirty-five, handsome, with eyes just like his mother, dark and intense. If there was a flaw in his good looks, it was around the mouth, which showed a certain weakness, but he was very attractive for all that.

His voice was low and deep.

"Aren't you going to introduce me, Mother?"

There was the briefest pause, then Peggy smiled.

"My son, Malcolm," she said. "Malcolm, this is Lucy Gilbert, from Brampton Hall. She is looking for a cottage in the area, and I have been lucky enough to find something which might suit."

"Oh, well done." He smiled at Lucy, and took the papers from his mother. "Are these they?"

He ran his eyes over them as Lucy waited.

"Yes, dear," Peggy said. "I – er –"

"Well," Malcolm said, "there's no time like the present. I should be delighted to escort you, Miss Gilbert. There's nothing like a bit of experience when it comes to choosing a home."

"Oh. Well, I –"

"Do you have the keys, Mother?" He towered above her and looked down upon her warmly.

"Well, of two of them – not the apartment."

"Then that will do. Come, Lucy, my dear," he said, and she found herself escorted down the path.

"We'll go in my car, shall we?" he asked, while Peggy, for once in her life lost for words, stood behind the curtain in the drawing room, biting her lip.

Out through the village and on to the open road, Malcolm felt the old thrill of the chase. Beside him, this deliciously pretty young girl – somehow all was right with the world when he had a girl at his side. Sort of thrown into his lap, far too young for him, but what the hell? He was only trying to help. Impossible to imagine this young thing looking about on her own.

"It's awfully kind of you," Lucy said, unsure whether she was pleased or not. "I hope I'm not being a nuisance?"

Malcolm laughed out loud. "My dear young lady, it's the

least I can do. I am in my own field, you see – as an estate agent."

"Oh." Lucy was surprised. She hadn't expected that somehow. "Are you in business around here?"

"In town – in the West End. Brook Street to be exact." It always sounded good when he said it.

"So what are you doing down here?"

"Visiting the parents – ah, this looks like the place." And he pulled up in front of what looked like a derelict cottage on the Milney Hatch road.

It looked as if it were falling down. Boarded up windows and the path to the door almost completely grown over. Lucy looked at it in horror. There was nothing else in sight.

Malcolm smiled kindly at her and patted her hand.

"Don't worry, my dear. This is not for you. No point in getting out – I'll turn round and we'll go and see this one in the village."

Back into the village and up narrow Shoe Lane where a row of cottages faced each other, built of mellow stone, and looking slightly tumbledown. Lucy's spirits began to rise. This was more like it.

Malcolm stopped the car, and looked at the particulars. "Number four – a few doors up, I think. This is it."

Lucy thought it was just what she imagined, and hoped that the interior would be just as nice as outside. Malcolm unlocked the door and they were inside a small front room which was fairly awful. It smelled musty, lino on the floor and tattered home made rugs, two wooden armchairs and a little black fireplace, a mantelpiece full of odds and ends and a black marble clock. Lucy felt a twinge of pity for the old soul who had had to leave it.

Malcolm's fine nose twitched slightly, but undaunted he went through another small room to the kitchen which was minute and held a yellow stone sink and had a back door into a small garden. Going outside, there was a privy covered with virginia creeper, a lilac tree, and masses of flowers.

"Oh!" Lucy cried. "This could be quite sweet."

"Hmm," Malcolm said severely, back in the kitchen, his frown showing his real feelings. "This, of course, is a scullery, no more no less. Let's go upstairs."

A door in the kitchen led to a narrow staircase at the top of which were two bedrooms, one either side of the top of the stairs. Lucy looked around in confusion. "No bathroom?" she asked. "No loo?"

"My dear young lady," Malcolm admonished, "You expect too much." But he smiled at her, and wondered how much money she had to put things right, for of course it could be made into a super little property.

Downstairs again, he looked around, taking it all in and making rough estimates as Lucy went outside again.

"Keen on gardening, are you?" he asked when she came back in.

"I don't know – I never realized I was, but somehow having a garden is important."

"Let's go and see The Grange, shall we? We can't go over it, but at least we can see the set-up."

The Grange was exactly as Lucy remembered it from seeing it when she came down into the village. A large rambling old house, with overgrown shrubberies and laurels, a driveway up to the house which was almost concealed from the road.

He parked the car and they got out. Referring to the agent's blurb, Malcolm looked up. "Well, it's on the first floor, up there, where the bay windows are." He walked to the front entrance, the door of which was open to expose a large hall. On the side there was a list of three names and a bell beside each one.

He looked at her, and she turned from the house to look at him, then slowly shook her head with a smile.

"Not for you," he said, and Lucy shuddered. "No, I just couldn't live here."

"Then hop back in the car, my dear," he said. "It seems that out of the three, only one is a possibility – what do you think?"

She put on her seatbelt. "And even that's doubtful."

He glanced at his watch. "Half twelve," he said. "What about a pub lunch in the village?"

Lucy, about to refuse, wondered why.

"That sounds tempting." She smiled. "As long as you let me buy the lunch – it's the least I can do after all your help."

"Nonsense," he said. "My pleasure. After all, you are my first client."

She stole a glance at him. "Really? How's that?"

"I've just sold my business in Brook Street, and I'm thinking of opening up down here."

"Goodness, that's brave of you."

"Well, I can't say I haven't had the experience – there's nothing like a stint in the West End to sharpen the old wits. Ah, what about this? Will it do?"

He had stopped outside The Jolly Farmer, and Lucy remembering past meetings there with friends after riding, smiled up at him.

"Super."

They found a corner in the dark oak-panelled little pub, and Malcolm handed Lucy a menu.

"I think I'll have a roast beef sandwich and a glass of red wine," she said, handing it back to him.

"Good choice. So will I," he said, and went to the bar to get the drinks.

Looking at his back view Lucy thought what a fine figure of a man he was. Broad-shouldered, straight-backed with a good head of dark hair. Not in the least like his father, though.

"Here we are then," Malcolm said, putting down the glasses. "Let's drink to success in finding what you want."

"And to yours as an estate agent," she reminded him.

"Thanks – yes, it's just an idea at the moment, I haven't thought it through yet, but it's on the cards. And what about you? How do you feel about the cottage in Shoe Lane?"

"I think it's a great idea," Lucy said as the waitress brought the sandwiches. "Of course, I have no idea what it would cost to do up."

"No, but you could leave that to me to sort out. I've had a lot of experience in renovating and doing over properties."

"Oh," Lucy said, impressed.

"Again, it depends how much you're prepared to offer," he said, his fine dark eyes looking into hers.

He had nice eyes, she thought. It was a pity there was something about him she was not quite sure of. He was a charmer, even her inexperience told her that.

"You mean, it's not necessary to give the asking price?"

"Good Lord, no!" he laughed. "You must take into consideration the money you would have to spend on it. If you are seriously interested, I'd deal with it for you."

"Would you? You've been very kind, giving up your time which I'm sure must be valuable."

"Not at all," he said warmly.

"Are you married?" Lucy asked casually, finishing her sandwich and wiping her hands on the paper napkin.

"Divorced," he said ruefully. Once, twice, what did it matter? he asked himself.

There was sympathy in Lucy's grey eyes. "I'm sorry. It must be a traumatic experience."

"It is," he said sorrowfully, and his brown eyes darkened. "You go into marriage, hoping that it will be forever, but somehow, and it's neither's fault . . ." Which was nice, Lucy thought, that he didn't totally blame his wife. He sat staring into space for a moment, before turning to her with a smile.

"And what about you – are you engaged? A boy friend?"

"No."

"A pretty girl like you?" He shook his head in disbelief.

"Another wine – sandwich?"

"No, thank you, really. I must be going. Thank you for lunch."

"I'll run you home," Malcolm said.

When he had dropped her at the hall, he got back in the car and drove himself post haste to Cheltenham where he called at an estate agent's on the other side of the town.

Handing in his card, which seemed to impress them with its Mayfair business address, he withdrew from his pocket the particulars of the apartment in Smethwick Grange, Ainswick.

"Still available, is it?" he asked.

"Yes, sir,"

"I'd like an appointment to view," he said. "As soon as possible."

"It's empty – we have a key," the agent said. "If you'd just give me your name and address?" And looked at his appointment book.

"Four this afternoon?"

"Excellent," Malcolm said, "I'll see you there." And he left, climbing back into the scarlet Porsche, watched by many envious eyes.

Chapter Eight

Malcolm dropped his bombshell over dinner that evening. He waited until they were eating one of Mrs Dinsdale's excellent apple pies before telling them.

"I'm thinking of buying an apartment at The Grange," he said. "Ainswick," he added, so that there would be no mistake.

His father poised, his fork halfway to his mouth, while his mother stared at him in disbelief.

"Ainswick?" she found herself saying just in case she had misheard him.

He finished his apple pie and put down his fork and spoon. "Yes, Mother. The apartment at The Grange – the one you mentioned to Lucy – Lucy Gilbert."

"Oh," Peggy said, for there seemed nothing else to say.

"Well," Dennis said at length, "with the idea in mind, I imagine, of not returning to London?"

"Exactly," Malcolm said, glad to have got that quite straight. When his father said nothing, he realized that it was up to him to give an explanation.

"I think I told you, Father, that I had accepted an offer for the business?"

"Yes, you mentioned it," Dennis said drily. "I had no idea it had progressed so far."

"Oh, yes, it's been going on for some time but I finally clinched it last week, and then when Janice walked out, I thought, oh, what the hell – what has London ever done for me?"

He looked from one to the other but they apparently had no answer so he struggled on.

"Anyway, I've been giving it a lot of thought, and I came up with the idea of opening up here."

"What – here?" Dennis asked.

"Why not?"

"Well, for one thing, I doubt if there is sufficient business here. Also at the moment, with a deflated market . . ."

"Oh, that'll pick up," Malcolm said complacently, and Peggy thought that was one thing about Malcolm, he was a born optimist.

"You'd have to get planning permission," Dennis said. "Had you anything particular in mind?"

"Yes, that little corner shop – a gift shop. Didn't the old man die, I seem to remember?"

"In that case, you'd want permission for change of use," Dennis said.

"Naturally. But there's no problem, is there?"

"Well, your mother's chairman of the planning committee, and you can't ask for more than that."

"Also I've done a few deals – had a hand in a few developments – the sort of thing which has come off."

"Then you've been lucky," Dennis observed.

"After all, I've got to have a base somewhere, and I feel I am due for a change."

But not right under my nose. Peggy could almost hear Dennis's unspoken thoughts.

"Look," she said, getting up from the table and collecting the dishes, "I'll get coffee and you can both sit and talk it over. I'm all right dealing with financial problems if I am not directly concerned, but when it comes to family . . ." She smiled apologetically.

Malcolm threw her an indulgent smile, as she disappeared into the kitchen.

After she had taken the coffee tray into the dining room she made her way to the study with a cup for herself, and sank into the big leather armchair. Stirring the coffee, she gazed out of the window, not seeing the horse chestnut trees with their spires of pink blossom, the vivid yellow of the brooms and laburnums and the white lilac of which she was particularly fond.

Instead, she saw herself as a girl of almost eighteen, living at St Luke's Vicarage with her parents, without a care in the world, soon to be going to university. All the world lay in front of her. To pass the few weeks she had to spare, she had taught English at the local village school to older children, and it was there that she had seen Robin Spick for the first time.

He was fifteen, big for his age, and handsome as only a gypsy can be, with jet black curly hair which he wore long, even in those days. He had dark olive skin, and wore a single gold earring. The most arresting thing about him were his eyes, of a strange gold colour, with the longest and thickest lashes she had ever seen.

Looking young for her age, even then, she was petite and small-boned. The class must have thought she was ripe for a ribbing, and had been a little surprised when she managed, through sheer force of character, to keep them under control. But she was always aware of the boy, as she called him. Indeed the headmaster had thought it prudent to warn her.

"They're quite a handful," he had said. "Especially young Spick. So don't put up with any nonsense, Miss Durrant. Just refer them to me."

There was something about the way the boy kept his eyes on her during class. Intently, as though he was absorbing every single thing she said. Sometimes the glimmer of a smile would come to that beautiful mouth, and Peggy felt a stab of pleasure.

She discovered that he belonged to one of the worst families in the village. His father had ostensibly been a farm worker, but when he was sacked, refused to give up the tied cottage and lived there with his wife and lots of children as squatters – all of them, so the teachers said, as good-looking as the boy. The mother was thought to have been Irish, for she had the Irish colouring of green eyes and black hair. Now her hair was grey and she had grown very fat, and went from village to village selling pegs and dusters.

A dreadful family, was the general summing up.

But the boy disturbed Peggy, especially when, after class, he waited behind and asked her questions, standing next to her, closely, and not taking his eyes off her face. It was as if he was too near, certainly too near for comfort, but she couldn't interpret her emotions. It was seldom she found herself at a loss, but she did whenever Robin Spick was near and didn't know why. She as not a sexually aware girl, yet he disturbed her, and once or twice his lips would curve into a smile as if to say, Don't think you can teach me anything – you're not much older than I am.

Which was true. So that when the time came to leave, she was sad yet pleased to have that small part of her life over and done with. His face would appear to her every now and then at first, from out of nowhere, which disconcerted her. Then with college, and working hard and exams, Robin Spick faded from her mind . . .

She looked down at the empty coffee cup, surprised to find she was holding it, and put it down, so carried away with her thoughts she had forgotten where she was. She could still hear them talking in the dining room, and almost as a kind of self-punishment, brought out from her memory things she hoped she had forgotten.

It was seven years before she saw him again. She was twenty-six and had been married to Dennis for five years – years when she had been busy at first with teaching and then throwing herself into the work of helping the village in any way she could. Charities, the Church, local clubs, committee meetings; she had a natural flair for organization and helping others.

In the autumn term, she had been holding an evening class for adults who wished to improve to read their English and the small class met on Tuesday evenings at the barn. Dennis never minded when she was out of the house in the evening, he had so much to do himself; like her he was on various committees and the local council. So that when one late-summer evening she saw this very expensive-looking car driving through the village – she learned later that it was a Bentley convertible – she was shocked to hear that Robin Spick had returned to the village and that the car belonged to him.

She was not surprised, though, when the following Tuesday he appeared in her class and explained that now he had got on in the world, he was anxious to learn, to be educated.

He belonged to a family who never put anything more than a cross when asked for a signature, and she had thought that Robin would carry on the tradition. There was a limit to what a certain kind of mind could absorb, and she had thought he belonged in that class.

But it seemed that she was wrong and he had other ideas, for he explained that he had made a great deal of money doing various deals, and assured her that knowing how to read and write was the least important part of that – but now that he had established himself as a rich man, he needed to be educated. He felt, he explained, that she would be the right person to teach him.

Trying to regain her composure, for he had disconcerted her more than somewhat, a fact that she was only too ready to admit, Peggy suggested that he went to adult evening classes.

That's what he thought he was doing, he explained, and she could not put the thought from her that this was not the sole reason for his being here.

Now that she had fallen in love and married, she knew what fatal attraction was, and recognized it in herself and suspected it in him.

There was a sheer animal magnetism in him that sparked off something in her, but for a long time she fought with herself. She could do no more than accept him as a pupil anxious to learn. After all, the class was made up of adults from various walks of life, there was no good reason why she should single Robin out and refuse to teach him.

Sometimes the sheer proximity of him was enough and she wondered how long she could go on, short of resigning as a teacher to that particular class. Sometimes she caught him looking at her with a kind of challenge, daring her to back out of what seemed an impossible situation. He knows, she thought, he knows what I am going through. I am like a fly caught in a spider's web.

All this time she kept the home going, doing her good works and keeping busy, yet praying for Tuesday evenings to come round so that she might see him again.

As the evenings got darker, and October made way for November, she had reached an almost impossible situation.

She could not fault his behaviour as a pupil for he absorbed avidly everything she had to say, concentrating hard, his wonderful eyes following her, then the blackboard. He seemed genuinely to want to learn. But it was the undercurrent, the things unsaid, that were the worst.

As the nights drew in and darkness fell, it was not long before he was giving her a lift home, although at first she refused. But not too strongly, she thought now. He had been circumspect, opening the door for her to alight before driving back to Cheltenham where he apparently lived.

She could remember that evening as though it were yesterday, and the date. A misty evening, the twentieth of November – she should know, it was important. He had driven past her house and up the lane, and she hadn't stopped him, her heart beating fast enough to choke her. It was an inevitable as night following day.

What followed she would remember until the day she died. Never had loving Dennis been like this – and yet she had known it would never happen again. There was no way she would allow it to. It had been so overwhelming, so passionate, arousing depths in her she had never dreamed possible. Had it been the same for him?

She would never know, for after that night she never saw him again. He disappeared, forever it seemed, out of her life, and sometimes she wondered if that was all he had ever wanted. To tame her, to bring her to heel, much as he might a tinker's dog. She, the vicar's daughter. And through that one act of folly and lust she had ruined three lives. Her own, Malcolm's and Dennis's.

For, of course, she found herself pregnant, and could only wonder through those long months of waiting whose the child would be, knowing deep down that it was Robin Spick's, the gypsy's child. Dennis was overjoyed at the news, but so guilty had Peggy felt that her whole attitude towards him changed.

She had gone to church and prayed for forgiveness for her wantonness and unfaithfulness, and explained to Dennis that, owing to certain physical problems, they would be unable to make love during her pregnancy. He accepted this quite naturally. Only after the birth, when she told him that having a child had put her off the physical side of their marriage, did he find difficulty in accepting her decision. For a long time things were strained between them.

The baby, a fine boy, looked like his natural father, as Peggy had known he would. But her own father had had the same kind of looks, so it was not unreasonable to suppose that the boy took after him. Dennis was delighted with his son, overjoyed, and then came the hardest part of living a lie, times when she thought she would have to run away, so deep was her guilt at her deception, so much did she despise herself for her deceit.

They continued to live separate lives, working for others, the boy taking his place in the community with no one ever having any suspicion. He went to boarding school, with Peggy dreading any signs from him that he was going to be like his father.

It was inevitable that he would be. Malcolm was in one scrape after another, causing concern to his parents from the time he went to school until he left to make his way in the world.

She couldn't count the number of times Dennis had got him out of trouble, and each time the agony for Peggy was worse. She made a vow that if Malcolm ever did anything really to disgrace Dennis's name, then, and only then, would she tell him that Malcolm was not his son.

It was like something you read in a book only you might not believe it, she thought, staring out into the garden. Far-fetched, you'd have said. Yet truth was stranger than fiction, and it was Dennis her heart went out to.

She stood up wearily, her back and legs stiff from sitting down so long, and could hear that the conversation was more desultory now. She was full of aches and pains. I'm getting old, she realized. And we need rain. Everything is so dry. A good downpour – we need the rain. It would freshen everything, especially the lilac. You couldn't have lilacs without rain, it just wasn't right.

"Well?" she asked brightly, returning to the dining room. "Got it all sorted out?"

Malcolm was looking pleased, which meant he had talked his father round into agreeing with whatever he had in mind.

"Yes, I think so," Dennis said, but he looked tired, Peggy thought. "He might be on to something, I suppose, and The Grange seems a good idea. It seems a reasonable price for what it is."

"Oh, that's good," Peggy said, her heart sinking at the thought of Malcolm being under their feet.

"Well, I'm for bed."

Long after they had gone to bed, Peggy lay awake, thinking. And yet, as she knew, there was nothing she could do. Once a thing was set in motion it would carry on in its own inexorable way. Try as she would she could find no good reason for Malcolm's re-appearance, and knew without doubt that he was up to something. Yet, was she misjudging him? Perhaps it was the girl he was after? She wouldn't put it past him even though he was so much older, but she was sure of one thing. Malcolm had something up his sleeve.

Chapter Nine

Beth Pennington made neat little piles of the church magazine on the hall table, ready to be distributed. Marcus had gone over to his other church, the small and ancient St Paul's in Milton Hatch, which was in his parish. She hoped one at least of the church ladies would help her with the magazines for she was short of time with the one act festival taking place at the end of the month. Marcus was right, there was precious little time for rehearsals with all that she had to do.

June had come in, as sunny as the end of May, and Ainswick promised to be a riot of colour. Outside on the rotary drier, the clothes she had put out early were ready for ironing, and she collected them in the basket and put them on the washing machine. Tonight was rehearsal night for the Ainswick Players and fortunately her part was so small. She'd had no difficulty learning the lines. But she still had to be there, to turn up for rehearsals; it was of paramount importance.

Glancing at her watch, she saw that she had almost an hour before picking up Freddie. She collected her magazines and made her way to the front door.

When she opened it she was surprised to see Jackie Hetherington standing there, rosy-cheeked and a little flustered.

"Oh, Beth, I am so sorry to trouble you, but I had nowhere else to go."

"Jackie! What is it?"

"Could I come in?"

"Of course you can." And Beth closed the door behind her.

Jackie glanced about her, wild-eyed. "Oh, you were busy, I shouldn't have . . ."

"My dear, it's quite all right," said Beth, feeling at her most maternal. "Come in and sit down."

Jackie gave a little sniff and dabbed at her nose, her lovely eyes filling with tears.

Beth waited, gaze full of sympathy.

"Well, you see," Jackie gulped, "I don't know if I will be able to go on with the play . . ."

"The festival play? Whyever not? What's wrong?" Beth asked, full of concern.

"It's a long story," Jackie said, and took a deep breath. "You see, my husband, Tony, is very difficult – he's forbidden me to act or do any stage work." And the tears ran freely down her face.

"But, Jackie!" Beth cried. "Why? What reason does he give?"

"Jealousy," Jackie said simply. "Pure jealousy."

"Oh, surely not." Beth said, although what other reason could there be?

"You have no idea what he can be like. When we came here it was only because he would have me tucked away, in a country village, and I wouldn't be able to do anything like this. And then when he found out –"

"What do you mean – found out?"

"Well, I had to tell him. He's away a lot, travelling in the States, the Far East – you name it,"

"So what does he expect you to do while he is away?" Beth was outraged.

Jackie shrugged. "Stay home and keep house."

"But that's archaic," Beth said. "You've no children?"

Jackie shook her head. "We had a little girl – she died."

"Oh, I am sorry!" Beth got up and went over to the sofa. "I had no idea. My dear, how awful."

"Oh, it was a long time ago – five years – in the States, but ever since then he's become more and more impossible. He won't allow me to have a job."

"Jackie! That's dreadful. Why do you put up with it? Why don't you leave him?" Beth asked. There were limits, she thought.

"I've tried, but he always brings me back."

She raised great green eyes and damp lashes to Beth, who found it almost impossible not to give her a hug as she would have Clarrie, her daughter.

She sighed.

"Oh, Jackie, I am so sorry – I had no idea."

"No one has any idea," she said, sniffing into her hankie. "I've tried, Beth, honestly, but I get so bored. He won't even let me have a dog."

"Good Lord!" said Beth. "He may be your husband, Jackie, but he sounds like a monster. Tucking you away – burying you. That's no good. How long have you been married?"

"Ten years."

"And you've stayed with him all this time? Jackie, I can't help feeling the law would be on your side." She had a sudden thought. "Do you love him?"

"I did. I suppose I still do in a way."

"He has no right to monitor your every move. What do you do all day? Have you tried to get a job?"

"He wouldn't hear of it! You don't need it, he says. We don't need the money."

"That's not the only reason," Beth said.

"Well, he's right of course. We don't need the money, he has a well paid job – but it's not that. I need an interest – that's why I joined the Ainswick Players without telling him."

"How did he find out?"

He came back unexpectedly one evening and found me learning my lines."

Had he – could he – have come back to trap her? Beth thought, outraged. Surely this sort of thing didn't go on in this day and age?

"You see, I don't know how I am going to carry on with rehearsals. I knew I was taking a chance at the time, but I thought I could manage to fit it in. Once or twice I told him I was going to aerobics – he doesn't mind that."

"Oh, I see. That's all right. In other words, he has to vet whatever you are doing? That's no kind of marriage."

Jackie suddenly collapsed against Beth. "Oh, I'm so unhappy!"

Beth put an arm around her. "I can well believe it!" she said grimly. "Look here, I'll go and make us some coffee – I think we both need it."

Drying her eyes Jackie sat up, and Beth thought she had never seen a prettier picture. Of course she was a beauty, that ghastly husband could well be jealous of her every movement, but in this day and age that sort of behaviour didn't have to be tolerated.

Shuddering to herself, she went out into the kitchen.

"I've been thinking," she said when she returned, putting the tray down, "why don't you consult a marriage guidance counsellor?"

Jackie's eyes were wide. "He'd go mad! He would be furious. I couldn't possibly –"

Jackie really seemed afraid of him, Beth thought. She poured out the coffee and handed it to her.

"Whereabouts do you live in Milney Hatch?"

"In Manor Lane – one of the new houses."

They were very nice, Beth thought. Expensive, Tudor-style houses with every modern convenience. Jackie probably got through her chores in no time. What did she do with herself all day?

"Do you like gardening?" she asked presently.

Jackie shook her head. "No, no interest at all."

This seemed an impossible situation, Beth thought. How did one deal with it?

"So what are you going to do about rehearsals? There's one this evening."

"I know," Jackie said. "There are only two more before the dress rehearsal – I suppose I'll just have to play it by ear." She sipped her coffee. "He's gone off today to London where he has various meetings. He won't be back until Saturday."

Beth was thoughtful "You know, amateur dramatics aside, marriage shouldn't be like this," she said. "I know every marriage has its problems, but yours seems particularly fraught. Especially as you're only doing what you are good at – it would be a terrible waste to have to give it up now." She smiled. "I think we stand a good chance of winning the festival with this one."

"Really, Beth, do you?" Jackie's eyes shone.

Poor little thing, Beth thought, feeling quite motherly towards her. What a terrible life.

"Where did you meet him – Tony?" she asked.

"Well," Jackie said, almost guiltily, "That's part of it, you see. I was an orphan . . ."

Beth's eyes were wide.

"And I went to him for a job – he was in charge of an hotel then, and gave me a job on the reception desk. I'd had no experience, but he took a chance, and we've – he has never looked back. He's in charge of the Grandida Hotels Group."

"Golly!" Beth said, impressed. "That's quite a job."

"Yes. So you see, I owe him. I know I do, I realize I wouldn't be where I am today if it weren't for him."

"But that doesn't give him the right . . ." Beth bit her lip. "You don't come to church, Jackie, do you?"

"No," she said. "I don't have any beliefs. Besides . . ." And she hesitated.

"Besides what?" Beth asked.

"I couldn't very well. Tony is Jewish."

"Oh," Beth said. "And you didn't –"

"Become a Jew? No."

Beth brought herself back to earth with a jolt, and glanced at her watch. "Gosh, is that the time? It's almost twelve. Jackie, I'm sorry, I have to fly."

"Of course," she said, getting up swiftly. "I shouldn't have stayed so long – thanks for listening, Beth."

"It's the least I can do," she said. "I'm glad you told me, and if there is anything else I can do – do you think you will be along this evening?"

"Yes, I'm sure I will. Tony's away until the weekened, so I'm quite safe."

Beth gathered up her purse and cardigan. "Look if you think it might help, have a word with Marcus – my husband. He's a dear when anyone needs a spot of help, and he would be only too glad to listen."

"I'll remember that," Jackie said, her green eyes on Beth's. "But you won't tell anyone, will you? I'd hate anyone to know."

"Of course not," Beth assured her. "Your secret is safe with me. Except for Marcus. You wouldn't mind if I wanted to have a word with him about it, would you?"

"If you think it would help," Jackie said, her lip quivering, and bent quickly to kiss Beth's cheek.

"Thanks again. I'll see you this evening."

Beth walked along to the nursery school, totally preoccupied with the story she had just heard. When she saw Freddie standing with his hand in the teacher's waiting for her, she felt a surge of thankfulness for all that she had. A loving husband, two nice children. What bleak lives some people led.

Later that day, when she had bathed the children and put them to bed, she went into the study where Marcus was dealing with church matters. He looked up, his pleasant face breaking into a smile.

"Are you off, then?"

"No, darling, I have a quarter of an hour yet, if you have a moment to spare? Something happened today. You remember I told you about Jackie Hetherington, the new girl, the one with the leading part in our play?"

"I do indeed."

And she told him most of what Jackie had told her, and watched his face grow more and more serious with everything she said.

"I felt I wanted to help her, but how, Marcus? What could we do?"

He looked at her. "Not a lot," he said. "Her best bet would be the Marriage Guidance Council."

"I said that, but she was horrified. She said he never would forgive her."

"I think," he said slowly, "you are also hearing one side of a story."

"Marcus! How can you condone behaviour like that? The poor girl is almost out of her mind."

"Yes, I can imagine. But, Beth . . ." He looked at her pretty face, saw the consternation written there, the depth of feeling that had been aroused by the girl's story, and knew that this would not be the first time she would be tormented by concern for others, it would be something as a vicar's wife she would have to learn to take in her stride. In a larger parish, like the one he had held briefly in Stoke Newington in London, she had not been called upon for personal help, she had merely been one of the women church members who worked on behalf of its parishioners in the best way they knew how. To pacify her was the best thing he could do now.

"I'll give it some thought, darling," he said, "and of course, if she would like to come and have a word with me, I will only be too glad to help."

"Bless you, Marcus," she said, kissing him swiftly. "I knew you would."

They were all there, the members of the cast of *The Twelve Pound Look*, and other members besides. The props girl, the prompt, the secretary who was to order the costumes for the play, the member who worked in a printing firm and who ordered the programmes and tickets, Arthur Lang, looking very important in his navy suit and cravat, his silver hair gleaming, and, Beth felt, wearing a little stage make up to subdue his colouring.

When they had all finished talking, Peggy regained order and you could have heard a pin drop.

Beth, her mass of fair hair pulled back, stood on the stage, Geoffrey kneeling at her feet as she held a stick over him, about to tap his shoulder. On the night, it would be a handsome sword. Glancing towards the wings, she saw Maggie sitting there. She winked back, prompt book in her hand. Was Jackie here? There was the sound of a door being closed and a muttered apology.

"Sorry, Peggy. I got held up."

Beth heaved a sigh of relief as she saw Jackie make her way behind the stage.

"Arise, Sir Harry," she said, only to be stopped by Arthur who promptly explained how it should be said, then the play went on. Beth's part was small and she quickly retired and sat watching as Jackie made her entrance, announced by the butler.

Beth was engrossed. Jackie was magnificent. Just the right kind of smile as she peeled off her gloves – not pretend gloves, she was wearing real ones – and Beth realized you could have heard a pin drop. Even Geoffrey's performance was better than she had ever seen him give. Oh, she was sure it was going to be a winner!

During tea break, she had a word with Maggie. "Jackie's good, isn't she?"

"Yes, she is," Maggie said. "And word perfect – she doesn't give me anything to do. I might as well get off the stage."

"Oh, don't do that!" Beth laughed. "You never know with Geoffrey . . ."

She saw Peggy watching, her dark eyes intent on the performance, and her approval as with each line Jackie made her point, scoring over the pompous new knight to be.

Arthur Lang's face wore a look of triumph.

I bet he never imagined we'd be as good as that, Beth thought. Let's just hope Jackie can go through with it.

Chapter Ten

A builder's skip stood outside the little cottage in Shoe Lane which had recently been purchased by Lucy Gilbert. Inside, the dividing wall had been knocked down to make a through room, and the skip was full of rubbish: old lino, mats, bricks and old pipes. A WC sat in all its dubious glory on top of the pile, leaving passersby in no doubt that the little house had been gutted.

From time to time Lucy went along to see how things were progressing, but most of the work was being organized by Malcolm, who had been, she had to admit, a tower of strength.

It was halfway through June and the country had continued to enjoy lovely weather. The sun shone every day, the tourists flocked to the village, and there was a warning from the local water company that water would be in short supply that summer if the dry weather continued.

Every evening, people could be seen with watering cans spraying fuchsias, geraniums, window boxes and baskets, for by the end of the day the flowers were wilting and it wouldn't do for visitors to Ainswick to be disappointed at what they saw. It was one of the picture postcard villages of the Cotswolds, and it behoved the residents to be proud of it and present it as such.

Lucy was on her way to the solicitors to finalize all the business transactions which she had made in her own name. The purchase of the cottage had gone through with no setbacks, and now she had the final sorting out of her private affairs. She was a little disappointed to find that Mr Mansfield had deputed the appointment to Philip Sanderson, his junior partner.

Oh, well, she sighed, can't be helped, and thought of the weekend visit to her mother in town. Ariadne had thought Lucy quite mad. First of all to stay in Ainswick, then to buy a miserable little cottage. What could she be thinking of? Well, on her own head be it, was her mother's final comment.

Strange, Lucy thought. She had never been close to her mother, perhaps because they were so different in temperament. After all, she would have felt stiffled where Ariadne lived in London, although it was a luxurious apartment and close to Hyde Park. But the air was different there, and whenever Lucy went to London she couldn't wait to get home.

She was shown into Philip Sanderson's office to wait when she arrived, since he was just seeing off another client. She looked around her curiously. It was a nice office, with his name on the door and the shelves lined with books. He had a very fine old desk which was leather-topped, there were filing cabinets on one side of the room, and two large comfortable leather chairs.

Lucy, however, sat in a high wing back chair. She felt more in charge of the situation that way.

"I'm sorry to have kept you waiting, Miss Gilbert," Philip said, coming in and holding out his hand. She took it, and found her hand gripped firmly, somewhat to her surprise.

"Don't apologize – I'm sure you must be very busy," she said politely. His very presence did something to her, made itself felt, she thought, and she wasn't sure whether she felt dislike or interest.

He sat at his desk where, she thought, he looked quite impressive, every inch the solicitor, with his horn-rimmed glasses, the grey eyes behind them impersonal yet intelligent as they looked at her across the desk.

"Well," he asked in a very avuncular way, "and how are you getting along?"

Perhaps he is one of those people who have never been young? thought Lucy, thinking of the difference between him and Malcolm who at thirty something or other managed to keep a juvenile outlook and was always ready for a bit of fun. This young man couldn't, she thought, be much more than twenty-six or seven.

"Very well, thank you. Thanks to Mr Mansfield's son, who has been most helpful with the cottage." And she saw a very disapproving look come over Philip's face, and wanted to smile. What a stuffy thing he was!

"Yes," she said, warming to her subject and wanting to tease, "I don't know what I would have done without him."

"Oh – good," he said. "You seem to be happy with your purchase of the cottage?"

"Yes, it's sweet," Lucy said. "I know I'm going to be happy there. It's a dear little house."

"Quite a change after Brampton Hall?"

"Oh, not to be compared," Lucy agreed. "My life has taken a very different turn since my father died."

"Now, there are one or two things – you will be glad to know that the sale of Brampton Hall has gone through without any problems – the purchasers, a Mr and Mrs Blakeney from London, being delighted, so I am told. They intend to move in on completion day."

"I'm so glad," Lucy said, feeling desperately unhappy at the thought of strangers living there.

"We have written to your mother to notify her of the situation, and of course this all helps the liquidators."

Lucy sat silent. I suppose he had to mention them again, she thought.

"Now – about your own affairs. Fortunately, you are in an advantageous position thanks to your paternal grandfather who left you various legacies, the main one of which is due when you reach the age of twenty-one."

Lucy nodded

He consulted his files. "Just around fifteen months to go."

"Yes."

"Until then, you might find yourself a little hard pushed, although now you have bought the house, at least you will have a roof over your head. Are you still working at the riding stables?"

"Yes, temporarily," she said. "I shall have to find myself a more lucrative job, I think."

"Perhaps that would be wise. In the meantime we are holding the deeds to your cottage, and if there is anything we can do to assist you, please let us know."

He actually smiled at her across the table.

Lucy stood up. "Thank you for your help."

"Not at all, Miss Gilbert," he said, and walked her to the door, shaking hands once again.

Outside the door, Lucy felt like stamping her foot. What was it about him that annoyed her so?

She got into her car and drove round to Shoe Lane, her eyes lighting up as she saw the men carrying hods of bricks on their brown shoulders, burned by the sun which shone down full strength at midday. She wouldn't get out now but carry on to the riding school, where she knew Jack was taking four children from a Cheltenham home for the handicapped. The look on their faces as they sat on a horse was something to see, and she knew Jack would be glad of some assistance.

Outside the riding stables a large yellow notice had been pinned. Parking the car, she got out to read it. It announced that the Festival of One Act plays was to be held on the twenty-ninth of June at eight pm. The Ainswick Players were entering *The Twelve Pound Look* by James Barrie and the adjudicators were three famous names.

Well, Lucy thought, that might be interesting. She would make a note of it. After all, she was going to have to get down to life as it was lived in the village, and the sooner the better.

Peggy Mansfield made her way home after pinning up the last notice about the festival. It had been quite a walk, but the riding stables was the last call. They had already sold a lot of tickets, but you could always do with selling more.

Walking through the High Street, she stopped for a moment outside Ye Olde Village Gift Shoppe which had been closed now for some months, ever since the owner, old Bill Purchase, had died and his widow moved away. It was a nice little shop, single-fronted and not very big inside. Still, if that was what Malcolm wanted, she supposed it would do. An estate agent didn't require much room, and it would be good to see the shop in use again. An empty shop window was inclined to look depressing, and thank goodness there were not many in Ainswick. She hoped for Malcolm's sake that he was on to a good thing. All the property sales in the area had been covered by large agents in Cheltenham, but there was no reason why that should always be. Malcolm must have made a success of the Brook Street business to have been able to sell it for a profit.

A lot of the briskness had gone out of Peggy's step, for until he got settled, she seemed to be walking on hot bricks. Dennis had taken the idea very well, considering all things. His only stipulation was that Malcolm's new business did not bear the name Mansfield. He said it was not a good idea for established solicitors in the village to have a connection with a house agent.

Peggy wasn't sure about that. Still, if that's what Dennis wanted, Malcolm would have to agree. "As long as you have the certificate up in your place of business," Dennis said. "Malcolm Mansfield trading as . . . whatever you want to call the business."

"Right," he had said. "Will do."

A week to go, Peggy thought, and she was getting really excited. Saturday week, with two rehearsals to come, the final one on Friday. Oh, it was all going to be fine. She was willing to bet that the Ainswick Players would win. How could they not with their newest star, Jackie Hetherington in it? She had even brought out that ghastly little Geoffrey Latimer. Peggy would never have suspected he had it in him. Alistair, of course, was always excellent, and Beth quite delightful.

"Well, Mother," Malcolm said, when she reached home. He looked pleased with himself, she saw. Father has received the contract for me to buy the apartment in The Grange. It's not bad at all: two bedrooms, a very large living room, kitchen, bathroom, and garage which is a boon for the old Porsche in the winter. And I knocked them down ten thousand."

"I'm sure you did."

"It's freehold, you know, which is quite unusual in that situation," he went on. "They've left the carpets, which are not bad, so –"

"You're on your way," Peggy finished. "Will you bring down the furniture from your flat?"

"Of course," he said indignantly. "If Janice walks out on me, what else does she expect me to do?"

"I just wondered," Peggy murmured.

"And what do you think of this?"

He drew out a card.

Brooke & Street, she read. Estate Agents. High Street, Ainswick, Glos. And looked up to see him grinning.

"How about that?" he asked.

"I think it's called 'jumping the gun', but I have to hand it to you, Malcolm. When did you have those done?"

"Collected them this morning from the printer's," he said. "What do you think?"

"An inspired choice," Peggy commented.

"How long do you think I shall have to wait for planning permission? It can't take long, surely?"

"No, I'll try to bring it up at the first opportunity. I can't see any problems.

He came over and hugged her. "Good old Mum," he said. "What would we do without you? Got to pop out for a bit," he continued. "I'll be back about six."

He was probably going to find Lucy, she thought, and that was another worry. Still, she must stop fretting – no good would come of it. It was a fruitless pastime.

Malcolm walked briskly along the High Street until he came to the avenue where the new development was taking place. They had made remarkable progress; of course, the hot dry weather had helped. Up to roof height, rows of holes for windows, nicely laid red brick, and openings for doors. My word, it would be finished in no time.

It wasn't the first time he had been along here. He had spent quite a few hours surveying the area, especially the house next door, which looked ripe for developing. God, what a dingy place. Surrounded by trees, dark and depressing, and a hideous old house – he knew because he had gone farther up the lane and looked around it. If he remembered correctly, a retired general had lived there. Surely he must be dead by now?

As he saw it, the place should be pulled down. A handsome block of flats could be built on the site. It wasn't as if they hadn't already started to develop. Or, come to that, four or five new houses. Smart modern homes. He was sure there would be a demand for those. Two or even three bathrooms, double garage . . . he could just picture it. Yes, he would think there would be quite a demand for those. Or perhaps flats. Less aggro with a block of flats . . . Well, there was no time like the present.

He smoothed his hair and straightened his tie, and made his way up the drive of The Cedars. It got worse, much worse, as he went on. The house itself was almost submerged in shrubberies and laurels. He found himself in a huge porch, tiled, with a mansard roof. Pulling himself up to his full height, he rang the bell.

He had a long wait, but eventually he could hear low voices in the hall, and presently the door was opened by two elderly women who looked as frightened as a pair of mice.

He gave them his best smile to inspire confidence. It usually worked and he saw one of them relax a little.

"Yes? What do you want?"

"I am so sorry to trouble you, ladies, but I wanted to speak to the lady of the house."

"Didn't you see the sign on the gate?" Lydia asked. "No Hawkers, No Circulars."

"No, do you know, I didn't see it," he explained regretfully, "and I do apologize for the intrusion." He looked across at the development. "That must be ghastly for you," he said sympathetically.

"It is," Edith agreed, and Lydia threw her a warning look.

"What do you want?" Lydia pressed.

"My card," he said, handing it to her as though on a gold plate.

Lydia read it while Edith tried to see. Then Lydia looked up at him enquiringly. "What is it you want?"

"Perhaps I could come in and have a little chat?" he said, and knew he had done the wrong thing for Lydia held the door firmly and almost began to close it.

"Certainly not," she said. "And if you don't go at once, I shall call the police."

Malcolm gave them his most winning smile.

"I can see I have called at an awkward moment. That was not my intention." And he looked so sorrowful and so apologetic that Edith almost gave him a comforting word, but one look at Lydia's face and she knew that wasn't on.

"I am opening up an estate agent's office in Ainswick, there has long been the need for one," he said confidentially, "and if I may be of any use to you in the future, ladies, please let me know. This house, for instance, would command a high price – a very high price," he said, with a knowing look. "And if you needed someone to negotiate the figure – after all, ladies must be protected – there is nothing like a local man. By the way, the General, God bless him . . ." and waited for them to tell him that he had passed on. But at that moment there came the sound of banging on the floor above the hall, a rapping peremptory noise, and Malcolm realized that this was not the case. The General was indeed still with them.

Now they looked agitated, and Lydia handed back the card as if it were a hot cake.

"Oh, please keep it," Malcolm said politely. "You may –"

"No thanks," Lydia said abrupty. "Good morning." and closed the door in his face.

Well! he thought. What a pair of harridans. Still, you never knew. Stranger things had happened. And he made his way back up the drive not in the least put out. Homework, he told himself. The most important lesson he had learned. Always do your homework. An optimist by nature, he had high hopes. The old dears couldn't last forever.

After they had seen to their father's needs, and scuttled back down the stairs, they sat in the kitchen.

"Do you think he really was an estate agent?" Edith asked fearfully.

"Don't be stupid – there isn't one in Ainswick," Lydia said.

"But his card, and he did say he was starting up . . ."

"A pack of lies, I daresay," Lydia said grimly. "I'm wondering whether I should call the police. I would if it weren't for Father getting into a paddy."

"Oh, Lydia, we don't want that," Edith pleaded.

"No, you're right."

They busied themselves in the kitchen preparing their father's midday meal.

Presently Lydia said, "I have been toying with the idea of extra locks and bolts on the front door for some time."

"Oh, have you, Lydia?"

She did so admire her sister's strength.

Chapter Eleven

"So how many tickets do you want for the festival?" Peggy asked, coming across Malcolm in the kitchen busily talking to Mrs Dinsdale. He was such a social animal, she thought. He'd make conversation with anyone.

Malcolm frowned.

"The what, Mother?"

"The festival of one act plays – Ainswick Players – Saturday," she explained succinctly.

"Oh, I don't think so. I've got –'

She looked genuinely sorry. "That's a pity, I only have about ten left of our allocation. They've sold quite fast."

"Well, it's not really my kind of thing, Mother."

"Nonsense," Peggy snapped. "You should support your local societies."

"It's just that –" He hated to disappoint her.

Now she looked annoyed. 'Very well, Malcolm. But I think you would have enjoyed it. We have quite a bit of local talent in the society, especially the new girl – Jackie Hetherington. Every bit as good as anyone you might find on the professional stage."

"All right, Mother, give me one."

"Two, surely? You wouldn't want to go on your own?"

He smiled. "I'll have two. I can always give them to someone if I can't use them."

"That's the spirit," she said heartily, "and I'll have the money now, please."

She gave him the tickets, and he read them.

"Oh, very swish. Cheque do?"

"No, dear. Cash only."

He stuffed his hand in his pocket and brought out the money. Come to think of it, he might just as well use both tickets. Perhaps Lucy? The girl in the bar at The Lamb? No, perhaps not. Everyone knew her.

Peggy sailed on with her eight remaining unsold tickets. Philip Sanderson . . . now there was a young man good for two, even if he did only bring his mother.

"Good morning, Philip!" she said brightly when his secretary showed her into his office. "Isn't it a lovely morning?"

"Good morning, Mrs Mansfield. Yes, it is. "And he wondered what she could possibly want with him.

"Philip, I'm sorry to intrude but I wondered whether I could persuade you to buy a couple of tickets for the festival of one act plays in Cheltenham?"

His heart sank. "When is it?"

"This Saturday at eight o'clock," Peggy said. "The Ainswick Players are entering the competition, and we need all the support we can get. Can I persuade you to buy a couple of tickets – more if possible?" And her small bright eyes smiled into his.

To buy two, he supposed, would let him off the hook even if he didn't go, which he had no intention of doing anyway.

"Yes, I'll have a couple," he said, and Peggy was delighted. "Oh, thank you, Philip!" Only six more to go.

"I think your mother would enjoy it," she said happily, and he was immediately annoyed that she would think he had no one else to take except his mother. He would see about that. He might just shock her by taking a girl – Lucy Gilbert? – and was irritated yet again by the amount of time he spent thinking about her.

"Well, here you are then, Philip. I hope you enjoy the show."

Humming to herself, she went on her way. Now for a call on Marty Forsdyke who lived a way out of the village in St John's Farm.

No longer a farm, only the farmhouse itself remained, surrounded by a small pretty garden. It was one of Peggy's favourite places in the village, and although she'd had misgivings when she heard an American had taken over the farm, she was more than pleased when she met Marty and her husband. They took an enormous interest in the old building which dated back to the fifteenth century, and had spent a great deal of money on renovations and repairs.

When Marty opened the door, Peggy's nose was assailed by what she always called the American smell, a mixture of apples and polish, scented candles and dried flowers. The vaulted ceiling held up by ancient oak beams housed a minstrel gallery and the great room below was furnished with old colonial furniture and some early-American pieces from Marty's home town of Blessings, in South Carolina, while the walnut furniture came from Alistair's former home in Devon.

The great front door opened straight into the big room, and just inside was an early-American oak cradle on rockers which Marty had filled with African violets in all shades of mauve.

"Oh, Marty!" Peggy cried with delight. "That is simply lovely – how clever of you. And how on earth do you get them out all at the same time?"

"No problem," Marty said. Peggy had grown very fond of her, for she was forthright and called a spade a spade. You knew where you were with Marty. Plump to the point of being fat, she was casual in her dress and manner, and defied anyone to be shy or nervous with her.

That, though, had never been one of Peggy's problems.

"Marty, my dear, you mentioned an after the show party."

"Why, isn't that on?" she asked.

"Of course – I'm delighted. But it is rather a lot to do. You'll be busy watching Alistair, and then . . ."

"I have wonderful help as you know, Peggy, and I shall have prepared it all by then. You just have to tell me roughly how many to expect. I don't need you to count them exactly."

Peggy laughed. "Well, the cast, and whoever else you might like to come."

"Oh, everyone!" Marty cried. "I love giving parties – the more the merrier. I shall have open house so that anyone who wants to come, may."

Peggy was shocked. "You might be sorry! No, I think you should limit it, to say friends and relatives of the cast. And allow for a few extra. Say . . ."

"Great," Marty said, her round face creased into a wide smile, her babylike skin slightly flushed. "That's that, then. Any more questions?"

"No," Peggy laughed. "It's very nice of you."

"My pleasure," she said. "I do hope it goes well. It should, don't you think? Arthur seems pleased."

"As well he might," Peggy said.

"And that girl – Jackie – she's a real find," Marty said. "I just hope . . .'

"What?" Peggy said curiously.

"Oh, nothing."

"You must have meant something."

"Well, I feel she is in some kind of trouble – no, not that, but there's something . . . she is a little fey, wouldn't you say?"

Peggy thought for a moment. "I don't think that, although I agree she is unusual. But she *is* an actress, and we all know what that means."

"I think what I meant," Marty said slowly, "was that I hope she is dependable."

"Oh." Peggy fell silent. The thought had never entered her head.

"Do have some coffee," Marty said. "I'm just going to make some."

But Peggy got up. "No, thank you, dear, I must be on my way."

What did Marty mean – dependable? That Jackie might let them down at the last minute? Oh, surely not? How awful . . . I didn't bear thinking about.

But then the final rehearsal came round on Friday, and everyone was there, full of nervous tension and pre-show nerves, any tickets Peggy had had over were sold, and any doubts that Marty had sown in her mind disappeared.

Beth took Jackie to one side before the rehearsal.

"You were marvellous on Wednesday evening, but how is it going? You know –" She kept her voice down.

"Well," Jackie whispered slowly. "I'm keeping my fingers

crossed. Tony flew off to Hong Kong on Thursday and won't be back until Tuesday of next week. And she gave a great thankful sigh. "Oh, so he won't be able to see the show?" Beth was disappointed. She had hoped to see this husband of Jackie's.

"Oh, my God, no!" she cried. "He wouldn't have anyway – you know how he is," she whispered in Beth's ear.

Beth bit her lip. It seemed to her such a strange way of going on.

"Good luck for tonight, Jackie."

"You too."

Peggy sat entranced, watching them go through the play word perfect, with no hitches. She knew Arthur would say that was a bad sign, but she had no such misgivings. People in the acting profession were notoriously superstitious.

She found Malcolm at home when she got there, talking to Dennis about his new apartment.

"How did it go?" he asked. "The play?"

"Well, it was wonderful – quite the best thing we've ever done. I think so anyway," she added hastily. "I really have enormous confidence in it. I'm sure it will win."

"Then if you say so, Mother dear, it will."

He was in a good mood, Peggy thought.

Later, going to say goodnight, she found him in the living room watching a late-night film on television. "You are coming tomorrow, aren't you?"

"Wouldn't miss if for the world," he teased.

"Who are you taking?" she asked.

"Little Miss Lucy Locket," he grinned, and saw the look of consternation that crossed her face. "Why, Mother, do I sense disapproval?"

"Malcolm, you're not being very sensible. Lucy is a very nice girl, but she is young – and vulnerable. She's had a rough time since her father died. I hope you won't start up anything foolish? She's far too young for you anyway, and I'm surprised that –"

He stopped her. "Mother, as if I would! She's a child."

"I'm glad you understand that. Poor little thing, she has been very brave – and I feel responsible for her in some way."

"Knowing you, that's not surprising. But have no fear, Mother, she'll be safe with me. I merely thought she would enjoy the thing."

"Yes. Well," Peggy said. "Goodnight, dear."

Oh, Malcolm, would he ever change? Then she consoled herself with the knowledge that Lucy was sensible, like her father – but look what had happened to him!

Philip Sanderson toyed with the idea of telephoning Lucy Gilbert for most of the evening, almost picking up the telephone on several occasions but finally deciding that he simply couldn't bear the idea of her refusing him, as he was sure she would. He could almost hear that well-modulated voice saying how sorry she was, could almost see the amused smile behind her words as she said it. Sorry, but she had a previous engagement.

Oh, what the hell! It was only a tuppeny halfpenny affair anyway, but he was determined to go. For one thing, he intended to show his partner's wife that he wasn't so hard up for feminine company that he had to take his mother. Mother, indeed! Still, he had to find someone, and it wasn't easy. He had spent so many long years studying to achieve his goal that all the girls he had known at school had either married or were living with someone or holding down high-powered jobs earning twice what he was. He made two calls on the off chance to old friends, with no luck, and had almost decided not to go at all when he remembered that Diana his sister, who was at university, was due home this weekend.

He sat thinking gloomily. Fat chance of her going anywhere with him. She always had heaps of dates, and anyway, he wasn't too sure he wanted to be seen with her. She was so way out, with her grungy clothes and hairdo and clompy shoes, she was sometimes not fit to be seen with.

But he finally decided that if she were amenable to accompanying him, he would take her. If not, he wouldn't go at all.

He waited until Saturday morning before he broached the subject, and then Diana looked at him in disbelief and said, "You have to be joking!"

"No," he said seriously. "I have two tickets, and I thought –"

"Sorry, brother," she said. "You can count me out."

Well, it was simple. He wouldn't go. The chance of Peggy Mansfield noticing his absence was slim, anyway.

It was just after two when Diana came in after meeting friends in Cheltenham. Throwing down her strange floppy hat on a chair, she glanced at him idly and began to examine her nails.

"What was that do you were asking me to?" she said.

"Oh, that," he said. "It doesn't matter. I'm not going anyway."

"Oh, I should, dear," his mother said. Her one prayer was that Philip would find a nice girl and get married.

"Well, I was just thinking – I wouldn't mind – be a bit of a laugh," Diana said.

"Really?" He couldn't believe it.

"Yes, why not?" she said flippantly. "What time are you leaving?"

"Around half-seven."

"Right. I'll be ready."

The car park was full, and so was the hall, with every seat taken and a general hubbub of excitement. The adjudicators' seats were empty for they usually arrived just a few minutes before curtain up. Most people were looking with interest at the programme. Three one act plays, to be given by the Ravenham Amateur Dramatic Society – and every one in Ainswick knew they were their biggest rivals – the Ainswick Players, and the Thespians, who were not quite so good as their name suggested.

There was a sudden hush in the hall as the adjudicators took their seats amidst applause, then the lights were lowered and there was total silence.

As the first play went on, there was much reflecting in the audience. Diana Sanderson was trying to catch a glimpse of Magnus Dimmock whom she knew was somewhere about. Earlier that day, in The Flagstaff in Cheltenham, she had heard him say he was going to the festival, and it was for that reason she had changed her mind and decided to go. She had always had a soft spot for Magnus, way back when she and a friend had played mixed doubles tennis with him and his partner. Would he remember her? She doubted it, but that didn't stop her from hoping he hadn't forgotten her. He had been with a different crowd in the bar at The Flagstaff that morning, but no one could help noticing that shock of reddish-blond hair, the fine eyes behind rimless glasses, the intellectual face.

At her side, Philip Sanderson was inwardly seething at the sight of Lucy Gilbert sitting next to Malcolm Mansfield. He had heard he was home, but to be escorting Lucy! Well, if that was her taste in men, it was a good thing he hadn't asked her himself. It was to be hoped someone had warned her against men like Dennis's son. Much as he respected and admired his senior partner, his approbation did not extend to the wayward Malcolm.

Lucy was wondering who the attractive girl was with Philip Sanderson. She was quite surprised to see him with someone so – well, so up to the minute with her mass of dark hair tied back, the black velvet band round her neck, the long dangly earrings. And she was pretty. Very pretty. When the lights went up in the interval she would get a good look.

She had seen Magnus Dimmock, too, one of her social crowd before her father's so-called disgrace. Strange how most of them had disappeared off the scene, but it was no loss. Magnus had always been on the edge of her small social circle. They rode sometimes, played tennis, his mother was a friend of her own mother. She wondered what he was doing now.

Gradually, her attention was drawn to the play, *The Fish*, which was coming over as an excellent production.

They were good, Peggy thought, as always, and hazarded a threat to her own players, as they always did. In her heart she thought there was no doubt about the outcome, but she could be wrong.

As the play came to an end there was loud applause, and presently the lights went up for the first interval. Most people kept their seats, especially the local Ainswick crowd who were feeling especially het up and impatient for their own play to begin.

When the curtain finally rose, there was applause for the set, a well-furnished drawing room, with the two players front left of the stage.

Watching her, Marcus thought Beth had never looked more beautiful. He had not yet seen her in the gown provided by Berman's, the theatrical costumiers, which enhanced her fair beauty. Her hair was swept up Edwardian-style, and her gown of ice blue duchesse satin was tightly waisted and floor-length. The bodice was encrusted with pearls and beaded embroidery, the sleeves tight, elbow-length and embroidered, while a lacy frill emerged from the cuffs. He glanced at his programme and saw that the period was 1912.

Over this Beth wore a floor-length sleeveless cape, heavily embroidered with coloured stones and velvet appliqué, and round her neck she wore a glittering necklace of fake emeralds. She was obviously intended to be the wife of a very rich man. In her right hand was a long paper knife which she held aloft, as her husband, Harry, soon to be knighted by the King, knelt at her feet.

He was a pompous little man anyway, and had been perfectly cast, but now he knelt at her feet in obeisance, head bowed, as Beth lifted the knife and tapped him on the shoulder.

"'Rise, Sir Harry –'"

It was obvious as the play went on that Harry thought himself the cat's whiskers, and that his wife was in awe of him. Beth played the part gently and diffidently as he showed off, watching him with nervous admiration. By the time the butler, Alistair Forsdyke, appeared at the door and handed him a card announcing the arrival of a young woman with a typewriter, the audience was enwrapt, and when Jackie came in as Kate, complete with typewriter, you could have heard a pin drop.

There was something magical about her, Peggy decided. You couldn't take your eyes off her. She drew you like a magnet, to the exclusion of anyone else on the stage – which wasn't always a good thing. She was a perfect contrast to Beth, the woman who had everything: money, jewels, a husband soon to be knighted. Kate, the typist, had obviously the need to earn a living, and that was no mean feat.

She wore a black bombazine suit, ankle-length, the jacket brief and tightly waisted, with a peplum. The sleeves were just below elbow-length to expose tightly buttoned white sleeves to the blouse which had a frilled bodice and high neck. She wore a black silk hat with a brim which had a frilled net edge, and below it her green eyes shone with confidence. Her bearing was regal, and she captured the audience's heart and sympathy.

She left both Sir Harry and Lady Sims far behind, never losing her confidence, aware of her superiority over them even as a mere typist. When the play came to an end, there was a moment's silence then the audience burst into rapturous applause and Peggy knew, without even seeing the next production, that the Ainswick Players would win.

In the interval most people got up and went for refreshments, talking nineteen to the dozen about the performance of the Ainswick Players' production.

Malcolm sat back in his seat, quite overcome with the performance he had just seen from Jackie Hetherington. What had his mother said? As good as any professional actress? Well, he would back her on that. Those eyes! The girl had a kind of animal magnetism. Now what could he find out about her – and how? Well, he would find a way, for to ask his mother too many pertinent questions would only alert her.

"Yes, wasn't it good?" he said to Lucy at his side, who by comparison was like a pink rose to an exotic orchid. Nice little thing.

"Shall we go for wine or coffee?"

"Yes, thank you. I'd like that."

They pushed their way to the bar, Malcolm some head and shoulders above many of the men, Lucy looking surreptitiously around for a glimpse of Philip Sanderson's young lady.

"Lucy!"

She turned to find herself confronting Magnus Dimmock who bent and kissed her cheek as he held out his hands to grasp hers. "Lucy, how nice to see you. Where have you been hiding yourself?"

"Oh, here and there," she said as Malcolm returned with two glasses of wine.

She took one. "Thank you, Malcolm. This is Magnus Dimmock, an old friend. Magnus, Malcolm Mansfield."

The men shook hands, Malcolm giving his smile to inspire confidence. He had many assorted smiles, and used each one accordingly.

"What are you doing these days?" Magnus asked.

"Moving house, mainly," Lucy said with a smile. "I'm buying a little cottage in the village – Ainswick village. Mother has moved up to London." And she sipped her wine. "And you, Magnus?"

"I'm busy with the gallery."

"Gallery?"

"I've opened an art gallery in Cheltenham. Doing quite well – modern art, you know."

"No, I didn't know, how interesting," Lucy said.

Malcolm had the sudden feeling that he could be better employed. "Excuse me," he said, and wandered off to look around.

"We must get together," Magnus said.

"Yes, that would be nice," Lucy said. "Presumably you're interested in amateur dramatics?"

"Yes, quite," he said. "Backstage, of course. The scenery, that sort of thing."

"Of course," Lucy said, suddenly realizing that there was much more to this acting thing than she had realized, and then the bell went.

She put down her glass and looked around for Malcolm whom she saw coming towards her.

Smiling, they walked together back to their seats.

After the excitement of the previous play, it was difficult to settle down and get involved in the last one, which was excellently done but not a patch on *The Twelve Pound Look*.

Then suddenly the suspense was over, and the adjudicators announced that the winners of the evening were the Ainswick Players with their submission of J. M. Barrie's play. Applause resounded and the cheers seemed to go on for minutes as the cast reassembled on stage and took their bows.

Peggy drew a deep breath. Her eyes misted over. Oh, she had waited and worked for this day!

Afterwards they all made their way to Marty and Alistair's house. Everyone seemed to be congratulating everyone else on a fine performance, and there was a mood of great hilarity.

"You're coming back with us, aren't you, Malcolm?"

"Thanks, Mother. Lucy?"

"Yes, please," she said, eyes shining. She was really looking forward to it.

"Do come," Peggy said to Philip. "I know Marty will love to have you."

"Oh, I don't think . . ." he began, but Diana interposed. "If you're sure, we'd love to."

She nudged him. "Don't be such an old stick in the mud!"

"Come on, everyone," Marty cried, gathering Magnus on the way. She put an arm around his shoulders. "He's a special friend of mine. I bought a picture from him the other day and he gave me ten per cent off."

Once back at the house Alistair opened champagne and they raised their glasses, all eyes on Jackie and the rest of the cast.

Lucy quite forgotten, Malcolm couldn't take his eyes off her. At the first opportunity he would go over to her and make himself known. She caught his eye and a look passed between them. Had it been possible, Malcolm would have rubbed his hands together. As it was, he licked his lips and broke into earnest conversation with his neighbour.

"Help yourselves, everyone – over here," Marty called, where a long table had been spread with a buffet meal. Her help from the village, Mrs Manson, stood at the top of the table to give everyone a hand.

At first everyone seemed reluctant to move away from Jackie who was the centre of attention. Don Frobisher, Maggie's husband, seemed quite taken with her, until Maggie pulled him away. "Come on, darling." Marcus put his arm around Beth and kissed her. "You looked so lovely in that wonderful gown," he said.

"Fine feathers make fine birds," she laughed. "Mrs Dinsdale came?" She usually babysat for Beth when needed.

"Yes everything's fine," Marcus assured her.

Philip watched Lucy, who had her eye on Diana, who waited for an opportunity to speak to Magnus. Beth went over to Jackie and took her arm.

"Are you all right?" she asked. Jackie looked at her, eyes wide.

"Me? Oh, yes – I'm fine, thanks. It was a wonderful evening, wasn't it?" she said wistfully.

"I think it was such a pity that your husband, Tony, couldn't have seen it," said Beth. "You really were quite super."

Jackie sighed. "Thanks. Still, I was lucky he was away, otherwise you know, Beth, I never could have done it."

"I suppose it's an ill wind," she said as they joined the queue.

There were dishes of salad and stuffed eggs, cornbread and waffles, southern fried chicken casserole, prawns and French bread, sliced cold meats and home made chutneys – a spread fit for a king, Peggy said.

Lucy found herself sitting next to Magnus on one of the old oak settles.

"I was sorry to hear about your father, Lucy," he said presently, and she looked at him gratefully.

"Thank you," she said. "Yes, it was awful."

"What are you going to do?" He seemed genuinely concerned.

"Well, I have to find a job of some sort – and that's difficult, never having had to do anything. I'm working at the riding stables for Jack, just temporarily until something crops up."

"And you're buying a cottage in the village? That seems a good idea. You didn't want to join your mother in London, then?"

Lucy shuddered. "No, thanks. I'd hate that."

"Me, too," he said, and moved up to make room for a pretty girl with long earrings and a floor-length waistcoat. He liked arty girls, and quite approved of this one. "Sorry," he said, "can you manage?"

"Yes, thanks." She smiled and they looked at each other.

"Don't I know you?" Magnus said, and Diana smiled again. He had remembered – well, a little.

"I'm Diana Sanderson. I'm here with my brother – over there, Philip."

Magnus glanced towards the corner and Lucy felt a strange sense of relief. Philip's sister!

"Didn't we play tennis together, a long time ago?"

Diana thought hard. "Yes, I believe we did." And they talked for a little as Lucy speared her cherry tomatoes and salad.

When Magnus turned back to her he looked serious.

"Do you know, Lucy, I've had a thought. How would you like to work for me in the gallery, say three days a week? Does that appeal?"

She was really astonished. "Well, of course it does, any job does, in that sense, but I know absolutely nothing about paintings – art –"

"Oh, that doesn't matter," he said. "You'd learn as you went along, and it's not boring, quite interesting really. You get some odd bods in a gallery – you might enjoy it."

Lucy was warming to the idea. She had to do something, after all.

"Come and see me next week and we'll talk." Magnus dived into his pocket and brought out a card, "Here's where I am. Say Wednesday – any time."

"Thanks," Lucy said, reading it. "I shall look forward to that."

Looking around to find her escort, she saw Malcolm making a bee line for Jackie Hetherington. She saw him look down at her where she sat, and Jackie look up at him with those wonderful green eyes that now looked inscrutable, although her lovely mouth broke into a smile.

Lucy scanned the room. Which one, she thought, was the husband?

Chapter Twelve

Sunday dawned with the promise of yet another warm and sunny day. The people of Ainswick were making their way to church and it was a day Granny Dorrington especially enjoyed, seeing them pass her cottage in their Sunday best, although things had changed. Nowadays they wore anything, often no hat at all, not like it used to be when she was a girl.

She would have liked to have gone, for she liked a church service and 'specially liked the young vicar, Mr Pennington, and his pretty wife. That was another thing. Vicar's wives when she was young all looked the same. Sensible women, middle-aged, you couldn't tell one from another. But this one was young and pretty – and kind. Beth often brought her a cake or something from the church sale, seeing as how she couldn't go herself. That was the trouble with growing old. If your legs got bad and you couldn't walk, what was left to do but to sit and look out of the window?

She saw Peggy and Dennis Mansfield pass by. She'd bet that son of theirs didn't go with them, although she'd heard he was home again. And that was another funny thing . . . And there was Mrs Pennington and the two children, young Freddie and the little girl. She looked forward to having grandchildren, though at the rate young Kylie was going on, she might never get any. Girls didn't seem to want to settle down these days. All they cared about was having a good time and their freedom.

The two Misses Pargeter . . . now they always looked nice, with their felt hats and tweed suits. Ladies, both of them. They were followed by Colonel Forsdyke and his wife. She'd heard they'd had a right royal party up at their house the night before, or so Shirley had said.

Not everyone in Ainswick was at church on Sunday morning. Lucy Gilbert was already up and at the stables with her mare Daisy who was so pleased to see her that she nuzzled into Lucy's neck every time she came near, as she groomed and brushed her down, and smoothed her lovely velvety coat.

"We're going for a ride this morning," Lucy told her, for of course Daisy understood every word. "Across the fields, and into the woods."

There was no one more surprised than Lucy when a figure walked alongside, drawing Fanfare behind him, Fanfare's black coat and the white blaze on his forehead making him an animal of some distinction. The rider was Philip Sanderson, dressed in jodhpurs and jacket, carrying his riding hat.

Lucy was so shocked to see him that she was speechless, and it was left to him to say, "Good Morning, Miss Gilbert," as he stopped beside her.

"Hallo," she said, still pulling herself together. Philip Sanderson – a rider? Yet he looked the part, very much so, and handsome, too. Away from the office, he looked like any other presentable young man.

She dimpled suddenly, and smiled. "I didn't know you rode?"

"Yes, it's my favourite relaxation at weekends."

"But you don't usually ride from here?"

"No, I learned at Cubitt's Riding School just this side of Cheltenham. I suppose I didn't want the local people to see me make a fool of myself if I fell off." He smiled ruefully.

Heavens, thought Lucy, he's actually human.

"Where are you off to now?" she asked him.

"I came to see if they had a spare ride, and ended up with Fanfare," he said. "He's a beauty." And he stroked the animal's nose.

"Yes, he is, and quite a handful."

He looked at her. "Oh, I think I can handle him." And the grey eyes behind the glasses seemed to see so much more than she wanted them to.

He took the plunge. "If you like, we could ride together? That is, unless you . . ."

"No, yes, that would be nice," Lucy said, preparing to mount.

In a flash he was up beside her, Fanfare with his head held high beside Daisy who whinnied and shook her head as they rode together, out of the riding stables and across the wide path at the side of the meadow.

The sun was warm on their backs as they rode slowly, each busy with their own thoughts.

Not for worlds would she ever know that his sister was responsible for his being there. Long after Diana had gone to bed, Philip had sat and thought about what she had said.

"You're keen on her – the Gilbert girl – aren't you?" she had said with sisterly candour. "Why on earth don't you ask her out – do something? Are you going to sit forever working in that damned office and seeing life go by for other people? You know, you've got a chip on your shoulder. I can't think why – after all, I come from the same family and I don't feel it. What does it matter if we come from another world? It's what we are that counts – look at me. I'm clever, and I shall do well at university. You're a qualified solicitor and junior partner in a good practice. Get out there and show them!"

She was right. He did feel bitter sometimes, about his father dying so young and his mother having to work, mostly in other people's houses. At the way she had had to scrimp and save to give them both an education. How guilty he had always felt at her having to. He'd worked extra hard to achieve results and compensate her. It was the old old story. Yet Diana didn't feel as he did. Perhaps it was because he was a man?

He had seen many girls and boys like Lucy while he was growing up. Good schools, fine homes, friendships with the right people – Philip had always felt an outsider. But Diana was right. He had to put a toe in the water to test the temperature.

As the path widened, he drew alongside, seeing the lovely profile, the small, straight nose and the fringe of dark hair above her eyes. After all, she had had her share of bad luck. It must be harder to have had everything and then lose it as she had done.

"What did you think of the play?" he asked, determined that he would keep Malcolm's name out of it.

"I thought it was wonderful – very professional," Lucy said.

"So did I. I must admit, I wasn't expecting anything quite so good from a bunch of amateurs."

"One of the things I enjoyed most," Lucy said, "was meeting people I had never met before – it was like another world. The generosity of Marty and Alistair, their friendliness." She didn't add that she had found precious little of that among their own friends since her father died.

He threw her a sidelong glance. Perhaps things had not been quite so comfortable as he had always thought?

"Have you got a morning off?" he asked. "I thought you worked at weekends?"

"I do usually," Lucy replied, "but Jack knows it's only a temporary thing, and I felt I must get away and have a real run out – it's such a wonderful day." She took a deep breath, for, suddenly, it did seem like a wonderful day.

"Shall we?"

Philip looked at her, his grey eyes actually smiling, and she nodded, giving Daisy a little shove with her heels and off they went, Philip reining Fanfare so that he wouldn't pass her.

The ride was exhilarating, across the fields until they reached the edge of Dorcas' Wood and reined in, both breathless with exertion. For a few minutes they sat silent to regain their breath, saying nothing, Lucy feeling as happy as she had ever felt since the death of her father. Presently, they rode side by side along the dappled path, where the sun made a pattern on the soft brown earth, and the trees joined above them in an arch.

Emerging from the avenue at the other side they blinked at the sun which, coming up to midday was now quite hot.

"I could do with a glass of water," Lucy said. "I think I'm feeling the effects of the wine I drank last night – I'm not used to it."

He smiled. "Let's go back, shall we? Perhaps we could have a drink?"

"Why don't you come up to the house with me?" Lucy

asked. She was tempted to tease him after his last visit to her home to see if his reaction was the same. "I won't be there much longer – and we might as well enjoy it. Mrs Clayton is staying on until I move out. That has to be the day of completion, doesn't it?"

"Yes, I think about the middle of July. Will your cottage be ready then?"

He wanted to keep off the subject of the cottage, knowing that Malcolm Mansfield had been responsible for a lot of the organization.

"I hope so. I can't wait to move in."

They arrived back at The Hall just before lunchtime, and Lucy poured them both a drink, sitting in the garden underneath a striped umbrella.

They sat for a long time saying nothing.

"This is beautiful," Philip said at length. "It must be very sad knowing you have to give it up."

He certainly has changed his tune, she thought, but appreciated it just the same.

"Yes. I've tried not to think about it – it hasn't been the same house since Daddy died, anyway."

"And your mother – how is she?"

"Settled in London where I suspect she would rather be, anyway." Lucy smiled. "I do hope the new people will take care of it and love it as much as we did. They are very lucky."

"Yes, they are," Philip said, surprising himself with the sympathy he now felt. It was almost as if she were alone in the world, though she certainly hadn't been through such a hard school as he had, having to fight his own battles and any odds that came along . . .

"So what are your plans?" he asked. "After you move in to the cottage?"

"I'm not sure. Magnus Dimmock – he's an old friend who was there last night – has opened a modern art gallery in Cheltenham, and asked me if I would like to work there for three days a week."

Philip felt a stab of envy, and frowned. "Does that interest you?"

"Not particularly, I know nothing about modern art. Still, it's a job, and a fill-in until I decide what to do with my life."

She turned to him and smiled.

"And what are your plans – are you satisfied with being a country town solicitor?"

"No, not totally. I intend to go into politics."

"Politics!"

"Yes – are you surprised?"

She thought for a moment. "No, not really. In what capacity?"

"As the next local socialist candidate," he said.

She laughed out loud. "Oh, Philip!" And his name came easily before she realised.

He smiled stiffly. "Have I said something funny?"

"No, of course not – I'm sorry – it's just that I suppose you didn't have to tell me, really." She bit her lip. "I suppose you feel you want to put the world to rights? It's very commendable."

"I just think there are a few things wrong with the present system," he said. "I'm all for fairness –"

"And justice," Lucy finished.

"Aren't you?" he asked.

"The terrible thing is, I've never really thought about it – never had to. I suppose if I did, yes, I think there are lots of things wrong – but can you fight them on your own?"

"I wouldn't be on my own," he said doggedly.

They were interrupted by Mrs Clayton telling Lucy that there was a telephone call for her.

"Right, I'm coming," she said, holding out her hand to him.

"Goodbye, Philip."

He looked straight into her eyes. "'Bye, Lucy. I hope we can do this again?"

"Of course," she said, and he watched her go before returning to his car parked in the courtyard.

His thoughts were mingled as he drove down the wide carriage drive. She had taken hold of a corner of his heart, he knew that now, and she was not at all the sort of girl he had always envisaged marrying – when the time came, much later on. But, well, there it was.

Waiting to pull out into the main stream, he stopped to allow a red Porsche go by. It had the roof down, and sitting by Malcolm's side was the green-eyed beauty of the evening before. He didn't waste much time, Philip thought wryly. Typical Malcolm.

Malcolm also had seen the car with Philip in the driving seat coming out of Brampton Hall. So that was the way the wind blew . . .

Well, he had other things on his mind, mainly the delectable little beauty at his side whom he had persuaded to go for a drive and a pub lunch. Poor little thing – some men were such rotters!

He glanced down at her. Her face had a nun-like quality under that headscarf – but there was nothing nun-like about that provocative mouth or those eyes. He wondered if she realised how ravishing she was?

He had persuaded her the night before to come out – and if her husband was away, well, more fool him. Leaving a wife like Jackie. But, of course, business was business, as every man knew. However, Malcolm doubted if he could have left her alone for long.

"I thought we'd drive a bit farther out – there's a nice little pub about five miles on."

"Whatever you say, Malcolm," she breathed in that dead sexy voice. It was enough to make a man tingle with desire. Low-pitched, soft and seductive.

She seemed almost lost, he thought, and so grateful for someone who took an interest in her. Just as she had been last night, pleased at all the adulation, yet never giving herself airs.

"Here we are," he said, stopping outside a delightful little pub, creeper-covered, with baskets and urns of flowers. It would have earned a prize in any competition.

Inside, Jackie toyed with the stem of her glass of red wine.

"I do appreciate this, Malcolm," she whispered, looking up at him with wide eyes. "You can't believe how boring it is being alone for days at a time."

He was going to joke: "And nights", but thought better of it. It was too early.

He touched her hand lightly in sympathy, then withdrew his own.

"And what about you, Malcolm?" she asked. "Is your wife . . ."

"I'm divorced," he said sadly, a small, rueful half smile on his lips, then putting up his hand to stem the flow of sympathy. "No, don't be sorry – it was one of those things. Not her fault." He sighed. "We were young, just not compatible."

Jackie looked at him sadly. "I do know," she said, and turning her head, bit her lip.

"You mean . . . ?"

Jackie looked down and nodded. "I'm afraid so."

"My dear," Malcolm said, "are you – er– going to divorce him?"

"I wish I could. I'm desperately unhappy."

"No children?"

"No," Jackie said sadly.

That was a consolation, Malcolm decided. It didn't do to have complications. Neither did he want to become involved in what might become a rather nasty divorce case. Play it carefully, old chap, he told himself.

Presently, she put a small white hand over his, causing his heart to lurch.

"Let's not talk of depressing things," she said. "Let's just enjoy the lunch and the drive."

Her green eyes were sparkling, now lifting his spirits which had begun to sink at the thought of possible difficulties. At first, he had thought she might be out for a good time, but now he wondered. She seemed genuinely unhappy, and it wasn't his particular forte to comfort damsels in distress – not unless there was something in it for him.

When he left her an hour later to get back into her car which she had left parked in The Lamb car park, she reached up on tiptoe and swiftly planted a warm kiss on his cheek.

"Thank you, Malcolm," she breathed, long lashes sweeping demurely down over those eyes.

He eased his collar.

He'd never met anyone like her before, and he'd thought he knew it all. Life was full of surprises.

He glanced at his watch. Just after two on a Sunday afternoon. Perhaps time to lay a few more trails . . .

He drove towards The Grange, quiet and deserted now with no sign of life, and no bicycle outside. He had made enquiries about the flat below and was told that an elderly widow lived there, a Mrs Hemingway.

He brought the Porsche to a standstill quite noisily, as he had intended, right beneath the front bay window, and rang the bottom bell.

The door was opened by a woman in her late-sixties, perhaps seventies, dressed in a nice afternoon dress, much as his mother might have worn. She had curly grey hair and bright inquisitive eyes which now looked a little irritated.

He leaned towards her. "Mrs Hemingway?"

"Yes."

"Good afternoon. I'm Malcolm Mansfield. My parents live in the village and I am in the process of buying the flat above."

Enlightenment dawned. "Oh, how do you do? Will you come in?"

"Thank you," he said politely as she closed the door behind him. He found himself in a large comfortable hall with a black and white tiled floor, leading through to a spacious drawing room.

"Do sit down," she said, indicating a deep armchair. "It's very nice of you to make yourself known. I had wondered when I saw the agent bringing people."

"Oh, I think it's necessary these days – one never knows," Malcolm said. "You can't be too careful." And his warm brown eyes looked at her kindly.

"While you are here, I might mention your car – that is your motor car?" she asked him, looking outside.

"Yes, indeed," he said with a proud smile.

"And very nice, too – but rather noisy," she said. "It is a sports car, isn't it?"

Malcolm nodded. "Yes, it is."

"Will you be putting it away every night in the garage? There is one, you know, did they tell you?"

"Yes, I did know that."

"Only if it's not put away, it might get stolen. Also –" and she paused before going on "to park it outside in the drive would be rather noisy, and as I don't sleep very well . . ."

"My dear Mrs Hemingway, say no more. Of course I shall try to be as little nuisance as I can." He looked around the room. "You have no burglar alarm or special locks. Is that wise?"

"Well, I have lived here a great many years, and up until recently I felt perfectly safe."

He shook his head sadly. "I'm afraid I would recommend all people living alone to have locks fitted, and an alarm." He could see now that he had her worried.

"Oh," she murmured, "do you think so?"

"If I may say so, I think you're jolly brave to live alone," he said. "Did you never think of moving up to the next floor?"

"No," she said. "I couldn't tackle the stairs."

"I see," he said sadly, and stood up. "Well, Mrs Hemingway," and he held out his hand, "nice of you to ask me in, and I can assure you that I shall be as little trouble to you as I can."

She seemed reassured by this, and led him to the front door.

"By the way," he said, "the people at the top of the house." And leaned forward to read the name. "The Littletons?"

"Oh, there's no one there," she said. "They left long ago. That's up for sale too."

"But you leave the name there . . ."

"I think it's safer." And she smiled confidingly. "People will think there's someone else in the house besides me."

"Good thinking," he said. "Well, thank you. I expect I shall be moving in some time in July."

"I shall be glad to see you, young man," she said, and looked quite pleased.

He started up the car with a roar, and as he waved saw the frown cross her face again.

Well, he had done the groundwork. There was no one upstairs, and she didn't like the noise of his engine – that was too bad. And he had certainly sown the seeds of doubt about her security on the ground floor. The next step was to enquire about the flat at the top. If he could buy that, he would be halfway there, but that would mean more borrowing. And in order to get the whole house he would have to suggest to the old lady that she would be more comfortable in a home or something of that sort. After all, he had no wish to be unkind.

He hummed a little tune on this fine Sunday afternoon. The Grange might be a better proposition than The Cedars for conversion. It was impossible to say how long the General would go on and those two daughters might well remain impervious to offers. He wanted to get his teeth into something big, and it was a strange thing but there was more going on up here than there was in London. He didn't think he'd had a dull moment since he'd arrived.

Chapter Thirteen

The fields surrounding Ainswick were parched and dry, large cracks appearing in the soil, while the gardens showed a lamentable lack of water in this hot July. Already there was a listlessness, a longing for a heavy downpour, and it showed in the windowboxes and tubs which needed to be watered so often, even the flowers that liked it dry like geraniums and petunias.

There was, despite the lethargy, a considerable amount of energy being expended, however. Up at Brampton Hall it was moving day for Lucy Gilbert and Mrs Clayton.

The small removal van had come to take the rest of Lucy's things and deposit them in the cottage, which at last was hers. Carpets had been laid over the wooden floors which had not been nice enough to leave bare, and the tiny back garden had been dug over by Charlton, the gardener up at the Hall.

Almost everything had been organized by Malcolm Mansfield, who since his return to Ainswick, had made himself known throughout the village and was a mine of information as to where to get things done.

His application for change of use from a gift shop to an estate agent had gone through with record speed, owing to the auspices of his mother who had pushed it through the council planning committee at the earliest opportunity. He had opened the small premises three days before, and already had an enquiry from a gentleman who wished to let his house on a six-monthly basis.

Now the name Brook & Street appeared on the window in

gold lettering, for Malcolm never did anything by halves, while inside was a desk for himself and one for staff, as he put it, although up to now he couldn't see his way clear to taking anyone on. All in good time, he told himself.

Peggy Mansfield passed the shop with misgivings. She was still not used to the idea of Malcolm's living under her nose. She couldn't wait for him to move into the apartment at The Grange which would be anytime now as there seemed to be no complications. And sometime this week she would call on young Lucy Gilbert. She was looking forward to that.

Lucy had been excited up to now about her new home, but when she saw the van depart with her personal possessions she shed an unexpected tear, much to her own surprise. She had dwelt so long on her new home that she had not given proper thought to leaving The Hall, but now, seeing her bedroom empty and awaiting newcomers that she didn't know, she felt a pang of emotion. Mrs Clayton too wept as Lucy bade her farewell at the railway station in Cheltenham en route to her sister's home. Having locked up the house, Lucy drove round to the estate agent and handed in the keys, then indeed feeling as though she was on the brink of a new life, she drove back to Shoe Lane.

The cottage seemed so tiny, especially with the furniture inside, and Lucy realized that she would probably have to let some things go. But it was pretty, and cosy, and the first thing she did was to take out the urn from the boot of the car and fill it with compost and plants that she had bought from the nursery. Standing it outside the front door, she thought, well, this is it. I'm in my own home, and we'll see what Ariadne has to say about this when she comes down on Saturday!

Going into her tiny kitchen she put the kettle on for tea, then gave Henry his meal in a new dish. He eyed it without interest, eyes drooping, and looking up at her reproachfully.

"Oh, Henry!" she cried, hugging him, and presently he sank down beside her, occasionally looking at her as though he depended on her to find the right answer to this strange sequence of events.

She was used to driving back and forth now, having started work at the gallery and finding herself quite enjoying it. Puzzled though she was by most of the paintings, she found them interesting, and the gallery itself was very pretty and inviting. Customers were few, but occasionally someone came in, and when they did they usually knew what they were talking about. Magnus himself was always out doing something or the other, he seemed to have his fingers in so many pies.

She sat in the gallery on the day after she had moved into the cottage, her elbows on the table, reflecting as she seemed to have had no time to do before, and facing yet another problem.

Up to now she had kept Henry, her beloved Labrador, but now that she was in the cottage, it seemed hardly fair to leave him so much on his own. The garden was tiny, and not at all what he had been used to. She needed a dog for company, but a little dog, perhaps. Henry was so big and lumbering now. What a pity that the new owners of The Hall couldn't have had him. After all, Daisy was all right at the stables, but Henry looked like a small horse in the cottage, and the thought of him being shut up in the house or left in that tiny garden worried her. When she'd left this morning, he had looked up at her with those great soulful eyes – oh, it was horrid, Lucy thought. She couldn't do it it him.

She sighed as the door opened and a customer came in, and wished in her heart that she had something more active to do for the gallery was a little boring. Anything would be better than moping about her past life at Brampton Hall.

Camilla Blakeney was already up there, seeing to a small army of electricians, men from the water company, gas meter men, carpet delivery vans from London firms – all in preparation for their move the next day – while Nick was in the solicitor's office.

She had decided to keep all the curtains and pelmets just as they were, and had had to buy several rugs since the flat in town had been close carpeted. The house seemed huge once the men had left, and she felt a brief moment of trepidation, wondering if she and Nick had done the right thing. It was such a contrast to where they had lived before. The very first thing she must do when they moved in was to find a housekeeper, or failing that a daily woman. Never keen on housework, the last thing Camilla intended to do was to try to keep house. The gardens, though, were another matter.

The gardens surrounding the house were a picture, thanks to Charlton who had agreed to stay on. A magnificent herbaceous border faced her, alive with colour. There were shrubs in every shade of green, while beyond the formal garden were fields just made for grazing horses. To say nothing, Camilla thought with pleasure, of the pool. She looked round the property and checked in all the rooms, setting the burglar alarm as she had been told to and closing the door behind her to drive down to the village to see Beth. Nick would arrive in his own good time, then they would drive back to London, to make the final preparations for tomorrow. It was found at the last moment that they could not afford to keep the flat, which had to be sold in order to buy the Hall. If Nick wanted one so desperately, he would have to rent a small one for a pied-à-terre.

She found Beth in the garden with little Freddie, who was riding around on his three-wheeler, red hair glinting in the sun.

"Camilla!" Beth cried, seeing her. "I had a feeling you might call in – how's it going?"

Beth's fair skin was sunburned just from being in the garden for there was nothing she liked more than to spend time outdoors.

"A treat, as they say." Camilla bent down and gave Freddie a kiss. He turned away, embarrassed, and put his thumb in his mouth.

"I do that to all the fellas," she said, "render them speechless." And Beth laughed. To her, Camilla was like a breath of fresh air, redolent of the past when she had been young and dizzy herself, without a care in the world. The days before she became a vicar's wife with children and a home to run. She was more sensible now, she knew, and just a little bit boring – it was a good thing Marcus didn't find her so. The strange thing was, she was happier than she had ever been in her life. She hoped Camilla would be. She still couldn't get used to the idea of their buying Brampton Hall

– but time would tell. Which one of them had wanted it most?

Camilla slumped into a garden chair and eased the tee shirt off her suntanned shoulders, closing her eyes against the sun. She was seldom without sun glasses. In fact, Beth couldn't remember the last time she had seen her without them. Of course, she was myopic, so that her glasses were real ones, darkly tinted. Her ash blonde hair, cut short and simple, suited her strong face with its large well-chiselled mouth and good teeth.

"You know, between you and me, I can't believe all this," Camilla said, taking out her cigarettes and lighting one. "The house has been left in immaculate condition, there's hardly anything to do except move in. Which reminds me, you don't happen to know offhand of a house keeper, cleaning lady – whatever?"

"There are plenty about," Beth said. "I don't know about a live-in housekeeper.'

"That's what Nick wants, but I'm not sure. I don't much like the idea of someone else in the house. Still, whatever turns up. Where do I find them?"

"Mostly adverts on the boards in the High Street, or there is a domestic agency in Cheltenham."

"Right, I'll go there, although if you hear of anyone . . . I want someone as soon as possible."

"Of course you do," Beth said. "As a matter of fact, I could mention it to Mrs Tomkin, my help, who might have some time to spare on a daily basis."

"That would be great," Camilla said.

"Keep an eye on Freddie and I'll go and put the kettle on," Beth said.

When she returned, she thought Camilla was asleep but she was only dozing.

"Aren't you too hot in the sun?" Beth asked. "I shall have to sit under a tree, it's much too hot for me."

"Do that then, and I'll stay out in the sun."

"I suppose there was no one there when you arrived? The housekeeper gone, and Lucy –"

"No, they went yesterday. I must say, I felt a little sorry for the girl, whoever she is."

They had just finished their second cup of tea when they heard a car draw up outside and Nick walked across the front lawn. Beth had always had a soft spot for Nick. He was a warm comfortable person and a little shy, considering he wrote thriller bestsellers and now was a successful film and television producer.

He kissed Beth then went over to Camilla, bending down low to kiss her too, afterwards lifting Freddie high up in the air over his head.

"God, he's grown," he said. Freddie was delighted. He was happier with men than women.

"Just in time for tea," laughed Beth. "Let me go and make some fresh ."

Nick sank back into the chair next to Camilla's and reached out to take her hand.

"I've just been up to the house," he said. "It's great, isn't it? Did the men come?"

"Every one of them," Camilla said. "They turned taps on and off and checked meters – that sort of thing. In other words, it's all ready for us to move in."

He looked across at her with the fine brown eyes which were his greatest attraction. Camilla always said she had married him for his long lashes. "Happy?" he asked.

She just smiled at him. There was no need for words.

"Me, too," he said, as Beth returned with a fresh pot of tea.

"I thought you and Marcus might like to come out for a meal this evening?" he suggested, seeing Beth's eyes widen with pleasure.

"Oh, that would be lovely – we so seldon go out – but I'm not sure whether Marcus can. He has several commitments on a Thursday."

"See if he can put them off, just for once," Nick said. "I noticed a very nice restaurant along the road to Cheltenham and someone told me it was quite good. What do you think?"

"I think it's a great idea but we'll have to see what Marcus says. Oh, here's Clarrie. Hello, darling."

Maggie had dropped her off at he gate, and now she ran towards them, a pretty little girl with long fair hair, the image of her mother with her big blue eyes and friendly smile.

"Hallo, Auntie Camilla," she said, and shyly looked at Nick.

"You've forgotten your old Uncle Nick," he accused her, then smiled broadly. "It's a long time since we met, isn't it Clarissa?'

She liked him at once. She wasn't too sure about her aunt – sometimes Camilla said things that made people laugh and Clarrie didn't understand.

"Well, go in and change," Beth said, "and I'll find you a cool drink,"

Clarrie took off her school hat and pushed the hair back from her eyes.

"It was so hot in school today and Miss Mardon had to close the windows because there was a plague of wasps," she announced.

"Goodness. Good thing you didn't get stung," Beth said. "Now, come on. Excuse us."

"This is great," Nick said, leaning back. "The old country life – and the air smells wonderful." He drew a deep breath as the church clock struck four.

"I suppose you'd get used to that," he said.

"You'd have to. Still, I hope we can hear it where we are – I like to hear church bells on a Sunday morning."

"You're going to become quite bucolic," Nick grinned.

"What's that mean?" Camilla asked. She always pleaded ignorance, yet was as sharp as a button.

The vicarage sat in the centre of its own garden, so that visitors at the front could see through to the back, and now they saw a small elderly woman go to the front door delivering something. Beth saw her through the kitchen window and presently they both emerged from the house and walked over to Nick and Camilla.

"I'd like to introduce you to Peggy Mansfield," she said. "Peggy, this is Camilla and Nick Blakeney, old friends of mine, the new owners of Brampton Hall." Nick got to his feet.

"How do you do?" they murmured, shaking hands.

"Peggy is the mainstay of the village – no, don't argue,"

Beth said. "I don't know what we'd do without her. And, well, Nick, you've met her husband, Dennis, the solicitor."

"Of course." He smiled. "I saw him this afternoon,"

"I hope you'll be very happy in your new home," Peggy said, her small eyes shining like jet. "It's a lovely house."

"We think so."

"Well, it's nice to have met you – now I must fly," Peggy said. "Good luck!" she called out, and walked with Beth to the gate.

What charming people, she thought, making her way home. Young and well-to-do – just what the village needed. Brampton Hall needed new blood. Perhaps it had been in the Gilbert's hands too long?

Once home she made herself some tea and got out a pile of scripts which had been sent to her from French's. The amateur dramatic society started again at the beginning of September, but there was always lot of preparation before that. The three act play needed some thinking about, especially if it was to bring in the public who were fussy these days about what they paid out for. Understandably, when even amateur shows cost a lot to put on.

She sat down in the cool of the dining room and picked out *Abigail's Party*. That had been such a successful play on stage and television, she was sure it would be a box office draw, and there was no doubt what a splendid vehicle it would make for their new leading lady. Peggy began to read.

She was startled by a sharp ring of the doorbell, engrossed in the first act although used to people disturbing her peace and quiet. Frowning, she put down her book and went to the front door.

At first she did not recognize her visitor. It took a moment or two before realization sank in, and then with a shock she saw who it was.

"Miranda!" she cried, looking at the young woman who had been her son's second wife, the mother of Bobby, her younger grandson, whom she hadn't seen since he was three.

What had brought Miranda to Ainswick? Trouble, Peggy thought grimly.

"My dear, come in," she said, for want of something better to say.

"I'm sorry to call on you like this," Miranda said, finding her voice, "but I was desperate and didn't know which way to turn."

Peggy's heart sank as she led the way through to the study.

Miranda looked sadly around her before sitting down. "It's a long time since I've been here, and I wouldn't be here now if it weren't for . . ."

"How's Bobby?" Peggy asked, thinking of her grandson and fearing the worst.

"He's fine, with my mother," Miranda said. "She's taken time off work to look after him."

"I see," Peggy replied, feeling she knew what was coming. "What about your job?"

Miranda had held down a high-powered job with an excellent salary, much to Malcolm's delight, and Peggy sometimes wondered if that was the reason her son had married her. She knew the girl had gone back to work after the baby was born.

"I lost it six months ago, and I can't get another. It's not easy with a child."

"I'm sure," Peggy said sympathetically. "And what about your friend?" She could'nt remember his name, the man she had run off with – where was he?

"Matthew? He left me and I came back home. We went to Spain but it was no good – things didn't work out."

"Let me get you some tea," Peggy offered, feeling that the worst was yet to come.

"No – no, thanks. I really am sorry to bother you like this, but I'm looking for Malcolm. Is he here?"

Peggy's heart was hammering in her throat.

"Not at the moment," she countered.

"I've tried to find him. I went to his office, and to his flat but he's simply disappeared. He hasn't paid maintenance for Bobby since I left him. It's not for me, it's Bobby. I have a court order, but being unable to find him . . ."

Peggy bit her lip. It was not the first time she'd had to listen to the same story from other young mothers.

"It seemed to me at the end of the day he might have come back to Ainswick, so I thought as a last resort I'd try here."

"He did come back," Peggy said slowly, "although I can't tell you where he is at the moment."

"You would rather protect your son and see your own grandson go hungry?" the girl said accusingly.

"I'm his mother," Peggy said, "and I can't interfere. What I will do is tell him you have been to see me, and if it's in my power, force him to make payments to you. I can't promise more than that."

The girl gave an embittered smile. "As if that would make any difference! He's a bad lot, and you know it. I just hope Bobby doesn't grow up to be like his father."

What an indictment, Peggy thought sorrowfully, but the girl was right.

"I am going to make out a substantial cheque to you, to tide you over." She saw the girl's disbelief. "It's the least I can do," she went on. "In the meantime, I shall tell Malcolm, and you may rest assured that I shall do all in my power to make him see sense."

From a drawer, she took out a cheque book and wrote a cheque which she handed to the girl.

It was for a thousand pounds, and the girl's eyes grew wide. "All this?"

"It's for my grandson. I just hope in the future Malcolm will toe the line and see that you get the money due to you."

The girl's eyes filled with tears. "Thank you," she said.

"Now you must give me your address," Peggy said. "Will you write it down here for me?" And when the girl gave it to her she saw that it was somewhere in Battersea, where she seemed to remember Miranda's mother lived.

"How did you come up from London?".

"By train from Cheltenham – then I got the bus."

"I'll drive you to the station in Cheltenham," Peggy said. "Are you sure you won't have something – a cup of tea?"

"No, I have to get back."

"I'm sorry you had to make this journey."

I'd like to horsewhip him, she was thinking to herself as they walked to the car. Just wait until he gets in! But there was one thing she wouldn't do. She wouldn't tell Dennis about this. She could imagine his fury. Least said, soonest mended. But she would see that Malcolm knew. Oh, yes, she would see to that.

"Come along, my dear," she said. "Let's be on our way."

In Cheltenham, she let Miranda out of the car and watched her disappear into the station, a tall elegant young woman with beautiful legs, wearing a smart suit. She looked as though she hadn't a care in the world.

Appearances could certainly be deceptive, thought Peggy, remembering the strain on the girl's face, and the anxious eyes.

"Good luck," she called after her, then drove grimly home to Ainswick.

Chapter Fourteen

The end of July came and with it a drought which ended, with a mighty storm which raged for twenty-four hours and broke the long spell of dry weather. Afterwards the air smelled sweet and scented and fresh; it was like being given a new lease of life.

Steam rose off the pavements as the sun shone and drew out the damp. Dry weather was perhaps going to continue through August and the school holidays, Beth thought, knowing they were not going away this year. A week in Devon with Marcus's parents was the most they could hope for, but at the moment they must carry on parochial work with its attendant chores. She wished more than anything that Marcus could have a break. With two churches he was kept terribly busy, and always at the parishioner's beck and call.

This morning he had officiated at two funerals, and she had thought she might go into the churchyard to observe the flowers for one of them, that of an elderly man who had had a large family and was adored by all his grandchildren. Marcus had said the flowers were a sight to see. But now she was taking the children along to Maggie's for the afternoon, and hoped that her garden would not be swamped after the deluge to make it too muddy to play in. Maggie was such a help when Beth was inundated with work, like getting ready for the annual summer fair which was her particular responsibility. Of course there were always many willing helpers, but it was her job to get it off the ground.

On arriving at Maggie's house, she waited at the front door until it was opened.

"Hello, Beth, come in. What a storm."

"Just for a moment. I have to be at the church hall."

"Well, the children will be all right with me. Don't worry about them, they all get on like a house on fire, and if there are any arguements – I'll deal with them." Her pale blue eyes slid over Beth's face.

"Are you all right?"

"Yes, of course, why?"

"You look a bit pale," Maggie said. "Cup of tea?"

"No, I'll be off if you don't mind," Beth said. She did feel a bit washed out, and wondered if it were not the usual thing – or lack of it – and began to ponder as she had yesterday . . .

Maggie sent the children into the garden where there were squeals of delight. "I'm afraid it's a bit muddy. Still, I'll dump them in the bath before you get back."

"Maggie, you are a brick."

"My second name," she said. "Have you seen Peggy lately?"

"No, not since Wednesday – why?"

"Nothing, really . . . By the way, we had Jackie to dinner last night."

"Jackie?" Beth was surprised. She had no idea that Maggie even liked her.

"Yes, I bumped into her in the grocer's, and she looked a bit forlorn. You know, Beth, she's really awfully nice."

"Yes," Beth said, making for the front door.

"It must be awful being alone so much – and with no children. Her husband is in Hong Kong so I asked her round for a meal." Maggie had her hand on the door handle.

"You know, I didn't awfully care for her at first but when you get to know her . . ."

She seemed to want to say more and leaned forward confidingly. "I suppose I shouldn't tell you this . . . still, I must say, I was very concerned. She's got a sod of a husband – an absolute swine. He treats her appallingly." Mistaking Beth's surprise for concern: "I shouldn't have said anything as she asked me not to – but, well, you know."

Beth managed a weak smile. "I won't say a word," she said. "Promise."

"Even Don felt sorry for her – I had to tell him. Her husband reminded me of Tony – my first husband, I don't envy her."

Well! Beth thought. At least now she knew she was not the only one who shared Jackie's secret.

She thought hard about her all the way back home and through the churchyard. The smell of the earth and the newly cut flowers was heady and as she neared a newly dug grave, simply surrounded by flowers and wreaths of every description, she saw a girl coming towards her and recognized her immediately.

As they drew nearer, there were smiles of recognition.

"Lucy Gilbert, isn't it?" Beth said. "We met at the party at Marty and Alistair's house."

"After the show," Lucy laughed, "where you wore that beautiful dress."

"Thank you. Yes, it was – and weighed a ton."

"I guess it did."

She was a pretty little thing, Beth thought, slight and very slim, almost waif-like, with that dark hair and grey-green eyes, pale creamy skin and a nose covered with freckles. "What are you doing here?"

"I came to put flowers on Daddy's grave," Lucy said. "Today is his birthday."

"Oh, I'm sorry," Beth said. "You must miss him."

"I do, more than I thought possible, but it gets better, doesn't it?"

"Yes, time heals, " Beth said. "I'm on my way to the church hall to arrange the summer fair – would you like to come with me?"

"No, but I'll walk a way with you. As a matter of fact, I wanted to see you. I was going to telephone."

"Really?".

"It's about Henry, my Labrador. I've had him since he was a puppy, he's nine years old now, and moving away from The Hall has simply broken his heart. He tends to be cooped up in my small house and garden."

"Yes, I can imagine," Beth said sympathetically.

"What I was wondering was, I hope you don't think I've got a cheek, but I did wonder if your friends up at The Hall might like him?"

Beth stood still.

By a strange coincidence, Camilla had been talking about getting a dog, but she mustn't pre-suppose she would like Lucy's.

"Why don't I mention it to her?" she said. "I'd have him myself, but I already have a dog – blessed not with a noble temperament, but one that would most definately shoo off all newcomers."

Lucy laughed. "They're the best kind," she said. "Well, if you would."

"I'll give you a ring – what's your number?" And Lucy told her.

"Have you settled in now?"

"Yes, it's great."

"Oh, that's good. Well, I'll be in touch."

"Goodbye, Beth."

Another friend, Lucy thought, and hoped something would come of her suggestion.

Three days later she was on her way up to The Hall with Henry in the back of the car. As she went through the gates, he sat up straight and cocked his ears. She could see in the mirror that look of excitement around his nostrils as they went up the drive. When she arrived at the front door, he barked to be let out. She put him on a lead and saw Camilla standing at the front door, wearing white pants and a white sweater and dark glasses. There was no doubting her pleasure at seeing Henry.

"Oh, he's lovely!" she cried, bending down and stroking him, and Henry looked very pleased with himself, wagging his tail.

Camilla held out her hand. "I'm Camilla Blakeney – do come in and meet my husband, Nick."

He was coming into the hall and Lucy felt instinctively that she would be happy if Henry could come and live with them.

"Nick, this is Lucy who used to live here."

"Hallo, Nick," she said, and felt her hand grasped warmly.

"Does it feel strange to be back?" Camilla asked.

"Yes and no," Lucy said untruthfully, surprised at the depth of her feelings. If she had known it would be so nostalgic, she might not have come.

"So this is Henry," Nick said bending down, and there was no doubt about the dog's feelings.

"I expect he feels quite at home," Camilla said. "Oh, he's a lovely boy, aren't you?" And she petted him while Henry obviously enjoyed himself hugely.

"Come in and sit down then we can have a chat. Where's he going – in the garden?"

"I expect he'd love a run," Lucy said. "He knows every inch of it."

"Come on, Henry," Camilla said, and Lucy went with her to the back door where they let him out. He stood for a while as they waited.

"Go on, boy," Lucy said.

And he ran. Chased across the lawns and into the field beyond, where he suddenly stopped and looked about him. "I expect he thinks he's found a rabbit," Lucy said.

She felt quite sad, knowing that she couldn't take him back – if only these nice people would have him. Whether he would be so happy to leave her, she wasn't sure. He obviously thought he had come home.

"We'll have tea on the terrace," Camilla said, and Lucy was astonished how quickly they had made themselves at home after living in London for so long.

Over tea they talked, mostly of the house and how long Lucy and her family had lived there, what she was doing now, and about Nick's work.

Lucy found herself wanting to stay on, and when Henry raced back to them and lay panting at her feet, bent down and patted him.

At the end of an hour, Camilla, a proprietary hand on Henry, looked up and said, "Well, what do you think?"

"It's up to you," Lucy said. "I can't bear to give him up, yet I know this is where he belongs. He's a country dog. He likes the land and the space which I can't give him."

"How do you feel about it, Nick?" Camilla asked.

"I think it's a great idea," he said. "Why don't we give it a whirl and see how he gets on."

Lucy suddenly felt totally bereft. Was she doing the right thing?

"Well, I didn't bring his basket or anything. I just thought if we could see his reaction to you, then perhaps we could play it by ear, if you are willing?"

"Would you feel happy about us having him?" Nick asked. "It's quite a big thing to do – give up your dog."

"It's for him," she said. "I'd get another, smaller dog. I don't think I could bear to live without one, especially on my own."

"That's settled, then," Nick said. "We'll give it a try. So what are you going to do now, Lucy?"

"If it's all right with you, I'll take him back now then bring him again tomorrow with his basket and things, and his toys."

"And you know you can come up and see him anytime," Camilla said. Already, Nick thought, she sees the dog as hers.

Lucy drove home with mixed feelings. In her heart she knew she was doing the right thing – Henry belonged at The Hall. And so do I, she thought angrily, and with a twinge of jealousy. Oh, perhaps it wasn't such a good idea after all!

Once home, she perked up at the thought that Philip was coming round this evening. She had seen quite a bit of him since she had moved in, and less, she thought, of Malcolm. Not that she minded not seeing Malcolm, but he was always good for a laugh whereas Philip tended to be serious-minded. He had suggested going for a meal at the new Pekin restaurant which had opened in Ainswick, much to the older residents' disgust.

"A Chinese restaurant in Ainswick?" They were horrified.

It was charming inside, restful with a tiny water garden and trickling water. Green ferns and trellis. Lucy thought it delightful. Philip sat opposite her, watching her eyes shine with pleasure, and thought he had never seen a prettier girl. The problem was, they were so different. They had nothing in common, and in his saner moments he wondered if attraction was enough.

She stood for all the things he despised. A family who had indulged themselves, had everything they wanted, spent money like water. Even Lucy admitted that she had never wanted for anything. And that ghastly mother! It was her fault that Alec Gilbert had died – well, she had contributed largely to his downfall. Was Lucy going to take after her mother?

A sensible man had to ask himself these questions even though he had fallen in love. If they were not compatible, how would they fare when married? If he decided to ask her, that was.

He had to admit she had behaved splendidly since her father's death. Shown great courage, living on her own after the Hall. It couldn't have been easy. But even so, she had managed to buy herself a cottage, she still had her mare, and was about to come into an inheritance when she came of age – and he knew, having seen the private papers, it was quite a considerable sum. After all, most men wanted to be the breadwinner, he wasn't unusual in that, and he'd never liked the idea of having a wife with money of her own.

But tonight he would think on the positive side and forget his doubts. Marriage was a big step, and he had no intention of jumping into it without some serious thought.

"Well, Lucy," he said. "What shall we order?"

She studied the menu. "Why don't we have the suggested Pekin meal for two – that is, unless you know about Chinese food and how to order it?"

"No, I don't," he admitted. "I'm afraid I am not very adventurous with foreign food."

Or with a lot of other things, Lucy thought. Yet he was so nice, just needed to be brought out of his shell. He had had a different upbringing, she knew, which was why he had that chip on his shoulder. Sometimes she wondered if she could knock it off? Would she want to?

"Have you eaten much Chinese food?" he asked.

"Yes, I've been to Chinese restaurants many times, but I'm afraid it was left to other people to do the ordering." And she smiled.

That settled it, Philip decided. He didn't want to make a fool of himself.

"We'll have the Mandarin order for two," he said to the waiter.

They smiled at each other across the table, as Lucy toyed with her knife.

"You've quite settled in?" Philip asked.

"Yes. Today I took Henry, my dog, up to The Hall," she began.

"Was that a good idea?"

She ignored this. "I don't think I should keep him. He's too large for the cottage, and besides it's not fair on him. He needs to have space to run in – and, well, it seemed a good idea. I spoke to Beth Pennington about it, and she said she'd mention it to the Blakeneys, and the upshot of it is that they're prepared to give him a trial."

He frowned. "You'll miss him."

"Philip, of course I will, but I'll get a smaller dog – after all, I'm out of the house most days now."

"That's true. Are you keen to stay at the gallery?"

"Until something better turns up. Magnus knows that. It's not really my cup of tea. I'd like to do something more worthwhile."

This was more like it. He had never approved of her working at the gallery any more than he approved of his sister mooning about the house when she was at home and hoping Magnus would ring.

"My mother is coming down to see the cottage tomorrow," Lucy said as the food arrived.

"What do you think her reaction will be?"

"If I know my mother, she will disapprove heartily." Lucy laughed. "It's not her cup of tea at all."

Afterwards, Philip drove her home, and as she watched his fine hands on the wheel, Lucy wondered yet again what it was about him that she found so attractive. She couldn't begin to think like he did, and yet the physical affinity was there.

"Will you come in for coffee?" she asked him.

"Thank you, yes," he said, and followed her into the tiny sitting room.

It was so Lucy, he thought. Neat and tidy, he approved of that, yet cosy and inviting. He knew that the furniture had come from The Hall, some of the smaller chairs, for she hadn't wanted to buy new. Everything blended in so well with the plain carpet, and she had kept the small fireplace in which now sat an arrangement of dried flowers.

Lucy put on a tape, and they drank coffee and sat and talked and listened, and as it grew darker, she lit a lamp.

By the lamplight, she looked almost ethereal, and Philip went and sat beside her and put his arm around her. She made no demur when he kissed her and she was surprised to find how much she liked it. She returned his kiss with ardour, feeling his warmth and closeness after being alone for so long. It was lovely to be held tightly and ages since she had been kissed, and then only by the young men who formed part of her social life up at The Hall.

When he caressed her, it seemed as if her body suddenly became alive of its own volition, and she wanted it to go on. She felt the tip of his tongue and as he became more ardent, was slightly shocked that it was Philip who was doing this to her, a kind of kissing that she had never experienced before. Her body seemed as if it was on fire and almost out of control, and when he put his hand on her breast, she pushed him away, a little scared of what she was getting in to.

"Philip . . ."

"I'm sorry," he said, a little stiffly, and she knew that she had upset him. Couldn't he understand that she just wasn't used to it, that she was out of her depth? It took time – he was rushing her. Perhaps he didn't realize that there were girls like her who really had had no experience of men, even though this was the age of women's freedom?

She saw his face in the lamplight, and he wasn't looking at her. She took his hand. "You swept me off my feet." she smiled, hoping to make a joke.

"I didn't realize that you didn't like it, or I wouldn't have –"

"Oh, but I did," she reassured him. "You just went a little fast for me."

He managed a smile, and she felt once more at ease.

"I must go, thank you for the coffee."

"Oh, but –" She felt she wanted him to say something more, to stay and talk, explain.

One look was enough to tell her that that wasn't his intention.

She stood up and brushed down her skirt, holding out her hand.

"Thank you for the Chinese meal," she said. I enjoyed it immensely."

"Good," he said formally, and made for the door. He kissed her lightly on her cheek. "Will you be riding on Sunday Morning?"

"Yes, hopefully." She smiled, wishing they could get back on their old footing.

"I'll see you then," he said. "Goodnight, Lucy."

"Goodnight, Philip." And she closed the door behind him.

She washed up the coffee cups, saw that Henry was in his basket, and went to bed, where despite the food and the wine which made her drowsy, she lay awake, trying to understand the relationship between her and Philip.

She supposed he would think her a prude. Perhaps she was? Still at boarding school at eighteen, where of course there had been jokes, ribald jokes some of them, and tales which made your hair stand on end about men, especially from some of the girls who were really way out. But she had never been one of them and had never had brothers; she had loved her father and her home and Daisy and Henry – her life had always seemed full. The boys she had known were more like brothers. One went to the theatre, or rode, or played tennis with them. They were all busy carving out careers, and almost none of them was studious – not like Philip, really having to work hard for a living.

She sighed. Well, she had got it wrong and had upset him. What had he expected? That she would go the whole hog, as they said at school?

No, Master Philip, she told herself. If I was madly in love with you I might. But I'm not. Although when she remembered his kisses and the effect they had on her, she admitted that there was a strong physical attraction between them.

Presently she slept, and woke late with the sun streaming in through the window. She leapt out of bed and pulled back the curtains, hurrying down the stairs to find Henry still asleep in his basket.

"You lazy old thing," she said, hugging him, and opened the back door for him to go out. She followed him out to the tiny garden, enjoying the scents of summer, until she suddenly remembered that Ariadne was coming down to take her out for lunch.

"Henry!" she shrieked. "Mother will be here soon – and you didn't wake me."

She hastily ran a bath and had breakfast, then walked along to the newsagent's to buy the Sunday Paper, something she had enjoyed doing since she had a home of her own.

Afterwards she sat in the garden with coffee to await her mother, due at Midday. Almost on the dot of noon, Lucy heard the BMW pull up behind her own small car in the street, and looking through the window, saw Ariadne alight and lock her car with the air of a woman who wouldn't trust anyone in sight. Lucy smiled to herself.

Opening the door, Lucy greeted her. "Hullo, Mummy!"

Ariadne twitched a perfect nose, and managed a weak smile.

"Darling –"

"Come in, come in." Ariadne followed her, blinking after the sunlight in the small, dark and cool sitting room.

"Well, what do you think?"

Her eyes shining with excitement, Lucy had waited for this day.

Ariadne walked through to the kitchen/dining area, then out into the garden where Lucy had placed two chairs round a very small wicker table. On the table was a pot of mixed flowers.

"This is it?" Ariadne asked. "All of it?"

"'Fraid so, Mummy," Lucy said. It was, after all, the reaction she had expected.

Ariadne placed a foot gingerly on the narrow staircase and went upstairs while Lucy followed her. At the top of the stairs she peered into the pretty bedroom and then into the white bathroom.

"There's only one bedroom," she said in a shocked voice.

"I've turned the other one into a bathroom," Lucy explained.

Ariadne brushed past her and went back down the stairs where she collapsed into a cosy chair.

"Well, Mummy? What do you think?"

“What do I think?” Ariadne repeated, settling herself and crossing her legs to expose acres of thigh. “I think you are absolutely mad, darling. Aren’t you going to offer me a drink?”

Chapter Fifteen

Another warm day, Peggy sighed, making her way downstairs. Really one shouldn't complain about this summer which went on and on, seemingly without a break, yet there was an overall feeling of dryness, of parched earth, which even in a village in the Cotswolds was making itself felt. Water was at a premium; the sheep were grazing dry grass, and the farmers moved them from field to field in order to give the pasture a chance to recover. Nurseries were kept busy watering and sales had gone down, for gardeners were wary of planting lest plants were lost in the drought.

She was surprised to find Dennis already downstairs; she was usually the early riser. He had taken to getting up earlier this past week or two, and she wondered whether he might be sleeping badly.

Glancing through the kitchen window, she saw him standing looking up at the apple trees where the fruit was ripening fast but was undersized owing to lack of water. The apple trees were Dennis's pride and joy – pratically the only thing in the garden he was interested in.

She prepared breakfast, her mind busy with all that she had to do today, as was usual on a week day.

She eyed Dennis as he spread his toast liberally with marmalade – and saw that his hair, still thick and wavy, was even more silver now than it had been. He looked what he was, a man approaching sixty-five, although he was a fine figure still and enjoyed good health.

Thursday morning he often played a round of golf, and

once or twice a week he went in to Cheltenham. Like her, he always had plenty to do apart from his business.

"Are you golfing?" she asked. "It's another beautiful day."

She seemed to startle him. He was deep in thought.

"What? Golf – er, no, not today. I have one or two things to do."

She glanced at her watch. "Mrs Dinsdale isn't here yet – she's late." She got up and took the dishes out to the kitchen.

He followed her out with his coffee cup and saucer.

"Peg, I may be late this evening. I have to –"

But she didn't wait for him to finish. "I expect I shall be, too. I thought we'd have salad anyway – the evenings are so warm, really, one doesn't feel like eating much."

He had gone when Mrs Dinsdale arrived, her eyes red from weeping, a large hankie to her face every now and again as she took off her woolly cardigan and hung it on the hook behind the kitchen door. This was unlike Mrs Dinsdale who rarely showed emotion about anything.

"My dear, what is it?" Peggy asked, going over to her.

"Oh, Mrs Mansfield, I'm that upset – I don't know what to do for the best."

"Is there anything I can do?"

"It's our Kylie." And she burst out into a fit of fresh sobbing.

"There's nothing wrong, is there? Is she all right?" Peggy was picturing that pretty if brazen little thing under a lorry or raped or murdered. After all, everyone in the village knew Kylie Dinsdale.

"Come and sit down, there's no need to start yet. Plenty of time."

Mrs Dinsdale blew her nose, then sniffed, wiped her eyes, and took a deep breath.

"She's pregnant," she said to Peggy's relief. She had imagined all sorts of dire things.

"Oh, is that all!" she cried, with an attempt at consoling Mrs Dinsdale who merely looked at her reproachfully.

"All!" she repeated. "And her not married, nor likely to be."

"Well," Peggy said mildly, "it's not uncommon today, is

it?" And went over to the sink to put the kettle on. She knew a cup of tea would help to pull Mrs Dinsdale round.

"I wouldn't mind, but I thought he was a nice chap. He was ever so polite – not like some of them."

"I don't suppose that makes any difference," Peggy said, thinking of some of the tales she had had to listen to.

"Who is he? Would he be anyone I know?"

"Oh, no, he's a tractor driver from Cirencester – been working at Little Field."

"Oh, I see. But wasn't she – er – living with him?"

"Yes, that's half the trouble. That's what they all do, then wonder why they get pregnant. Think they know all the answers, and it don't matter what you tell 'em, they know it all –"

"Yes, that's true," Peggy agreed.

"You're lucky you 'aven't got daughters, Mrs Mansfield."

"Oh, I don't know. I would have liked a daughter, but I suppose I might have had the same problems," Peggy said. Thank God, she thought, I only had Malcolm, though he's been nothing but trouble.

"She's only sixteen," Mrs Dinsdale sniffed.

Remembering the last time she had seen Kylie, Peggy was not worried. A big strong healthy girl – she'd be all right, she thought.

"I expect he'll marry her," she said comfortingly.

"That's just it!" Mrs Dinsdale declared. "She don't want to get married! No way, she says. What's getting pregnant got to do with it? Mind you, I think he'd marry her, but she wouldn't 'ave it. Can you understand it? It's not like when we was young. You'd have been thrown out of the village – well, p'raps not, but you'd 'ave 'ad to keep it quiet 'til your time come. And you dursn't go out . . ."

That's true, Peggy thought.

"It's her granma that worries me. Ow am I going to tell 'er? It's enough to kill 'er – Kylie's 'er pride and joy. Well she's the only granddaughter – me not 'avin' any more."

"I tell you what," Peggy said presently after making the tea, "I heard yesterday that the new flats will be ready by the beginning of September, and I don't know if they've told her yet but of course your mother is eligible, and they've allocated her a unit."

That was enough to shake Mrs Dinsdale out of her misery.

"Oh, there! Well, I never! Oh, that *is* good. She'll be pleased."

"I thought I'd go along and let her know, and if I do it today, I'm sure it will help when you go and tell her about Kylie. It will take her mind off it."

"Oh, you are good, Mrs Mansfield. You've made my day." And soon she had her apron on, and by the time Peggy left the house, she was washing up at the sink.

Peggy had hoped to find Malcolm in this morning, for she wanted to ask him what he had done about making payments to Miranda. It had been on her mind ever since the day her ex-daughter-in-law had arrived, and although she had given him a good talking to and he had made a solemn promise that he would do something about it immediately, somehow she didn't trust him, and wondered of he realized that he could be sent to prison if he failed to comply with a court order. She couldn't shake off a suspicion that if he could, he would lie his way out of trouble. She wondered now if she had done the right thing in giving Miranda money. It took the pressure off Malcolm, although he knew nothing about it, but Miranda would feel that much easier. Peggy didn't regret giving her the money, it was the least she could do for Malcolm's little son. She wondered now what Bobby was like. In her heart she would have liked to see him, but she had no desire to stir up any trouble.

On arriving at Malcolm's flat, she found he was out but as she was leaving she saw Mrs Hemingway from the flat downstairs standing on the porch, leaning heavily on her stick.

"Mr Mansfield is out," she said. "Would you be Mrs Mansfield – Malcolm's mother?"

"Yes, how do you do?" Peggy said, holding out her hand. "I don't think I know you – and I know most people in the village."

"I've only been here ten years, when they converted the house to flats, so I'm practically a newcomer." She smiled. "I saw Malcolm go out earlier."

"Yes, never mind, it wasn't important," Peggy said. "Well, I must be on my way. I'll see him later."

"So nice to have met you," Mrs Hemingway said, still leaning on her stick.

Watching Peggy's retreating figure, she was pleased she had spoken to her. It helped when you knew a young man's background – and his mother seemed like a very nice person. She had heard of her, of course, everyone knew her, but it was nice to meet her just the same.

Peggy made her way to Little Field and the new development, half of which was in the final stages of completion.

Passing the General's house, which she had long stopped visiting, for the Pargeters were not churchgoers and had no interest in what happened in the village, she noticed that it was as dark as ever, surrounded by trees which over the years had grown so tall that they met each other in the drive and made a canopy of dark leaves.

What must that house be like inside? she wondered.

And here were the new retirement homes. She had to say, they really fitted into the landscapes very well.

Two stories high, of warm red brick, they had modern latticed windows, so pretty for older people because they resembled a row of old cottages. Just sixteen of them finished, another sixteen on the way. The front doors were of highly polished wood, and walking across the dry and dusty earth Peggy made her way to the first one, calling out, "Anyone there?"

A man appeared from upstairs and called over the banisters.

"Ooisit?"

"I'm from the council," she said. "Just having a look round."

"Oh," he said. "That's all right then."

"You have got on well," Peggy said. She believed in giving praise where praise was due. "When will they be ready for occupation?"

"Mid-September, as far as I know. We've been helped by the weather."

"Yes, I'm sure." She nodded. "Will the gardens be done?"

"Yes, miss. As soon as we've finished, they'll be lawned and laid out."

"And very nice, too." Peggy was as pleased as if she was having one herself.

"Thank you. I'll come and see them again when they are finished – they're very nice." And walking back up the lane, she made her way to Granny Dorrington's little house. What sort of mood would she be in today? Better, Peggy hoped, after she had been given the news about her new home.

Malcolm, on the other hand, was feeling a bit fed up, despite having six properties on his books with a possible sale pending, and a couple of homes for rent. The reason being that Jackie's husband was at home this week, and because of that Malcolm wouldn't be seeing her. Not at all. The thought depressed him more than somewhat. Added to that was the worry of Miranda. It had been a damn nuisance her coming down like that. Thank God he hadn't been around to see her. Now he had to do something about finding some money – almost an impossibility with all his commitments. Of course, he had assured his mother he would see to it immediately, and there was no point in upsetting her. He had to thank her for not telling his father and was grateful for that. His mother was one thing, his father quite another.

He wondered just how far he could go in persuading Mrs Hemingway, his downstairs neighbour, to go along with buying the small bungalow he had on his books, and which he thought was eminently suitable for her. For if he could get her to move out of her flat and take it over, what with the top floor being empty, he was on to a good thing. The Grange lent itself to a luxury conversion, he could just visualize the plans. It was not necessary for anyone to learn that he was behind it. In fact, he wouldn't be, totally. He needed a backer, and who better than Leo Burns?

He and Leo had been partners before in quite a few business ventures which had paid off well. Pity, he thought, that he had not put some of the profits to better use instead of frittering the money away. Still, he wasn't going to grumble. He had had a good time on the proceeds, but now his need was more urgent.

It was almost closing time before he managed to get hold of Leo, who was always out and about doing some deal or another. Leo had earned Malcolm's utmost respect for the way he went to the heart of a business deal, never playing round the edges but getting straight to the point.

"So what's the deal?" he asked, and Malcolm pictured him at the other end of the line, puffing away at his cigar.

"I've bought this first-floor apartment – freehold – and the one at the top is empty. If I can persuade my downstairs neighbour to move, we're laughing. It's a fabulous apartment, Leo, high ceilings, marble fireplaces, you name it."

"So where's she going? You're not trying to do a Rachman, are you?"

"Good lord, no. I've found her a nice little place. The thing is to persuade her to buy it, but there's no point unless you can see what I'm driving at."

"So why don't you go ahead and buy it?"

"I haven't got the cash at the moment," Malcolm said. "This is where you come in."

Leo saw the warning signals but it wouldn't be the first time young Mansfield had put him on to a good thing. He seemed to have a nose for sussing out a possibility.

"I'm pretty tied up at the moment – cash flow-wise."

"Now you know I wouldn't bother you unless I was sure," Malcolm said, which Leo had to agree was true. "Why don't you come down and see my place? I can't let the old girl know what I'm up to, but you'd get the drift. The place is just ripe for conversion. These old houses don't grow on trees, especially in a place like Ainswick."

"All right, all right," Leo said. "How about lunch on Thursday?"

"Great," Malcolm said. "See you in The Lamb about twelve. You can't miss it." And he rubbed his hands together with satisfaction. He was on his way.

Later he sat in Mrs Hemingway's drawing room, having given her the particulars of the little place he had in mind.

"I wouldn't like to leave here," she said, "yet I know I'm going to have to soon. My husband was alive when we first came to Ainswick. Of course, he's been dead five years or more now."

"Yes, I'm sorry, and it's a bit of a barn for you to live in on your own. As I say, I've had heaps of people after

Woodbine Cottage, but when I thought of you, I said to myself, 'Malcolm, old boy, tuck it under the counter until Mrs Hemingway has seen it.' It seemed so right for you."

"How kind," she murmured.

"You can see the pretty little garden in the photograph, no upkeep, and you haven't a car so there's no problem there, and someone has modernized it beautifully – the kitchen is a dream. But there you are, if you're not interested." And he made to put the details back in his pocket.

"Wait a moment," Mrs Hemingway said. "Leave them with me – I'd like to think it over. I have to admit, I have often thought how nice it would be to be nearer the shops and the library, and no stairs –"

"Well, there you are then," Malcolm said triumphantly. "I'll leave these with you. If we can't help a friend in this life, what are we here for, eh?"

She looked at him fondly, this big hulk of man, tall and broad-shouldered. He might have been the son she never had.

"No, don't come to the door – I'll see myself out," he said, and humming away to himself, did so.

After lunch at The Lamb, and brandy and cigars to follow, the two men made their way back to Malcolm's flat in Leo's Roller. It pulled to a silent stop outside the front door, and Leo followed Malcom into the large and spacious hall.

Already Malcolm could sense that Leo was impressed.

Once inside Malcolm's flat, he looked around with interest at the huge drawing room with its painted ceiling, the linen-fold panelling in the dining room, the huge bedroom with magnificent views.

"What did you pay for it?" he asked, and Malcolm told him.

Leo whistled.

"You did well," he said, walking over to the huge windows and admiring the view. "I see velvet-covered banquettes in these windows, French furniture, the whole bit. Can we see upstairs?"

"No," Malcolm said. "I haven't got the key. It's smaller of course, but downstairs it's even better than this."

Leo drew on his cigar.

"With extensions, I should think we'd get six luxury flats, my boy."

"That's what I thought. All I have to do is to get the old sweetie to agree to sell."

"And to put your outline planning permission in – that's the most important thing."

"But not until she sells."

"Of course before she sells. Anyone can put in a planning application even if they don't own the property.'

"I know that," Malcolm said doubtfully.

"It's done all the time."

"There's the rub," he confessed. "I wouldn't want it put through in my name, old lad. My mother is on the council planning committee." And Leo whistled.

"That could be good – or bad," he said. "Is she – er –?"

"No, she is not," Malcolm said. The very idea was almost laughable.

"Pity. Everyone has his price."

"Not my mother," Malcolm said grimly.

Leo sat down at the desk. "I'll tell you what to do. Press on with the old lady – you're good at that – and I'll show you how to present the planning application. This is for outline only, before we draw up the plans."

He stuck his cigar in his mouth, gripped it, and wrote down what he was saying.

"Outline planning permission for six luxury flats at Smethwick Grange, Ainswick. Then my name: Leo Burns, 23, Gender Street, London, W1. Any queries and I'm their man. You don't have to be involved at all at this stage."

"How about buying her flat?" Malcolm asked. "If she'll sell. I haven't got the lolly at the moment."

"Leave that to me," Leo said. "Everything's going to be all right. We're on to a winner here, me lad, especially when you think that London's a dead loss at the moment."

"I tell you something, Leo," Malcolm confided, "I'm not sorry I came up here. "And he winked. "There's a damn' sight more going on in this village than you think."

"I can believe it," Leo said.

Chapter Sixteen

Lucy was on a stepladder dusting pictures when she heard the shop door open and turned to see both Nick and Camillia Blakeney standing there.

She jumped down at once, and put away the ladder and duster in a cupboard.

"Hallo, good morning," she said, eyes lighting up at the sight of them both. They made such a handsome pair, Nick darkly good-looking with those very nice eyes, and Camilla, always so elegant in white and the eternal dark glasses.

"Can I help you?" asked Lucy, hoping that they had come to buy.

"Yes, as a matter of fact, we've come to buy Camilla a birthday present. And I have a feeling that that's it, up there."

On the wall was a large oil painting, in mainly dark blues and black, modern but starkly realistic, of New York at night. It caught everyone's eye who came into the gallery, but although much admired it hadn't been sold.

"Camilla has set her heart on it," Nick said.

"It is lovely," Lucy agreed. "One of my favourites. Where would you hang it?"

"In our bedroom," Camilla said. "On the wall between the two windows, what do you think?'

"Lovely. I'm not an expert, as you know, I simply help out here, but I do think it's interesting. You can pick out all the landmarks, and see something different every time you look at it. Do you know New York well?" she asked, suspecting they did.

"Yes, quite well," Camilla said with a smile.

"She spent a week there on her own while I was in Hollywood, directing," Nick said. "She hated Hollywood, didn't you, darling?"

"I certainly did. Well, are we going to have it?"

"If you're sure that's what you want . . ."

"No question," Camilla said. "Thank you, darling," as he took out his wallet.

"And how is Henry?" Lucy asked.

"Oh, he's lovely," Camilla said. "Look, why don't you come up to the house this evening and have a swim? He'd love to see you."

"Oh, could I?" Lucy's eyes were sparkling.

"You're welcome any time," Camilla said seriously. "We mean it. Come soon after six and share our supper."

"Oh, no, I couldn't . . ." Lucy began.

"Oh, come on, it won't be a big meal. Just salad, that sort of thing."

"Well, thank you," Lucy said, taking Nick's cheque. Magnus would be pleased, it was for a large amount, her biggest sale yet.

"I'll have it sent up to you tomorrow.

"Fine, someone will be there," Camilla said, lighting her cigarette. "I've found an excellent housekeeper by the way, Mrs Tomkin from the village, do you know her? She works for Beth, too."

Lucy shook her head. "No, I can't say I do."

"Well," Nick said, "thank you for your help."

"I think that's the easiest sale I ever made," Lucy laughed.

"Confidentially, we looked through the window at it last week, and Camilla had quite made up her mind. We'll see you this evening then."

At half-past six Lucy drove up to The Hall and saw that the front door was open on this summer's evening, and Henry lay just inside on the cool tiles. As soon as he saw her car, he jumped up and began to bark, flinging himself at her when she got out.

She kissed him. "So you did miss me, you old silly," she said, as Nick came out to greet her.

"Hallo, Lucy, come through," he said. "We're in the garden."

"Hello, Camilla. "Lucy dropped into a chair while Henry lay down beside her.

"Traitor," Camilla said to him.

"How about a Pimm's?" Nick asked.

"That would be heaven."

They lay side by side while Nick went off to get drinks, not speaking for a few moments.

"I often think how awful it must have been for you, leaving here," Camilla said.

"Yes, it was, although I didn't realize how much it meant to me until some time after I'd gone. I think being in the cottage, sweet though it is, makes me realize how much I'm missing. Still, I'm jolly lucky to be nearby and have the chance of coming up now and again."

She glanced across at Camilla. It was so difficult to see what she was really thinking behind those thick dark glasses.

"How long have you been married?"

"Nine years," Camilla said. "Nick was a cameraman working on a film I was doing."

"Really?" Lucy was facinated.

"What did you do?"

"Make up – make up artist, that's my official job," Camilla said. "But don't let it fool you. It's a rather grand name for what is a very ordinary job. Mind, I was good at it."

"Like Barbara Daly?"

"That's it."

Nick returned with two glasses of Pimm's and a bottle of Perrier water, pouring out a glass for Camilla.

"You're not going to join us in a Pimm's?" Lucy asked.

"No, I can't take wine or alcohol," Camilla said. "Thank you darling."

"I seem to have lived such a very dull life, really," Lucy said. "When I come up against people like yourselves who've travelled and worked in exotic jobs."

"There's nothing exotic about film making," Nick said. "It's damned hard work. It can be worthwhile, but there's an awful long wait sometimes when you don't get a break."

"You can say that again!" Camilla agreed. "When we

were first married we didn't have a bean. In fact we went off to Canada for Nick to make a film which kept us going for six months until the next one came up. It was fairly steady being a cameraman, but now he's gone upmarket and produces, it's the luck of the draw. Still, the last one was hugely successful, wasn't it, Nick?"

"Yes, thank God," he said. "I got a nice rake off which is why I decided to buy something worthwhile – and Camilla always wanted a home in the Cotswolds."

"So did you," she said.

"That's true, but I thought later, perhaps when we were older . . ."

Nick was, Lucy thought, around thirty-eight or thirty-nine, maybe, while Camilla could be anything between thirty and thirty-five, it was hard to tell.

She lay beside Lucy, making Lucy's skin look quite pallid for her colour was a golden tan all over. She had shapely legs and arms, toned down and trim, where Lucy was just thin. Small breasts and trim waist – and she almost always wore white.

Lucy sighed inwardly. Not only did Camilla have everything she would have liked herself, she also had this good-looking, nice man for a husband.

"So what are you working on now?" she asked.

"It might look a bit ambitious but I'm looking at a Trollope novel, although I don't think Merchant Ivory have much to fear from me." And he laughed.

"I love the Forster films," Lucy said. "I usually go when there's anything worthwhile on in Cheltenham. The trouble is, there's so much that doesn't appeal."

"I know, but film makers have to make films for mass viewing, which is usually the young."

"Yet when they do turn out a really good film, people flock to see it. It's often hard to get in."

"A point I've made quite often," Camilla said, sitting up and pouring herself more Perrier. "I think," she said slowly, "we should give a house warming party." Lucy saw Nick frown.

"Oh, do you really want to, Camilla?"

"Why not? It could be quite nice to meet the neighbours –

not that I can see any from where I am – but Beth knows a few people. After all, darling, we don't want to live here in isolation," she said, winking at Lucy.

"If you really want it," Nick said, lying back and closing his eyes.

"Nick is really a natural hermit. I think he could be quite satisfied living alone on a desert island."

"Not so," he said, eyes closed. "I could be quite happy alone with Meryl Streep or Julia Roberts."

"See?" said Camilla. "The intelligent ones. He's never satisfied."

Lucy lay smiling at their banter. Presently she would get up and swim. Life seemed so leisurely here and it was certainly a change from sitting in the gallery or helping down at the stables, except that she liked that more.

Perhaps, she thought, she should be a riding mistress? She could teach young children to ride, she would like that. Her heart was more in it than sitting in a gallery, even if she was working for the eminently likeable Magnus. But he had quite enough young women eyeing him already. They usually came in at least once a day, dressed in long draggy clothes looking as if they came straight out of a Burne Jones painting, on the off chance of finding him there. How often had she seen the disappointment on their faces?

"I was wondering who we could ask," Camilla said, reaching for her handbag and cigarettes. "By the way, have you met a weird character called Jackie?"

Lucy thought. "Jackie . . . Wasn't she in the play?"

"I don't know, I didn't see it – but I met her at Beth's."

"Yes, she's the one. She was marvellous – quite stole the show. And of course, they won the shield."

"Why do you ask?" Nick said lazily. "Are you going to invite her to the house warming?"

"I might," Camilla said, smiling, as though she were up to something.

"Well," Lucy said, "anyone mind if I have a swim?"

"Do," Camilla told her, stubbing out her cigarette. "I'll join you."

Lucy dived in. It felt marvellous, to be back in the pool again. Closing her eyes, she floated and swam, length after length, and ended up by Camilla who sat at the water's edge, kicking her painted toes in the water.

"Oh, that was wonderful!"

"Yes, you looked as if you were enjoying it," Camilla said, making no effort to join her.

"Coming in?"

"Presently," she said, spreading a towel on the tiles and lying face down on it.

Lucy continued to swim, enjoying every moment of the luxury, until she got out and lay down beside Camilla. She lay for some time, lazily drying out, then sat up and not wanting to disturb Camilla whom she thought must be asleep, she was so still.

Lucy lay back, soaking in the lovely smell of the new mown hay in the adjoining field, the scents of summer. It was a beautiful spot with a view stretching a long way into the distance. So many times had she and her parents sat here in just the same spot on summer evenings. Perhaps it had not been such a good idea to come? She was just making life difficult for herself.

Presently she got up and put on her towelling robe and walked round to the back of the house, thinking to find Henry in the shade. She came across Nick coming out of the house.

"Hallo," he said. "I've just seen Mrs Tomkin off and she's left us a rather nice buffet in the dining room, so if we want to help ourselves we can grab a plate and what we want and eat outside. Where's Camilla?"

"Still by the pool," Lucy said, and watched him hurry over to her side. How he adored her, she thought wistfully. He didn't seem to like letting her out of his sight.

It was late by the time they had finished eating and the sun was going down in the west, making wonderful colours in the sky.

"We must do this again," Nick said. "You're welcome to come up at any time – don't forget."

"Thank you," Lucy said. "If you don't mind my coming up for the odd swim – but not to eat. Please don't feel you have to feed me."

"We like your company," Nick said, taking Camilla's hand.

She sat back and stretched her arms above her head. "Oh, this has been nice – a super evening, peaceful." Presently she took off her glasses and began to polish them, and looking at her, Lucy was astonished to find that without them she looked quite different. Her eyes were obviously short sighted by the way she screwed them up against the light, but it changed her face. She became almost someone else. Before Lucy could decide what it was, she had put them on again.

Lucy was somewhat embarrassed, although she couldn't have said why. It was as though she had seen something priveotic – a word she had made up and used as a child, much to her father's delight.

"Well, I really must be going," she said, getting to her feet. "Goodness, it's almost ten o'clock."

"Come again!" they called out, arms around each other, as they stood in the doorway of The Hall, waving.

The next evening, spent with Philip Sanderson, could not have been more different.

He arrived on Lucy's doorstep at six o'clock, carrying the most enormous bouquet of pink roses.

"Philip! For me?"

He nodded. "Just to say how sorry I am for the other evening."

"What other . . ." And suddenly she remembered. "Oh, Philip, it didn't matter, honestly. But thank you. Do come in."

"I thought you might like to come out for a meal," he said. "Nothing special. The Yew Tree does good evening meals – what do you think?"

"I think I'd like it," she said. "Sit yourself down while I put these in water – oh, they're lovely!" And she bent down to kiss his cheek, and to show him he had been forgiven.

He looked so young, she thought, sitting there, perhaps because she had been in the company of older people the previous evening. He was dressed casually in light-coloured slacks and yellow sweater which suited him.

"How's the gallery going?" he asked, determined not to say anything this evening that might upset her. He had given their relationship a great deal of thought over the past few days, and had decided that he would have to overlook many things which just slightly annoyed him. She was, after all, a young girl on her own, with no previous experience of how life could be in his sort of world, and it was up to him to protect her.

"Quite good," Lucy said, returning with a jug of roses and standing them on the low table in front of him. "Look, aren't they lovely? How kind of you."

He was pleased. He felt he had reinstated himself.

"Yes, I made a good sale, a very expensive picture, and Magnus was pleased. In fact, I didn't have to do anything, the couple just came in and bought it." Something told her you didn't broadcast who had bought what.

"What's he like?"

"Magnus? Very nice – has a wonderful sense of humour."

"My sister's dotty about him," Philip said gloomily.

"All the girls are."

"But not you?"

"Not in that way – you know."

He smiled at her indulgently. "Yes, I know, Lucy." And she wondered if he saw her as a child.

Just as long, he thought, as she didn't become embroiled with Malcolm Mansfield. He didn't trust him as far as he could throw him. It was a bad day for Ainswick, and for his father, when Malcolm came back to the village.

Life was quiet in the dog days of August as the sun continued to shine down. It was very quiet in the gallery with hardly any customers; in fact, Lucy thought, Magnus could quite well have closed the shop for the month of August for all the good it did.

She and Philip went riding on Sunday mornings, and had the occassional meal out. When he kissed her now it was with affection, although when he put his arms around her to say goodnight, she often wished that he would kiss her like he had the first time. Perhaps he was waiting for her to make the first move?

Towards the end of August he asked her home to meet his mother. She was asked to Sunday lunch, and it was obviously a very special occassion. He made no secret of the fact that he had never taken a girl home before.

He came to collect her in his car, and drove her to Dinhampton where he lived, ten miles away from Ainswick.

His mother opened the door of the neat little villa and gave Lucy a warm, shy smile. She was obviously proud of her son, and welcomed Lucy like a longlost daughter.

The lunch was excellent: roast beef and Yorkshire pudding and a delicious apple pie. Lucy could hardly move after she had eaten it and refused all Mrs Sanderson's efforts to press her to just one more helping.

She knew that she had made a good impression and that Philip was pleased. He held her arm tightly when he took her round the garden, and was more relaxed than she had ever seen him.

Only on the way home did she wonder if she was getting in too deep. Was she allowing Philip to read too much into their friendship? Had she egged him on by going out with him?

That night, when he kissed her, she didn't push him away but returned his kisses with an ardour he hadn't expected. This time there was no hurry, no taking her by surprise. He caressed her slowly, taking his time, savouring every touch, every kiss, until they both felt in deep waters. Presently Lucy broke away, conscious of the need to let her head rule her heart, or make a decision not to.

"Philip –"

He didn't restrain her, just let her go.

"I love you, Lucy," he said, and kissed her again.

Much as he moved her physically, she could not answer him honestly. She knew without a doubt that he was on the point of proposing to her, and she wanted to delay his asking the question. Much as she enjoyed being with him, she knew she was not ready for marriage, and was perfectly sure that she was not in love with him. There was so much more she had to know about him, the more she understood what made him tick. He was just different from anyone she had ever known.

"Philip, it's awfully late and we have to be up in the morning."

It seemed he didn't want to let her go without saying more, but she was firm. She put an arm through his. "We must do this again."

He hugged her tightly. "Goodnight, Lucy."
She saw him to the door.
"Goodnight, Philip."

It was during the last week of August that she had a telephone call from Camilla asking her up to The Hall. It seemed Nick had plans for something in the garden and thought Lucy might help.

Only too pleased to make another visit, she drove up on a fine Friday evening after dinner. Nick was waiting for her in the library, poring over garden designs and maps.

"Ah, Lucy, there you are."

"Where's Camilla?" she asked.

"Changing, I think. She's just had a swim."

How well he had settled in here. Casually dressed in jeans and sweater, he might have lived here for years.

"Lucy, I asked Charlton to clear out the shubbery fairly drastically, the one before you get to the vegetable garden, and he discovered what looked like a York stone terrace – do you remember anything about that?"

Lucy shook her head. "No, but I still have lots of old maps and photographs Father gave me years ago when I had to do a project of some kind or other on eighteenth-century houses. There might be something there."

"Oh, that would be great – do you think you could turf them out?"

"Of course. When do you want them?"

He grinned. "As soon as you can, would you mind?"

"Of course not, Nick. They might prove interesting."

"It would be great if I could find something original. There are signs that a great many yews were cut down at one stage."

"Really? I don't know anything about that. Ah, hallo, Camilla."

She was still rubbing her hair with a towel, then shook it about.

"Hi, there, Lucy. So he has this bee in his bonnet about hidden treasures . . ."

"No, darling, hidden gardens."

"You'd think he had enough to keep him occupied,

without going on about his secret gardens." But she smiled at him over Lucy's head.

"Lucy, come and have some coffee with me. I went down to Beth's this evening, and she's up to her eyes in the preparations for the September Fair. She's marvellous, all kinds of things she thinks up."

They walked together down the stairs and into the kitchen.

"You know, I went to school with Beth, and if you'd told me she'd end up as a vicar's wife, I just wouldn't have believed you. As it is, she does it so well, throws herself into it, body and soul. I couldn't do it myself."

"I suppose if you loved someone, and he was a vicar . . ." Lucy suggested.

"I couldn't fall in love with a vicar," Camilla said, and Lucy had to laugh.

Camilla made coffee for three and took it up to the library, where they all sat and talked for the rest of the evening.

Lucy was to remember that for the rest of her life.

Chapter Seventeen

The first of September, and this week Freddie would start school all day. Holding his hand tightly, Beth strolled along the High Street in Ainswick, taking him for a treat to see the work going on at Little Field, for if there was one thing he loved it was machines of any kind.

The first of the new residents was due to move in at the end of the following week, and the gardens were being prepared. Now the small garden tractor was turning over the land and preparing the soil for turves.

Freddie leaned his arms on the fence, totally absorbed in watching.

"Could we have a tractor like that in our garden?" he asked.

"We could if we needed it, but we already have a lawn," Beth said.

"I would like a tractor like that – it's not very big."

"And what would you do with it?"

"Plough up the garden, of course," he said scathingly.

"Come on, then, it's time we went. We have to do some shopping."

"When I go back to school, I'll be in class two," Freddie said. "And I hope Kafleen Palmer won't be there – I don't like her."

"Why? What has she done?"

"She pulled my face and made it hurt."

"Oh, dear."

"I didn't cry though," he said.

"So what did you do?" Beth asked.

"I would have liked to knock her down, but you can't do that so I told her to piss off," he said, as Beth gasped.

Controlling her face, she asked: "What does that mean?"

"That's what you say at school when you want someone to go away."

"Well," Beth said at length, "I don't think it's quite polite to say that to a little girl."

"She's not little, she's big!"

"Well, any girl then. It's not what a big boy would say."

"They do!"

"Well, it's not what a nice boy would say," she said, hoping he would grow out of it like all the other things he had learned at school.

In Mrs Patel's grocer's shop they made much of him, with his red curly hair and wide laughing eyes. He was helpful, too, in that he would go to the shelves and remind Beth of all the things she needed, and some that she didn't, especially the things that he liked.

This morning, not having the car, she only bought what she needed urgently, and put the groceries in a basket and began to walk home.

It was a lovely September day with lots of dried leaves about for owing to the hot summer there had been considerable leaf drop for lack of water.

She was walking up the wide garden path when she saw Mrs Tomkin waiting for her at the front door. She looked quite agitated.

"Oh, Mrs Pennington, will you ring Mr Blakeney up at The Hall? He said it was urgent."

Beth handed her the basket. "Thanks," she said, dialling Nick's number and wondering what on earth could be wrong.

He answered her in a voice she had never heard before.

"Nick?"

"Beth, I'm afraid it's bad news."

She went white. "What do you mean?"

"I don't know how to tell you, Beth, but Camilla – she's gone."

And still it didn't sink in. "Gone? What do you mean? Gone where?"

"Oh, Beth." And she heard his voice crack. "She's dead."

Beth felt faint and sat down abruptly on the hall chair.

"Dead? How can she be?"

"Look – Beth – can you come up right away? The doctor's already been – there'll have to be a post mortem."

"Of course."

Her legs like jelly, she turned to Mrs Tomkin who waited beside her. One look at her face told Beth that she already knew.

Mrs Tomkin nodded, her eyes filled with tears.

"I thought Mr Blakeney should tell you."

"I can't believe it," Beth kept saying. "How could she die? She was so young to die."

"I think she was ill," Mrs Tomkin said sorrowfully, "I thought so from the first."

"How could you think that? She didn't look ill to me – she was in good health . . ."

Mrs Tomkin shook her head. "There was something about her, poor lass." She dried her eyes. "You go on up to The Hall – the children will be all right with me. There's nothing I can do up there at present."

"Oh, thank you, Mrs Tomkin." And Beth, as if in a dream, got out of the car and made the nightmare journey up to The Hall.

They had only been up there six weeks. How could Camilla die – just die? She had never said anything about being ill. She had looked so well.

Beth parked the car and ran to the front door and rang the bell. Nick answered it and they fell into each other's arms.

"Oh, Nick!" she sobbed as he broke down.

"Beth –"

Presently they emerged from the embrace, and sadly, slowly, Nick led her out into the garden where they sat in garden chairs on the terrace.

"Where is she?" Beth whispered.

"Upstairs," he said.

"Can I see her?"

"If you want to," he said. "It's been an awful shock, I know, take your time." And he left her to go inside the house. He came out with a glass full of thick yellow drink which he handed to her. She looked at it with distaste.

"It's a brandy egg nog – drink it," he said. "It will help bring you round."

She sipped it slowly, not liking the unaccustomed taste.

"Tell me, Nick," she said presently, seeing his eyes were full of unshed tears. The lashes that Camilla had always admired were wet, and Beth burst into a bout of weeping.

"That's good," he said. "Better to cry."

When she had finished, he began to talk.

"She had an obscure blood disease," he said as Beth listened. "I can give you the name of it, but you wouldn't be any the wiser. They thought she might have picked it up in Kenya five years ago when we went, do you remember?"

Beth nodded.

"It may not have been then, but that's what they think. She's had two or three bouts of illness."

"Why didn't someone tell me?" Beth asked, angry that she had been kept in the dark.

"There was no point – it was at a time when you were busy having young Freddie, and after all, when you moved away, we didn't see you much."

"But to have such a serious illness and not let me know!" Beth was shocked and furious. "I was her best friend!"

He took her hand in his.

"Did you know?" she began.

"That she was going to die?" he nodded. "She had to have regular check ups and they told me a year ago, but Camilla didn't know. She knew she still had the disease, but not that she was going to die."

Beth sobbed.

"That's why you bought this place, isn't it?" she said, the light dawning.

"Yes. As soon as she saw it, she wanted it, and I thought, well, for whatever time she had left . . . Of course, I didn't think it would be quite so soon. I thought we'd have a few more years."

They sat in silence.

"What happened?" Beth asked at length.

"We went to bed at the usual time – young Lucy Gilbert had been up here. We'd been talking about a garden project I had in mind, and after she left we went to bed – Camilla was tired. When I woke early – about four, I think it was, I don't know – I had a feeling. I bent over to her – and she was –"

Beth put out her hand. "Don't," she said. "How awful."

They sat for some time, until Beth got up and said she would like to see Camilla.

She lay in her bedroom facing the windows, looking somehow different without her dark glasses. Beth caught her breath. She looked down at her for a moment, then bent over and kissed her lightly on the forehead. Biting her lip, she hurriedly left the room. Nick followed her after a time.

"They'll take her away, won't they?"

Later today – there'll have to be an inquest."

"Poor Nick," she said, holding his arm, and together they walked down the stairs.

She walked to the front door and stood there. "I'll have to go now, Nick, but I'll be back. If there is anything we can do, Marcus and I."

He nodded. "Thanks, Beth."

The tears ran down her face all the way home, but by the time she reached the vicarage, all trace of them had gone. Only her reddened eyes betrayed the fact that she had been weeping.

"Freddie, Freddie!" she cried, gathering him in her arms and kissing him. "Oh, how heavy you've grown."

"Put me down," he said. "I'm not a baby."

"Of course you're not," she assured him, going into the kitchen where Mrs Tomkin was preparing lunch.

"Mrs Tomkin said Auntie Camilla died," Clarry said, her blue eyes wide.

Beth was pleased she had been told.

"Yes," she said. "It's sad, isn't it?"

"She was quite old," Clarrie said, picking up her doll, Bessie, and taking her upstairs.

So much for Camilla, Beth thought. She still couldn't believe it.

"Why, Marcus, why?" she asked him in bed that night, as he cradled her in his arms.

"I can't answer that," He said. "If I knew all the answers, I daresay I should be at least bishop – all I can say is that in this profession you see so much sadness and get asked so many questions which can't be answered . . ."

"But you're supposed to know!" she said, quite angrily. "People come to you for comfort."

"And that's all I can do," he said. "Comfort. I can't give you any answers as to why –"

"Only to say it's God's will – and that's not enough," she said.

"How do you think I feel when a child dies? That's so much worse," he said. "Or a child is killed. There's no reason, no answer. With grieving parents who need solace, sometimes I think –"

"What, Marcus?"

"Nothing." he sighed. "I know no more now than when I was first ordained, but you just have to press on and trust in God."

"Dear Marcus," she said finally, drifting off to sleep but aware that he was still awake. She knew he sometimes did this, lay awake for long hours in the darkness, and there was nothing she could say that would help.

There were more celebrities at Camilla's funeral than the village had ever seen. The church was full of visitors from London, Nick's friends and business colleagues, and a few local people, including Lucy, who still couldn't believe what had happened. Why, she had seen Camilla only a few hours before.

Beth listened to Marcus give a moving eulogy on a girl he had known since he was twenty odd, who in a few weeks had re-entered their lives, only to depart so swiftly.

Through a haze of tears Beth listened, and none of it made sense. She hadn't Marcus's deep belief to comfort her, just a sense of loss that Camilla should have died so needlessly. Thank God they had had no children.

Lucy sat stunned. The second time in a year she had attended a funeral service, having never been to one before. All round her were famous faces, people she recognized from films and television, and the flowers were magnificent. She could only think of Nick, and what he must be going through.

When it was over, mourners gathered up at the hall, where Mrs Tomkin had prepared a light luncheon, but it was nothing without Camilla, Beth thought.

Seeing Lucy on her own, she went over to her. "I'm glad you came."

"I couldn't not. I thought of them both as such good friends – they were so kind, asking me up here." And she bit her lip.

"Camilla was like that," Beth said. "If she liked you, you could have anything – but woe betide you if she didn't!" And she managed a small laugh. "I've never really seen the grounds up here. Do you think we could take a walk?"

"Of course."

They wandered round the rose garden and the Italian garden which had been laid out by Lucy's grandfather.

"It's beautiful. And the pergola over there."

"My father had that built not all that long ago. Oh, Beth, life is so sad sometimes, isn't it?"

"Yes, it is," she said. "And I suppose I hear more about it than most, being a vicar's wife, but it doesn't seem to make any difference. You never get used to it. Tragedies, I mean."

They were walking now back towards the house.

"Of course you saw them only the previous evening, didn't you? Nick said you were helping them in a garden project."

"Yes, perhaps we could see where it is?"

Lucy led the way to the shubbery where they found a lot of ground dug up and below it evidence that there had been a York stone terrace.

"How exciting!" Beth said. "It's lovely to find something of the past in a place like this, isn't it?"

They walked back slowly towards the house, both of them with their own thoughts.

Catching sight of Marcus, Beth went over to him.

"Ah, there you are," he said, somewhat relieved. "I think I must go, Beth."

"Me, too," she said. "Just let's have a word with Nick, shall we?"

"Thank you for coming," he said gravely.

Beth kissed him. "What will you do?"

"I'm not sure. You think about these things when you

have to be prepared, but now that it's come – I simply don't know. I need time to think."

"Well, Nick, you know where we are," Marcus said, shaking his hand.

Walking back to the car, side by side with Marcus, Beth thought of the one bright thing that had come out of an unhappy week. She was carrying a new life inside her. Even Marcus didn't know yet, and she hugged the knowledge to herself.

She had a sudden thought of Maggie, and what her mother had said when Maggie's husband walked out on her. "One door closes and another opens."

It was true.

Chapter Eighteen

On this mid-September morning, Shirley Dinsdale was swanning around Peggy's kitchen in the very best of moods, even from time to time breaking into a little song.

Peggy was relieved after the disaster of Kylie being pregnant, although she was preoccupied with several other things she had on her mind.

"So your mother is pleased with the flat?" she said, coming into the kitchen with her envelopes of council business and prepared to do battle for another day.

"Oh, Mrs Mansfield, it's lovely, it really is," Mrs Dinsdale beamed. "Her own bathroom, hot water, lovely tiling. As for the kitchen, well, it knocks my old one into a cocked hat! They've give them everything, fitted cupboards, everything. I tell you, my old mum is as pleased as punch."

"I am glad," Peggy said sincerely. She hoped all the old people who had moved in felt the same about the Little Field development. It was a wrench in one way to leave their old homes, but the fascination of a completely new one was usually enough to make them feel they had a new lease of life.

"Well, I'm off now," she said. "I won't be back to lunch today."

"Right you are, Mrs Mansfield."

She might leave a few minutes early today and get the bus into Cheltenham. It was time she thought about buying a few baby things for the expected grandchild. Young Kylie hadn't a clue in this world about what you needed for a baby. All she thought about was that young man.

Peggy went on her way, immersed in thought. First, she wondered what Malcolm was up to. He had been very busy lately, dashing about with hardly time to pop in and see them, and without saying a word about what he was doing. That usually boded ill, but perhaps she looked too much on the black side where Malcolm was concerned? He had a nice little business going in the village – if he was to be believed. That was the trouble with Malcolm, she never knew when to believe him. Half the things he told her she didn't mention to Dennis, for fear of worrying him.

And that was another thing. Dennis. Of late he had been very preoccupied, so much so that she had wondered if he was ill and was keeping it to himself. Yet he looked well enough but he was out such a lot.

She should complain, she was out too much herself, but really today there was so much to do on local and civic business, one of the reasons being that there were no younger people to take over. They all had jobs with very little time for voluntary work.

On arrival at the local council offices, she went straight to the board outlining the forthcoming meetings and business. Complaints, complaints, not enough litter bins, another application for yet another public loo, could they have another bus stop halfway down the High Street, then looked at the planning applications which had arrived this week.

The Patels wanted a new fascia board, and someone a change of use from a sweet to a gift shop – oh, not another one! A new front entrance for the Hartlebury Hotel, some new steps, and down the list an address caught her eye. The Grange! An application to turn it into luxury flats. Her heart began to beat rather fast. Malcolm! But the name of the applicant was someone in London – well, she didn't know what that was about. Perhaps Malcolm would know? She couldn't believe it had nothing to do with him.

Malcolm at that moment was taking Mrs Hemingway to see Woodbine Cottage. She was thoroughly enjoying her trip, even though she had found it quite difficult to get into the Porsche. But what excitement! Her faded blue eyes shone at the prospect, which did sound rather exciting.

"There we are then," Malcolm said, holding out a strong hand for her to take. "Careful now."

Well, it was pretty and no mistake. Just off Shoe Lane, a bungalow with a dear little garden behind a chain strung along white posts.

She took Malcolm's arm as he led her to the door and inserted the key.

It was empty, but in a trice she saw it could be like home. A tiny kitchen and two living rooms which seemed rather small after the huge room at The Grange. She looked a little more doubtful.

"It's a bit cramped," she said peevishly. "I'm used to space. I don't think I could live without space."

"Yes," Malcolm agreed, for he thought it bad policy to argue. "You're right, but of course we could knock the dividing wall down , and hey presto!"

"I shouldn't like the work – so dusty, messy," she began, but he could see she was wavering.

"It would all be done before you move in," he confided in a whisper.

"Oh. Oh, I see."

She walked gingerly with her stick and came to two bedrooms and a rather nice bathroom, which someone had laid out rather well."

"Oh, very nice," she said. This was better.

"And cosy – don't you think?"

"Yes, it is," she agreed, looking out of the narrow window down to the garden.

"Oh, how pretty. It has an apple tree."

"And apples," Malcolm said.

"And a small pond."

"With fish and frogs, I believe," he said roguishly.

She went in both bedrooms and inspected the built in wardrobes.

"I have my own wardrobes," she said. "Inlaid mahogany from when I was first married."

"And I should bring them with you," Malcolm said indulgently. "These can be removed quite easily."

"So there would be quite a lot to be done?"

"Oh, no," he assured her. "Very little as far as I can see –

no problem at all. I'd see to that. If you were interested, of course. I'm afraid you would have to make up your mind rather quickly."

"Oh, dear," she said.

"Well," he sighed, "you know how it is. A little gem like this – everyone wants it! I have three people after it but I have given you preference because it seemed so right for you."

"Oh, you are a nice young man." She beamed. "Well, I have to say I'm interested, but I should have to think it over – sleep on it." Her blue eyes looked at him appealingly.

"Of course," he said. "I wouldn't dream of rushing you. Take your time over it – but I would have to know by say – Friday?"

"Of course," Mrs Hemingway agreed. "I expect I could let you know tomorrow."

"That's even better." He beamed at her. "Now, what else shall we look at – the garden?"

"Yes, please."

When they arrived home, she invited him in for a cup of tea, which he accepted.

"Now, young man," she said. "You do realize that I would have to sell this flat first before I could buy the cottage?"

"Of course," he said. "Naturally."

"Now, what are the chances of that?"

He concentrated hard. She must have no idea of the complexities of the situation.

"Yes, I agree, that is a problem." he said at length. "Still with a bit of luck . . ." And he appeared to be immersed in deep thought as she waited.

"I do have someone in mind. Mind you, it is a little doubtful at the moment since he has a house to sell – but he might, just might, be interested. Of course you must ask a reasonable price for this so as to make the offer tempting."

"Of course, of course – you must advise me."

"Leave it with me, and I'll get in touch with him right away and let you know."

Pleased with his efforts of his day, Malcolm drove back to the office where he got in touch immediately with Leo Burns.

"So far, so good, eh?" Leo said.

Malcolm let two days pass, then telephoned Mrs Hemingway from the office.

"Ah, Mrs Hemingway – I have some good news! In the first place, I have someone interested in your apartment, and secondly, Woodbine Cottage is yours if you want it!"

"Oh, that's wonderful!" she cried. For the past two days the apartment had seemed to get larger and larger and the thought of the little cottage so near to everything and so convenient had become a dream.

"Now between you and me, I'm being pressurized by the owner of the cottage, who has someone else interested – but I've managed to stave him off."

"Oh, dear!"

"Now don't worry, my dear Mrs Hemingway. Leave it to me. I don't want you fretting about unnecessary problems, so when I get home this evening we'll discuss it. I have to go now. See you later."

So far so good. And he picked up the receiver again.

" . . . Of course you can, Leo. It's in the bag. Be down here around eleven – you can be off again at twelve. It won't take long, and it's worth the drive . . ."

By the afternoon, Leo had seen Mrs Hemingway and left with a promise to buy the apartment at a much reduced price.

With slight and careful pressure from Malcolm, she agreed to this and later he called back to finalize the situation.

"Now I shall want the name of your solicitors," he said, and when she gave it, heaved a sigh of relief. They were in Cheltenham, thank God!

"Just as a sign of good faith, if you could manage a deposit?"

"Oh – now?" she asked.

"The usual ten per cent," he said with one of his most confidential smiles.

She went to the bureau and got out her cheque book.

"Eight thousand pounds," she said out loud as she wrote it, and signed it, and waved it in the air to dry before handing it to him.

"Now that ensures it is mine?"

"I certainly hope so!" he laughed, and stowed it away in his breast pocket.

Later he would have to think it all out. Work at it. But the thing was he had to put the wheels in motion. A bit of money to satisfy the vendor of the cottage. It was a little – well, it sounded complicated, but it wasn't really. At least it wouldn't be when Leo got down to it.

It was almost five-thirty when he finished business, and was just on the point of closing when he saw someone at the door.

It was Jackie Hetherington – and his heart missed a beat. He had not seen her for two weeks while her husband had been home, but now, here she was, live and well and calling in to see him!

She looked, as always, delicious. That long dark hair, the white brief suit, the skirt disclosing fabulous legs which were tanned and bare, and she wore gold sandles. But it was the look in her eyes as she closed the door and came towards him that unnerved him.

The green eyes flashed like emeralds as she gave him a brilliant smile.

"Malcolm," she said in that low breathy voice, holding out her hand. "You don't mind my calling in, do you? I simply had to see you."

"My dear, I'm delighted," he said, waving her to a chair. "Take a seat. This is a surprise – and may I say a very pleasant one?"

She sat down and crossed her legs. Malcolm could hardly take his eyes off them.

"Er – your husband – Tony – is he home?"

"No," she said with a sad little smile. "He has had to go to New York – without me, I'm afraid. He'll be away for ten days."

She gave him a more intimate smile.

"So you see I'm all alone – and I wondered if we could perhaps go for a drink somewhere, if you have time? It's a lovely evening."

Malcolm was already one jump ahead.

"My dear Jackie, that's a wonderful idea. Just let me lock up."

He followed her out of the shop as she walked a step ahead. "Where shall we go?"

Just behind her, he said, "The Watchmaker's Arms – do you know it?"

"I'll see you there in ten minutes," Jackie said, getting into her parked car.

She sat in the car until he arrived, watching him lock up the Porsche – always such a noticeable car – and walked over to her.

He opened the door of the passenger seat and stepped in beside her. She turned to him, her green eyes glowing, and moved towards him, face uplifted.

He kissed her hungrily, her warm soft mouth opening for his kiss, one hand on her silken knee.

He was breathless from excitement and anticipation as she gently eased herself away.

"Malcolm, later." And that was enough to steady him, to bring him back to earth.

He looked at her hungrily.

"God," he said. "You're a witch."

"I know," she said, smiling mysteriously.

Over drinks, they talked softly, hand in hand below the table top, Malcolm's mostly on her knee and moving slowly.

He swallowed hard, his mind racing with future prospects.

"Ten days, you said?"

"What?"

"Ten days your husband will be away?"

"I'm afraid so," she said softly, her green eyes gleaming wickedly.

"Look," he said, "why don't we go away for the weekend?"

"Oh, Malcolm, could we? Where?"

"Paris," he said, without realizing he'd said it, but having done so feeling a sense of elation at the prospect.

"Oh!" Her green eyes shone as she looked up into his and placed her hand on his thigh. He shivered at her touch.

"Jackie –" It was almost a groan.

"Darling Malcolm, it would be wonderful! When would we go?"

It was devilish difficult to keep an even keel, but he tried.

"Friday night until Sunday – what do you think?"

She squeezed his thigh and took a deep breath.

Malcolm had to admit that the knowledge that Mrs Hemingway's cheque was in his pocket did help.

"Will you get the tickets? And where shall we stay?"

He had no hesitation. "At the Georges V" he said, seeing her face light up.

"Of course!" she cried. "How shall we manage it?"

Malcolm was already there in his mind – way ahead of things. Still, they had to be careful, to plan.

"I'll ring you," he said.

"No, I'll give you a ring on Friday morning, then we'll both drive to the airport separately."

"That's it," he said.

Driving to Hunter's Lodge on his way home, he went straight in to his mother who was counting the collecting boxes for the Children's Union.

"Thirteen, fourteen – that's the lot," she said. "Ah, there you are – good day?"

"Very good indeed."

She could tell it had been. There was a lift to his shoulders and a roguish twinkle in his eye.

"Mother, I won't be here this weekend – from Friday night until Sunday."

"Oh?" she said vaguely.

"I'm going up town for the weekend."

"All right, dear."

"And how did your day go?" he asked her solicitously.

"Much as usual," she said. "Oh, I know – Malcolm, there was a planning application from someone for turning The Grange into luxury apartments – do you know anything about it?"

She would have to know sooner or later, but he couldn't go into it now.

He looked vague. "Luxury apartments? The Grange?" He frowned and shook his head. "Mother – how's Dad? I thought he looked tired when I saw him on Tuesday."

"I know," she said. "He works too hard. He's not getting any younger."

When Malcolm left, she sat down with a cup of tea. She

felt she needed pulling around. She was getting older and more tired, doing too much, she supposed. Like Dennis.

Dennis was late, very late. They usually dined at seven, but this evening it was eight o'clock when he arrived, and after taking off his coat and hanging it up, he went straight into the kitchen where Peggy was taking the casserole out of the oven.

"Could we leave that for a bit?" he asked. He was as white as a sheet.

"Of course we can," she said. "Let's go into the study."

He sat down opposite her as she waited. The sooner she knew what was wrong, the better.

"I have something to tell you."

She swallowed hard. "You're not ill, Dennis, are you?"

He shook his head. "No. Nothing like that."

"Thank God," she said. "Then nothing else matters."

"You might think differently when I tell you," he said, in command of himself now. "Peggy, you and I have lived separate lives for many years, and for a long time I didn't find that easy."

Now she was filled with compunction. Whatever he had to tell her, she had only herself to blame.

"For the past ten years, I have had a – friend, a mistress, I suppose you would call her."

She was shocked. She had never ever imagined such a thing with Dennis. The thoughts rushed through her head. How could she blame him? He was a man, like any other. What she had done had been cruel, but she had thought he'd accepted it.

"She lives on the other side of Cheltenham. I met her when her husband died, and I had to go into the question of his estate. We became friends. She has no children, and it went on from there. I have been seeing her a couple of times a week ever since then."

She was numb with cold shock. Oddly enough she didn't blame him, nor feel any sense of outrage. It was just that all this time he had been living a lie, and she had had no idea. That's what hurt. But how could he have told her? She wanted to be scrupulously fair.

Now he looked at her. "Peggy, I never wanted to hurt you."

She shook her head. "I know." How much had she hurt him, did he but know it, holding the biggest secret of all in her heart, and that was something she could never tell him. She could afford to be kind and generous after what she had done.

"Poor Dennis," she said.

He looked surprised and relieved.

"You mean, you don't mind?"

"Of course I mind – well, that you have gone on all this time without my knowing. But why are you telling me now?"

"She's very ill. She is not young – we're the same age – her heart isn't strong. She needs care. I think she needs me."

Now she did feel sad. He was slipping away from her Someone she had depended on for so long, never doubting always assuming – instead of which he had had a life of his own. And deep down she couldn't blame him.

"She – her name is Clare – has been in hospital for three weeks but now that she's home and rather frail she has help in the house."

Peggy felt a band around her heart.

"You want to be with her?" she said.

"Yes, Peggy, I do. We're all getting older, time become precious."

She leaned over and held his hand.

"Go to her, Dennis."

She saw his eyes fill with tears, and suddenly he buried hi face in his hands. "Oh, Peggy – I never wanted . . ."

"I know," she said, seeing that beloved silver-grey hea bent before her.

"If anything should happen, you will come back?" sh asked.

Her small black eyes were glistening like jet.

"Yes, Peg, I will." He blew his nose. "What will you say t Malcolm?"

"It's nothing to do with him," she said sharply. "He ha his life, and we have ours."

He went out of the room, shoulders bowed, and once h had gone she wept as she hadn't wept for many a long day.

Chapter Nineteen

They met in the departure lounge at Heathrow, a tall well-built man with eyes perpetually searching the crowds which seemed to increase by the minute, and the beautiful dark-haired woman. How could anyone not have noticed her? In tight black trousers and fitted jacket, her lovely hair tied back with a band, she carried a scarlet holdall and what looked to him like a small piece of Louis Vuitton luggage.

He breathed deeply and went over to her.

"Jackie."

She turned impish green eyes up to him, and smiled.

"Which way?"

"Over here."

Malcolm thought he had never seen a woman look so attractive as Jackie did, simply dressed as she was. She stood out by the very simplicity of her clothes, that and her beauty and self-confidence. More than one man turned to look after her. Malcolm couldn't have felt more proud.

In the departure lounge, he felt the air was electrified all around them. They had not spoken a word other than their greetings. It was enough to live on the promise of what surely was going to be a memorable weekend.

He ordered champagne on the flight, which they sipped slowly, and in no time they had arrived at the airport from where a hair-raising drive by taxi deposited them at the Hotel Georg V.

Once inside they went to the reception desk to obtain the key to their suite. The air was heavy and scented with roses and lilies; all around them liveried page boys and porters. An ornately carved wrought iron lift took them up to their floor where the porter showed them to the suite. Once inside, they looked at each other and fell into each other's arms, laughing.

Then Malcolm sank on to one of the two great Empire beds, while Jackie went over to the windows and pushed the floor-length silk curtains aside to reveal the beautiful courtyard outside where great urns were full of pink and red geraniums.

The Louis XV furniture was set on an Aubusson carpet in delicate pastel shades, while the beds were covered in crimson silk with masses of lacy cushions.

Jackie strolled back and took off her jacket to reveal a white silk top. He could see her breasts quite clearly beneath it, and suspected she wore no bra. Unable to contain himself any longer, he got up and put his arms around her, kissing her until she was like a rag doll, then pulled her towards the bed where he laid her down and began to caress her.

She struggled free and sat up. "I'm going to have a bath."

He had thought she felt like him, the same urgency, but with a laugh she went into the bathroom, leaving him to cool his heels and unpack, quite sulkily. Tomorrow, he thought, he would join her. They would bathe together.

She lay relaxing in the huge bath where soft fluffy bath towels hung waiting to be used, eyeing the enormous twin bowls, the jars and scent bottles which held every kind of luxury. Then wrapping herself in a bath towel, after spraying herself with perfume and powder, she went into the bedroom where Malcolm was standing by the window.

He turned and looked at her. Their eyes met, and as they did she let the bath towel fall, and stood there for him to drink in her beauty. She saw his eyes flame with desire.

"Jackie!"

It was almost a groan as he whipped her up in to his arms and flung her on to the bed, burying his face in the dark mane of her hair. She put her arms around his neck, drawing him down to her, and gave herself up to him, feeling the hardness of his body against hers, exciting him even more by her reactions. He kissed her slowly, lingeringly, as she held him tightly to her, feeling his strength, looking up at him, her green eyes glowing in the half light as she began to run her fingers over his body, teasing him, her movements joined with his in perfect rhythm.

He was exhausted and fascinated as it went on. He had known many women, loved a few, but never like this. There seemed nothing that she would not think up or do or experiment with, he wondered if he had the strength to keep up with her. She was the most beautiful women he had ever seen, and the most insatiable. More full of tricks than anyone he had ever slept with. Desirable, sexy, warm and passionate - there seemed no end to it, and he wondered how that lucky devil of a husband had the nerve to leave her alone.

It was late-evening when they emerged from the tumbled bed and bathed together. Even then, there seemed no limit to his desire. With her hair tumbled about her shoulders, soaking wet from the bath, he pounced on her, amazing himself that at his age he still had the strength to keep up with her.

Around eleven, they sauntered out of the hotel, Jackie in a long ankle-length silk skirt and brief top and shawl, and ate at a little restaurant by the Seine, toasting each other and gazing into each other's eyes.

Walking home along the river bank in the pitch blackness of the Seine, she drew him into the shadows against a buttress of a bridge.

"Take me – now," she said, putting her arms round his neck and drawing his face down to hers.

He lifted her skirt to find that she had nothing on underneath, which was enough to set his pulses racing yet again, wanting her.

"Here?" he said, not believing her.

"Yes, like a whore."

Afterwards they sauntered back to catch a taxi to the hotel and he marvelled that, with her, each time seemed like the first.

Back at the hotel, she fell like a kitten into bed, cuddling up, curled against him like a soft little animal, spent, her mouth soft with kisses, her cheeks flushed with wine. He bent and kissed her gently.

He lay back exhausted, marvelling that a woman like her existed when he'd thought he knew it all. There had been nymphomaniacs, greedy married woman, nice girls, all sorts of girls. But this one . . . she had it all. He was asleep before he knew it.

He heard a movement towards dawn as a sliver of light came in through the curtains, and saw a shadowy figure etched against the window.

Jackie stood there. She wore a nightdress of emerald green silk, heavy with lace. He could see even in this light every line of her body showing through it as in an erotic painting. He feasted his eyes on her as she turned and came back slowly to bed. He felt the soft shimmering silk as she lay down beside him, her soft lips on his shoulder, her soft hands on his body.

They breakfasted late, and afterwards took a leisurely walk through the park, seeing the trees with their autumnal foliage, the nursemaids and the dogwalkers, then they went along the Rue St Honoré, where Jackie was in her element.

Even Malcolm had to agree, there was nothing like the window displays in Paris. The exquisitely made suits, the soft leather shoes and handbags. He wanted to buy her everything she desired.

Her eyes were glued to the fabulous evening gowns, the silk hand made shirts – there was so much to see. He hated to put a damper on any of it, but this trip was already costing an arm and a leg, as he well knew.

They were outside a famous jeweller's when her green eye fell on an exquisite pair of emerald earrings. He had to agree they were beautiful – and, he would bet, a fair old price.

"Oh, Malcolm! Just look at those earrings! The setting – look." And she held out her hand with the emerald ring to show him how they matched.

"Perfect," he smiled. How he would like to buy them for her – he daren't even guess at the price.

She laid a hand on his arm and looked up at him wistfully.

It didn't need much imagination to see how wonderfu they would look near the green eyes, and after all, what wa money for but to spend? And after this weekend . . .

The commissionaire had ushered them in through the doc before he realized it.

It was sumptuous inside, ankle deep in carpet, polishe crystal counters and chandeliers, and there was Jackie a excited as a child. He looked down at her indulgently, smiled at the assistant as though to say, What can a man do?

The assistant smiled back, and went to get the earrings from the window, which took quite a time, what with the special precautions and burglar alarms.

By now Jackie was sitting on a chair, her silk-clad legs crossed, eyes sparkling with expectation, a hand on his knee.

The assistant laid the velvet box gently before her, lifted the lid with his long-fingererd, delicate hands, and waited.

Malcolm could see no difference between the emeralds and Jackie's green orbs. In fact, he thought hers were finer.

"Would Madam . . .?" the salesman suggested, handing one to her.

By the time Jackie had them on, and the mirror was being held up in front of her, Malcolm knew he was lost. Had known it, in fact, since he went into the shop, though he'd hoped somehow that something, someone, would come to the rescue.

When told the price, he inwardly passed out but surfaced again all in the space of a second. He knew, of course, that jewellery like this could cost the earth, but had never actually been involved in such a purchase. As it was, to hell with it. She was worth it, every penny.

Who knew what delights she would have in store for him after this?

Having committed himself, he felt as proud as a peacock. Like any other rich gentleman out buying his lover a gift, he strolled the streets of Paris like a millionaire.

Later, they dined at Maxim's by candlelight, where they sat on crimson velvet banquettes amidst art Nouveau decor. Malcolm's were not the only eyes on the green-eyed beauty who wore an off the shoulder black dress with a velvet band of jet beads around her creamy throat, her hair piled high, looking like the original of a Manet painting.

That night, when he came to bed, Jackie was lying on the bed waiting for him, naked but for the emerald earrings.

On Sunday, he hired a car to take them to the forest of Fontainebleau, where they dined at Barbizon in the summer sun under a rose-covered trellis next to a gnarled old wistaria tree. All around them were French families and young lovers. It was magical.

Sated beyond belief after an excellent lunch, Malcolm sat back, absorbing the beauty of the surroundings, knowing that he would find it hard to return to England, to a life without this beautiful girl about whom he knew nothing, except that she was the most wonderful girl he had ever had, that he adored her.

After lunch, they walked in the forest hand in hand, stopping now and again for a kiss like any young lovers before returning to Paris and thence to the airport.

On the flight home Malcolm seemed morose, miserable at the thought of leaving her, of her going back to her husband, however briefly he was in this country. But nothing seemed to quell Jackie's cheerfulness.

"Hasn't it been wonderful, Malcolm?"

He pressed her hand, deep in thought, recalling the week-end in the hotel.

"Shall we do it again sometime?"

"Of course," he said, wondering how he was going to pay for it all, and knowing that a second visit might not be possible for a long time. Thank God for Mrs Hemingway's cheque. Still, he had only borrowed the money temporarily, until he was in funds again.

"Tell me about your husband." he said suddenly. "I mean, what's he like?"

"Tony? You mean to look at? Fair, nice-looking."

"No, I don't mean like that – what sort of a man is he?"

"I supposed I'm biased," she said sadly. "I have to live with him, but he is selfish, almost cruel sometimes."

"Jackie." He gripped her hand suddenly. "Why don't you leave him?"

"I'd like to," she said wistfully.

"Then why don't you – you don't have to stay with him, do you?"

"I've tried once before," she said sadly, "but he came after me, I don't seem to have the courage to go it alone. I need a man – but not just any man." And her green eyes looked up at him beneath long lashes.

"But you would leave him to come to me?" he asked, pressing her hand and meeting her eyes.

"Of course I would," she agreed. "But that's not possible, is it? Is it, Malcolm?"

"Well," he said slowly, remembering his commitments, his two ex-wives, the mothers of his children, the outstanding child support payments that he hadn't got around to yet, "I can't think why not."

"Oh, Malcolm, could we? Run away? Elope?"

He was astonished. "You mean, you would? Seriously?"

"Of course," she said earnestly.

"But what about your husband? I mean, he must earn a good salary with his job – you have a nice home – what about all that?"

She waved it away. "It means nothing to me – nothing."

"Then I can't see why you stay with him. I mean, you have no children."

"What about you?" she asked suddenly. "You've been married before."

"Yes." He sighed. "It was a mistake."

"And with a child," she reminded him. "How did you feel about that?"

"Sad of course," he lied.

"Don't you miss him? Ever want to see him?"

"Of course I do, you can imagine," he said, his voice sounding hurt. "But he's best off with his mother, I know that."

"You're a very nice man, Malcolm."

They were silent for a few moments'

"I used to travel a lot with Tony in the early days of our marriage," Jackie said at length, "and the place I loved most was New Zealand. Oh, you'd love it, Malcolm! It's a wonderful place. I've always wanted to go back."

She squeezed his hand.

"Why don't we?" she asked him, looking up into his eyes.

"Why don't we what?" he repeated.

"Go to New Zealand, just the two of us – oh, Malcolm it would be wonderful! Leave everything behind us, start a new life together."

It was tempting all right. If they only could.

They were interrupted by the arrival of the stewardess with the duty free trolley.

"Is there anything you'd like?" He asked Jackie, hoping there wasn't.

"What do you have?" Jackie asked, looking at the list. "I think Van Cleef – have you the perfume? Not the toilet water. Yes, that and Chanel 19, and perhaps the Jolie Madame . . . I have a feeling you like that," she whispered as Malcolm took out his wallet.

"Oh, thank you, Malcolm darling." She snuggled up to him. Could he afford her? he wondered. But what a future! Jackie and him, they couldn't lose. She would be lucky for him, he knew it. She made him feel like a tycoon.

Too soon they had landed to find the tarmac wet where it had rained. Jackie shivered.

"Oh, how awful – after that lovely weekend," she cried.

Then, after what seemed like an age waiting for their luggage and getting through customs, they were in the car park, arms tightly around each other, then he saw her into her car and watched her drive off into the darkness.

Chapter Twenty

'hilip Sanderson read the letter the new girl had placed in 'ront of him, and looked up, his brows drawn.

"How do you spell admittance?" he said.

Her pretty face troubled, biting her lip, she looked up at he ceiling.

"A-d-m-i-t-t-a-n-c-e," she said.

"You have one 't' here, Miss Reynolds," he said. "Your pelling could be improved upon."

"That's a typing error, Mr Sanderson. I'm sorry."

He handed it back to her. "Amend, Miss Reynolds."

She didn't mind how often he told her off, she just adored he way he called her "Miss Reynolds". It made her feel nportant. In her last office, everyone had called her Angie.

Besides, he was really dishy. Miss Dickinson thought so oo, even though they laughed at his imperious ways They new he had a girl friend, but still, you never knew. He iight not look it, Angie thought, but he was a real macho ıan.

Philip sat deep in thought. Things around him were changıg fast. Something was going on with the old man. Dennis 'as keeping strange office hours, but he supposed that when ou reached the age of sixty-five you were entitled to. Any me now, he thought, Dennis surely must retire, thus leaving ıe field clear for him. Not a bad prospect, but deserved 'hen you think how hard he had studied to get where he 'as.

Also, and he began to relax a little, you needed added :curity when you were about to become a married man. Oh, yes. He had decided. This very weekend he was going to ask Lucy to marry him, and he grew quite warm at the thought. His mother had been delighted when he told her, but a little concerned. "Are you sure, Philip?" He knew what she was getting at, the fact that he was marrying out of his "class" as she called it.

What rubbish! That sort of thing went out with the ark.

When Angie returned with the letter, he was still sitting at his desk. She handed him the letter, waiting.

"That's better," he said, signing it and putting it in the post basket.

Angie just loved the way his hair grew with that curly bit in front and he had very nice eyes behind the glasses. She suspected his teeth were nice, too, although she couldn't really tell, because she had never seen him smile.

"That will be all, Miss Reynolds. Will you ask Miss Dickinson to come in?"

"Yes, Mr Sanderson."

Lucky Miss Dickinson.

"I can't do anything this weekend, Jack," Lucy said on Saturday morning.

It was seven-thirty, and she had already been for a canter on Daisy who had been delighted to be out in the meadows on this autumn morning. There had been a slight mist when they had first started but it had cleared, giving way to a fine late-September day.

"That's all right, Lucy," he said. "We're always glad of help when you can give it, we don't expect you always to have time."

"Thanks, Jack."

She went home to bathe and change. This morning, and it was something of a nuisance, she had promised Magnus Dimmock that she would work in the gallery unitl lunchtime. He usually did the Saturday morning stint himself, but today was going off somewhere for the weekend. Judging by his mood of exhilaration it was somewhere nice – and probably with someone exciting.

This afternoon she was going to stay in Cheltenham to shop before meeting Philip and going out for a meal. She had decided she would like something new for the occassion, and promised herself a new outfit. She couldn't remember spending much on clothes since her father had died, but then she already had quite a wardrobe. Now she longed for something new and trendy.

The customers were few and far between this morning, although there were a good many browsers just intent on looking.

She made herself coffee around half-past ten, and as she finished it the door was pushed open and Nick Blakeney walked in. A thinner Nick, who looked a little older, his mouth more set, but she was so pleased to see him.

"Nick, how nice!" she said, going towards him.

He kissed her lightly on the cheek.

"Sit down. I don't imagine you've come to buy a picture."

He shook his head.

"No. I haven't seen you since Camilla's funeral."

He could say it now, talk about it. Just six weeks ago, and he was already able to at least mention her name.

"I called round to Shoe Lane but you weren't there, and I had to come into Cheltenham on business so I thought I'd drop in."

"I got your letter – thank you," she said, and waited. "How are you, Nick?"

"Bearing up, I suppose you'd say. It's not easy. Life without her is bleak, as you may imagine. She was such a live spark."

She decided to let him go on talking if that was what he wanted, but he looked at her and smiled.

"I'm sorry if you haven't been able to swim, Lucy – it didn't last long, did it?"

"Oh, you mustn't feel like that." She said. "I don't mind, really. It's not something I have much time for nowadays."

"No. I expect you're always busy?"

"What are going to do, Nick?"

"About The Hall, you mean?" He took a deep breath. "I'd like to stay on, of course, but I have a few commitments. I shall be away on location in October and November, for something like six weeks – and that's what I wanted to talk to you about."

"Oh?"

"Henry. I won't be able to keep him – at least for the next couple of months."

"Oh, never mind, I'll have him back – between you and me, Nick, I've missed him."

"I'm sure you have. So, Lucy, if you won't mind – it need only be a temporary arrangement."

"I'll come up and get him. When would be convenient?"

"No need for a couple of weeks, I don't go until half way through October."

"If you are quite sure. Where are you going? You could do with a break, Nick."

"Yes, I want to get away. For a time at any rate, and there's nothing like work. The powers that be have decided to do a script of mine. I wrote it ages ago but they've just decided to pull it out of the rag bag, so I'm pleased about that. It's set in Canada, but we're going to use Norway for location."

"Sounds wonderful."

"It seems a bit mean to mess Henry around like this, but I have no option."

He stood up. "Well, Lucy, you've had your share of troubles this year, too."

"Yes, it's been quite a year," she said. "Still, it's amazing how one can adapt."

"Yes." He smiled. "Well, I must be off. I only came to say thank you and to tell you about Henry in case you thought I'd forgotten you. I'm afraid things like the garden project will have to be postponed." And he smiled ruefully.

"Never mind. There's always another day."

"Thanks again for all you've done," he said.

"If I don't see you – have a nice trip," Lucy said, shaking his hand and watching him go through the door.

He was such a nice man. She had liked them both, but felt more at ease with Nick. He was more natural, and so friendly.

She was glad when the morning ended, and spent the afternoon going from one shop to another before buying what she wanted. She decided she wasn't really a clothes shopper, she was far happier in jeans and shirts and casual clothes. Her mother had always been disappointed in her, even as a child. Poor Ariadne.

Those awful shopping expeditions when she had been taken round the shops to try on little girls clothes, as she called them. How she had sulked! Worst of all when Ariadne had ordered such pretty clothes from exclusive stores and had them waiting for her when she came home from boarding school, and there was nothing she wanted to do more than take off her school uniform, change into sweatshirt and jeans, find Henry and go for a run with him and Daisy. Oh, happy days. She couldn't believe they had gone forever.

She had tea in Cheltenham, then drove herself home to bathe and change into her new outfit and wait for Philip. Eyeing herself in the mirror, she saw a small slim girl with a piquante elfin face – wide eyes and a small nose. None of her mother's beauty there. Her mouth was nicely shaped, though, and firm, and her teeth were good. He skin pale and a little freckled. The outfit suited her, a long golden tan skirt and jacket with a cream top. The girl in the shop had been right.

She didn't look her age, she knew. She would be twenty in January, and she realized now that she had had to learn the value of money, and a lot of her newfound knowledge she owed to Philip who had been at pains to explain the intricacies of household accounting and many other things beside.

He had been a good friend, although she knew on his part the feeling went deeper than that.

He attracted her; she had never felt before the close proximity of a man and what it could do to a woman. It gave rise to feelings she had never known, emotions she hadn't realized she possessed. Was that what love was all about?

The more she knew him, the more she understood him and what made him tick. He wasn't like any of the young men she had known before, and had had to make allowances for that. She had to try to understand his background and how he felt he hadn't had the same chance as young men born into the upper classes, as he called them. It was a difficult subject, and one that she had never encountered before. There was also his desire to become a socialist member of parliament. She could quite understand that and sympathize with him although she sometimes wondered if his motives were a little confused. But would she want that? Her own political leanings were quite different – but why shouldn't they be? She was not going to feel guilty about that.

Philip arrived at six-thirty, looking very handsome in a new sports jacket and polo necked sweater, his fair hair brushed back, and carrying a huge bouquet of red roses.

"Oh, Philip, thank you!" He kissed her and she took the flowers. "Red roses."

He gave a special look, and she remembered red roses were for love – and her face coloured a little.

"Let me put them in water. If you'd like to pour the drinks?"

When she returned, he was sitting on the sofa, the wine poured, waiting for her.

"Well, and what have you been doing today?"

"I worked in the gallery this morning, then in the afternoon I shopped and bought this."

She twirled in front of him, still unaccustomed to wearing new clothes.

"And very nice too," he said. "You look lovely, Lucy."

"Thank you, sir."

"Here's to us," he said, raising his glass.

"Is it a special occasion?" Lucy smiled.

"I hope so," he said seriously, putting down his glass. "So you had to work this morning? I believe Magnus is out of town this week."

"How did you know?" Lucy asked.

"He just happens to have gone to York with my sister Diana for the weekend."

"Oh, really! I didn't know they were . . ."

"Neither did Mother until Diana informed us that she was going off with him for the weekend."

"Well!"

"She's been mad about him ever since I can remember – she'll probably end up marrying him."

"What's wrong with that?"

"What a waste! She's a real egg head, getting a degree in Philosophy and English lit. – and all she wants to do is to marry and have children."

"I don't see anything wrong with that, if that's what she wants."

"I can't see the point of all that studying if she's only going to . . ."

"But she'll be able to use it, work even if she does marry."

"Well, perhaps I'm jumping the gun, but it's just the sort of thing Diana would do."

They dined in a small restaurant near Cirencester, and afterwards drove home to Lucy's cottage where she made coffee. She wondered why it was that despite the excellent meal and the even nicer bottle of red wine, only half her mind was on the evening.

Philip held her close and kissed her which usually got a response though not tonight. Nothing daunted, he took her hands, held them tightly.

"Lucy, will you marry me?"

Although she had half expected the question earlier in the evening, she was still shocked when it came.

"Philip!"

"I'm asking you to marry me. You will, won't you, Lucy?"

She felt suddenly cold. It was her first proposal. She had imagined it so many times, and yet here she was with no feelings at all except one of sympathy for Philip, who had every right to ask her to marry him. They had been seeing so much of each other in the past few weeks.

"Philip, please –"

"I've taken you by surprise." He smiled. "I hadn't realized. I thought –"

"Please, Philip." It was as if she had been playing some sort of game all along, and now she wanted it over.

"Thank you," she found herself saying. "But –"

"I do love you, Lucy, and I think you love me."

She shook her head slowly.

"You need time to think it over, it's a big step," Philip said. "I realize that."

"Philip – I –"

"I'll go now," he said, getting to his feet. "You've had a long day. I'll see you at the stables tomorrow morning." He kissed her. "Goodnight, Lucy, sleep well. Sweet dreams."

When he had gone, for some unaccountable reason she burst into tears.

She lay awake far into the night, thinking. What was the

matter with her? Hadn't she realized that Philip was going to ask her to marry him – sometime, if not tonight? She was behaving in a ridiculous manner.

She took stock of her life over the last six-months: her father's death, her mother's leaving Ainswick, buying the cottage and staying on, her job at the gallery – what had gone wrong?

She saw her grandfather, a grand old man, successful owner of mills and factories, and how it had been when she was young. Being taken over the mills in Yorkshire and the factories in the Midlands, seeing the employees coming out from the great iron gates in their hundreds while she drove past them in her Grandfather's Silver Cloud, Dolen the chauffeur at the wheel. When she was a little girl both her grandparents had lived up at The Hall, and when they died, her mother took over the reins. She remembered, too, the dark days, when she was very small, when the baby boy arrived in the nursery, the baby brother who had died soon after he was born, her father's grief and the sadness which fell over the whole household.

After that, it seemed things began to move faster. The conservatory was built, and the swimming pool, and her mother seemed to change. From being young and happy, always laughing, she was always out, shopping or dining with friends, and her father seemed to be left alone more and more. But they got on so well together, she and her father, always riding together, swimming, playing tennis. She realized that she still missed him greatly. He wasn't just a father, he was a friend.

Philip had been a good friend too. The trouble was he felt romantically involved with her, and had stirred up emotions which she had never experienced before. When he touched her she felt a swift response; physically he was exciting. But wasn't it time she considered what he would be like to live with – permanently? Through sickness and in health, wasn't that what you promised? Hadn't she seen the mistake of her parents' marriage, two people with opposite views, little in common, unsympathetic towards each other? And children and their upbringing – that was important. The fact that she could coolly query this surely meant that she was not head over heals in love with Philip? Besides, there were things about him that she didn't like. His attitude towards women slightly riled her, that chip on his shoulder which may or may not disappear when they married. If they married. And thinking about not marrying him brought a sense of relief. There had to be more to it than this.

When she thought of being happy with someone, it was someone you wanted to be with – like Nick . . . The realization of this bought a flush to her cheeks. Nick. The mere mention of his name brought pleasure to her. She wanted to put her arms round him and comfort him. Her heart went out to him in his grief, and when he had told her he was going away, she had felt a sense of loss. She would miss him, his company, and the thought of how she would feel if he put his arms around her – if he was free – if he loved her, was almost more than she could bear.

That was what love was. The sheer ecstacy of thinking about him, the way he spoke, the way he looked, the way he was. But suppose he never grew to feel the same way about her? He was an older man. He met many women, beauties, glamorous actresses, girls who lived in his world, which was a complete mystery to Lucy.

She sighed, locking the secret away in her heart, and found that the realization that she loved Nick made everything easier.

When Philip arrived at the stables, she was there to greet him. The question in his eyes was uppermost, but she said nothing until they had galloped to the far corner of Munnings Field and were walking the horses through the glade of chestnut trees where the leaves had turned to gold, and a fitful sun dappled the ground beneath them.

He reined his horse, and she did the same. Turning to her, he smiled. "Well, Lucy?"

"I'm sorry, Philip," she said. "I like you very much, you know that, as a friend."

"But I thought . . ." he began. "I thought you felt as I did?"

"I do like you, very much, but I can't marry you. I'm not ready for marriage yet, Philip, it's too soon. My life-style has changed so much I can't bear the thought of yet another change."

"If I ask you later, give you some time . . ."

"No, Philip."

"Then there's not much point in our seeing each other, is there?" he asked stiffly.

She shook her head.

He sighed. "Well, if that's the way you feel, Lucy, there's nothing more to say."

"I still think of you as a friend, Philip."

"That's not enough," he said. "I was hoping for more." And digging his heels into the horse's flanks, he rode ahead as if someone was after him.

Lucy turned Daisy round and patted her. "Well, that's that," she said. "Perhaps I've been hard on him, but I had to be firm." Daisy snorted, throwing back her ears.

She understands every word I say, Lucy thought happily, feeling freer than she had for a long time.

After lunch she drove up to The Hall, ostensibly to see Henry but in reality to see Nick once more before he left.

Henry barked and licked her hands, tail wagging.

"No doubt about who's pleased to see you," Nick said, coming out of the house. How could she have ever doubted that she loved him? Lucy wondered.

"Oh, Nick, " she said. "I had to see him – I missed him today."

"Of course you did!" he said, putting an arm around her shoulders, much to Lucy's joy. "Come in and have some tea. Mrs Tomkin has just made a cake."

They sat outside on the terrace, looking at the huge swiss rolls of hay in the adjoining field, the short-cropped dry grass, the line of trees, red and gold.

"It is so peaceful here," Lucy said, closing her eyes, wishing it could go on for ever.

"I hate to think of leaving it," he said. "Even for Norway."

"So you don't want me to take Henry today?" she asked, smiling.

"Not today, Lucy," he said. "There's plenty of time."

"Of course. Well before I go, could we look round the garden?"

"Of course –"

"Did you ever see the remains of the Monk's Stone in the down field way over there by the hedge?" she asked him.

"No – I never did. I don't think I've been over the whole grounds since we came."

"It's a bit of a walk," Lucy said, looking down at her walking shoes, and then at him. "Shall we go now?"

"Let's. No time like the present," he said.

"It's such an interesting story," Lucy began, walking by his side. "Apparently, there was this monk – Dybol, according to legend – who decided to build this monument . . ."

Just to be with him, she thought happily, was all she asked.

When she left, Nick watched her go. He would miss her, with her stories about the house and her enthusiasm. Such a child – and yet, she was a woman by now, and an attractive one, at that.

A week before he was due to leave for Norway, he had an idea. It might be a good thing to start the garden alterations, so that work would be in progress while he was away – under Lucy's supervision. He thought, hoped, she would be pleased at the idea, and that way she could live here and it would mean that Henry wouldn't be disturbed.

Feeling more motivated than for a long time, he drove over to the cottage where he found Lucy digging up the geraniums in the front tubs to put away for the winter.

Seeing her there in jeans and old sweater, a scarf tied peasant fashion on her head, with an armful of pink geraniums, he felt a rush of affection for her. She looked so natural standing there, so much at home.

He got out of the car and kissed her lightly on her cool cheek.

"Nick!" Her heart leapt at seeing him. "How nice! Can you come in for tea?"

"Love to." And he found that he really meant it.

"Just let me put these outside in the garden," she said, leading him into the house.

"Are you supposed to do that?" he asked. "Where are you going to put them?"

"The gardener always used to over winter them in the greenhouse. Of course, I haven't that but perhaps . . ."

"Then put them in the greenhouse up at The Hall," he said. 'That's what it's for, isn't it?"

Lucy laughed. "Thank you, Nick."

While they were having tea, he looked across at her and smiled.

"I've had an idea," he said. "About the garden alterations."

"Yes?"

"I'd like to start the work now, before I go away. Then – if you'd like, of course – you could stay there to supervise."

Her heart gave a great leap of joy.

"Oh, Nick, how wonderful!"

"You wouldn't mind?"

"Mind – I should think not!" she cried."It would give me the greatest pleasure."

"It wouldn't take up too much of your time?" he asked, seeing the warmth in her eyes.

"Of course not."

"You could stay up at The Hall, have the run of the house while I'm away. I should feel happier then – and that way Henry would be pleased too."

"Oh, yes!" Lucy smiled. "You spoil him, Nick."

"No more than you."

He finished his tea and put down the cup. "As a matter of fact, I've already been in touch with Chalker Alley in Cirencester and they've agreed to start at the end of the week. I understand they are very good?"

"The best, so I've heard."

"Well, then?"

"Oh, it's so exciting, Nick. I can just imagine how nice it's going to look!"

"I do hope so."

He was halfway up a snow-covered mountain in Norway, surrounded by members of the crew, the sound of a rushing waterfall immediately behind him, the director trying to make himself heard above the noise, when he had a vision of Lucy, standing in front of the cottage with an armful of pink geraniums.

He would telephone her this evening, see how the work was getting on, he decided.

"Lucy?"
"Nick! How are you?"
"I'm fine – and you?"
"Great. How's the film going?"
"Very well. We've not been snowed in yet. How is the garden coming along?"
"Oh, Nick, it's looking super – at least, I think so."
"Are they doing a good job?"
"Everything as planned."
"Good. And Henry?"
"I think he misses you – I'm quite jealous."
Nick seemed pleased.
"Take care of yourselves. See you soon."
Lucy put down the phone and hugged herself. How kind of him to telephone. It had been wonderful to hear his voice.
She went back to the garden with renewed vigour.
It was while she was driving home from seeing her mother in town that she passed a specialist tree centre and, curious, went in. The nursery specialized in unusual trees, many full-grown, which though costly were quite fascinating. Her eyes were drawn to a golden tree, small and with a delightful shape.
"What is it?" she asked the man.
"A golden oak, Miss."
"Unusual, isn't it?"
"Yes, it is that."
"Could I get it in my car?" she said, nodding towards where it was parked.
"I think so."
"I'll have it," Lucy said. It would be her gift to Nick's garden.
She knew exactly where it would go – down in the corner where the ground sloped into a dell. It would stand there and grow – she hoped Nick would approve.
The next day she had the gardeners plant it. It might have grown there from an acorn, and she hoped it would retain its leaves until Nick came home.
Then she went back to he garden plan, and saw that they had made more progress, and at that point decided to chance it and put another of her ideas into practice.
Where the ground fell away, she planted a small bank of

heather at the foot of the bank, using all the winter and summer ericas that were still in flower and would be so when Nick returned. They rewarded her with a splash of colour. She hoped he wouldn't mind but it really did improve the bank. Even the gardeners approved, and when the heathers started to spread it would be a picture all the year round.

Nick telephoned her each week, asking her if she was happy with what she was doing, and each time her heart soared when the phone rang.

He found himself anxious to get home, not just to The Hall but to see Lucy again. Her enthusiasm was so infectious, but it wasn't just that – he kept seeing her face in front of him, the way she looked at him, her wish to please him.

She knew when his plane would arrive home, and wondered if he would drive straight home afterwards. She need not have worried. During the morning, she saw his car coming up the drive. Her instinct was to run out and hug him; instead she stood at the front door, holding Henry with difficulty. Finally she let him go and he made a bee line for Nick, jumping up, his tail wagging nineteen to the dozen. Nick, himself burned by the strong winds and sun at great height, looked as if he had holidayed in the West Indies.

He kissed her lightly on the cheek and put his arm around her shoulders to go into the house. Once inside, he looked around and smiled, he was obviously glad to be home, then turned his attention to the post which was considerable.

Lucy went into the kitchen to make coffee which they drank later into the huge kitchen.

"Well?" he asked her, blue eyes vivid against his tan.

"You look wonderful," she said. "Such a tan."

"Yes, amazing, isn't it? All that mountain air. You'd have loved it."

She looked, he thought, just as he had imagined her when he was away. A white shirt showing above her navy sweater, jeans, a vivid scarf tucked into her collar – her hair tied back, the dark fringe falling onto her forehead.

"Let's go outside, shall we?" he said. "This weather's nice – has it been all the time?"

"Yes, so the men were able to get on. I can't wait for you to see it."

The circular parterre looked as if it had always been there, edged with box and containing various herbs and old fashioned plants. The scent was aromatic. Nick took a deep breath.

"It's wonderful!" he said. "I didn't think it would turn out so well."

"I'm glad you're pleased. They did a good job, didn't they?"

"Excellent." He walked round it to where the ground dipped to form a bank, and saw at the foot to his surprise, a patch of bright colour: pinks, mauves, white.

"What's this?"

Her heart sank as he stood and stared. Now it seemed a presumptuous thing to have done; after all, it was his garden, she had no right . . .

He didn't look up for what seemed like ages – and she agonized until he did.

"It's a heather garden," she said lamely.

"Yes," he said in a muffled voice.

"Oh, Nick, I do hope you don't mind? It was very cheeky of me but you could always take it out."

He walked down towards the glade, where the little golden oak stood in the sunshine. He went towards it as if drawn – looked at it, then turned to her. "And was this your idea, too?"

"Yes," she said miserably, wishing now that she hadn't interfered.

He put his arms around her and drew her towards him.

"Oh, Lucy," he said. "My love."

Chapter Twenty-One

There was a desultory air in Dennis Mansfield's office on this fine September morning. Dennis had not yet arrived. Late again, Philip thought, frowning. He didn't know what had got into the old boy, leaving early in the afternoon and arriving late in the mornings.

He was due for a holiday himself, he thought. Since he had become friendly with Lucy Gilbert, he had put off any plans to get away – just in case. But now, having to accept the fact that she really wasn't his sort at all, he had had to begin his life all over again – even returning to his old riding stables for his Sunday morning ride.

He would have to put it down to experience, he decided philosophically. Lucy hadn't been for him, that was clear. He had to admit that it had, though, improved his confidence with girls, for he no longer felt shy with them, or nervous. In fact, he pondered slowly, he had it in his mind to ask Miss Reynolds in the outer office for a date at the weekend. He had delayed up to now, he didn't want her to get any ideas. Just as long as she realized one invitation didn't mean more.

When Dennis came in he looked awful, as if he hadn't slept all night.

For the first time Philip really felt sorry for him, he looked all in.

"Are you all right, Dennis?" he asked, going into his office.

"I will be – as soon as I've pulled myself round," Dennis answered, hanging up his raincoat on the stand. "I've been up all night – at the hospital – with a friend. It was touch and go but she's all right now, thank God."

"Oh, I see," Philip said. "That's good." Wondering who the friend could be.

Dennis wiped his brow. He had had hardly any sleep. When Clare was taken ill soon after she had gone to bed, he had managed to to get her to hospital where he had sat with her all night, but she really was rather frail this morning. Still in the oxygen tent, she looked ghastly. Her eyes were closed. She had no idea who he was, or where she was.

Well, he decided, down to business. There was nothing like work. Tonight was the local council meeting. Two members were on holiday, which left only seven of them. Peggy would be there – he would tell her about Clare then. She had been a brick, but then it was in Peggy's nature to help. Apart from the the physical side of their marriage she had been an excellent wife.

In the afternoon he drove into Cheltenham and bought some roses which he took to Clare, finding her just the same; still no improvement, no sign that she knew him.

He left a message at the desk that he would return later in the evening, then called in at the council offices before going home to give Peggy the news about Clare and take her to the council meeting.

She was sympathetic, and poured him a stiff drink.

"You need this, I think," she said, collecting her papers from the study.

"What's all this about an application to turn Smethwick Grange into luxury apartments?" he asked when she returned.

She always felt guilty whenever he mentioned anything Malcolm might be involved in.

"I don't know – Malcolm didn't seem to know anything about it," she answered, hoping she was telling him the truth.

"Hmm, well, we'll see. They're not likely to allow that in a hurry, are they. Before you know it, half of Ainswick would be developed."

"True," she said vaguely. "Well, I'm ready, shall we go?"

They were silent on the journey of some ten minutes and once there they seated themselves round the huge old table where decisions had been made long before anyone there could remember.

After reading the minutes, they sat back to discuss forthcoming applications. While there was some heated discussion about the proposed new steps for the hotel, the arguments really got underway when the proposal to develop luxury apartments at Smethwick was raised.

"Never," Arthur Blount said, thus revealing his feelings on the subject, no matter who was responsible for the application.

Joe Gregory thought otherwise, and they knew why. He was the biggest supplier of building materials in the area, so there was little doubt where his interests lay.

Harriet Peake, also a local magistrate, was in no doubt at all that it should be refused, simply because she was opposed to any sort of change, while Bert Peacock, the local butcher, couldn't see any reason why not.

Esther Rollinson thought it a good idea, because good modern buildings were a darn' sight better than old ones falling down. Besides, there was a demand for new homes; for too long people had had to put up with old-fashioned amenities. It was all very well for the townies who came in from outside the area and spent a fortune on restoring properties, but what about local people who were anxious to give up their large homes and move into something more modern? A converted grange was the best of both worlds.

Peggy sat silent, haunted by the idea that Malcolm was behind it. He had been ominously quiet on the subject, and it was a strange thing that he already had a flat there. Probably bought in the knowledge that he planned to apply for planning permission, she wouldn't put it past him. She was so anxious for Dennis not to know. She knew how furious he would be at Malcolm's doing anything behind his back.

Presently, as the arguments grew more heated, she banged her gavel on the table. As chair, she had the last word.

"We'll take a vote," she said. "Those in favour?" and three hands shot up.

"Against?" she asked, and three hands shot up.

"So I have the casting vote?" she said, feeling the tenseness all round her.

She took a deep breath. "Against," she said, and there was an audible sigh of relief.

The secretary wrote the result down in the minute book, and Peggy's feeling of guilt increased.

She collected her papers together. Well, what did it matter? They were leading such strange lives these days. Her world had gone topsy turvy, and she'd do well to hang on to the ordinary things, the day to day living. If she had scotched a plan of Malcolm's, she was sorry, but she had done it for the best.

When the evening came for the first autumn meeting of the dramatic society, Peggy was really looking forward to it. With her box of scripts of *Abigail's Party* she made her way to the old barn where they were all assembled and talking to each other in little groups.

She smiled with pleasure as they greated her, glad to see them all again after the summer break.

Beth, content in her knowledge of the coming baby, was enjoying the laidback feeling that nothing really mattered which she had experienced in her previous two pregnancies. It was even a relief to know that this season she wouldn't have to learn lines or get out on time in the evenings, although she intended to continue as club secretary. That and her parochial duties were quite enough at the present time.

She saw Maggie over in the corner talking to Marty, who had been in the States all the summer. Now she was back and already organizing a get together for the new season.

Maggie came over and kissed her. "Beth, you're looking wonderful! I wish I'd looked like that when I was pregnant – I *looked* ill, and *was* sick."

Beth laughed, and shook her head. "None of that, I'm glad to say."

"Oh, you are lucky, I envy you – although if I were honest, I'm far too old to have any more babies."

She looked around. "No sign of Jackie yet. I'm going to put in for the lead even though she will. What the heck?"

"Of course you must!" Beth said, wondering how Jackie had fared this summer. They had seen nothing of her in the village although Maggie had said she had gone with her husband on one or two trips.

"I meant to ask you, could Clarrie come to tea with Erica on Saturday? Just a few friends."

"Of course – it's her birthday!" Beth cried. "She'll be nine."

"Yes, a few weeks older than Clarrie, isn't she?"

"Clarrie will be nine in November."

"I say, look at old Geoffrey over there, preening himself. I suppose he thinks after his success in *Twelve Pound Look* he's one of the brightest stars on the English stage!"

Beth laughed as Peggy rapped the table and asked them all to sit down.

"Hallo, everybody, and welcome. We're all here, I think, no new members as yet – but I think we have someone missing . . .

"Jackie," they murmured.

"Never mind. We'll start without her – she's often a few minutes late."

She began to hand out the books. "Now, I suppose you all know the play? It's been done so many times. But I thought we would give a reading and see what you think. Perhaps, Maggie, you would read the part of . . ."

And the evening wore on, with everyone thoroughly enjoying it.

At the tea break, it was fairly obvious that Jackie would not be coming.

"What a pity," Peggy said. "I hope she knew we were starting this evening?"

"I sent her the usual notice," Beth said.

On the way home, Peggy consoled herself with the fact that Maggie really did read the leading part very nicely, and if Jackie decided not to come this season, Maggie would indeed do very well. Still, she hoped Jackie would turn up next week.

She was used now to arriving back at Hunter's Lodge on her own even though the nights were getting dark. A light which she had left on shone out of the hall window, and she always found these days that she was glad to get home. Old age again, she thought.

The first thing she saw when she opened the door was a huge basket of pink roses on the hall table and her first thought was: Dennis.

There was no card, but a sealed letter addressed to her and Dennis. In Malcolm's writing.

Her heart began to pound, she opened it.

Dear Mother and Father,
I am sorry if this is going to upset you, and I know it will be a shock, but I have to tell you that I am going away – abroad, New Zealand in fact – and Jackie Hetherington is coming with me. She is leaving her husband – not before time – and I know we are doing the right thing. We shall start a new life there, so wish us well. I shall be in touch about the flat and business matters.

Your loving son,
Malcolm

Peggy sat, stunned, in the hall chair. She read it again and still it made no sense. Why was he running off like this instead of seeing them face to face and telling them? Jackie Hetherington? She hadn't realized he even knew her, much less that they must have been seeing each other. And what kind of a mess would Malcolm leave behind him? She really couldn't take it in, even now.

With an effort she got out of the chair and made her way into the kitchen where she made herself a hot drink to take to bed. She left the letter beside the roses and climbed wearily up the stairs . . .

There, another surprise awaited her; a second envelope from Malcolm. Hastily, she tore it open.

Dear Mother,
This is my personal letter to you, to tell you how much I love you, and always have, even though I haven't always been a good son. I know I've caused you a lot of worry, and I regret that, but I would like you to believe that in Jackie I know I have found the one woman in the world for me. Could you, without causing Father

any worry, get rid of the apartment at The Grange for me and out of the proceeds give Mrs Hemingway, my downstairs neighbour, a cheque for eight thousand pounds which she gave me as a deposit on Woodbine Cottage? Tell her that the owner has decided not to sell, and I have been called away. The rest of the money you can give to my ex's for the boys. I'm really going to make a fresh start. Now you take care of yourself – and don't think too badly of me.

All my love,
Malcolm

Peggy sobbed as if her heart would break. How could he do this to them? New Zealand. Why, it was across the world, she would probably never see him again. As for Jackie – how could she be so deceitful? Peggy would have trusted her with her life. And Mrs Hemingway how awful if it got around that Malcolm had deceived her. Oh, it really was too bad. Perhaps it was the best thing for all of them if he did go away? Yet, with it all, he was her son and she loved him dearly.

She spent a fitful night, and woke in the morning believing it was a bad dream, until she saw the beautiful flower arrangement downstairs. She read the letter he had addressed to both of them again, and wondered whether she should get in touch with Dennis or wait until he next came home. She decided that to do nothing was the best policy.

But she had to get cracking. She must talk to someone, and she knew that someone would be Beth. She was a young woman, but she would understand. Besides, she knew Jackie, and perhaps could throw some light on the matter.

Peggy glanced at her watch and saw that it was eight-thirty, time for Mrs Dinsdale to arrive.

She was in good humour. Having got used to the idea that Kylie was pregnant, she now looked forward to the event. Yes, her daughter had been a naughty girl, but no naughtier than the rest of them these days. As for Granny, she was so delighted with her new retirement flat and the hot and cold running water that having a pregnant grand-daughter took a back seat. After all, young women became pregnant as soon as they were able, whether they were married or not, so what was the fuss about?

"I'll be back mid-morning, I expect," Peggy said, putting on her gloves. "There's some cold lamb in the fridge – I don't know whether you would like to . . ."

"I'll make a nice shepherd's pie," Mrs Dinsdale said. She almost added that Mr Mansfield would like that, but lately his bed had not been slept in. She had thought deeply about that. Either he slept in Mrs Mansfield's room, though there was no sign of any pyjamas, or he wasn't coming home.

Either way it was a mystery. Still, none of her business. She tucked her hair behind her ears and put on her apron. Folks like them did act strange. They weren't like other people.

"Lovely flowers," she said. "Is it your birthday?"

"No." Peggy suddenly remembered and tucked the letter safely in her handbag. Time enough for that when Dennis came home.

She did her usual walk along the village street, seeing it being swept of leaves by the council road sweepers, wishing them a good morning, and calling in at the post office.

She saw Beth leaving little Freddie at the village school, and wondered if she was going straight home. Who would have thought last night when Jackie didn't turn up that she was on her way to New Zealand with Peggy's son.

She simply had to get to the bottom of it all.

But first and foremost, without delay, she must make out a cheque for Mrs Hemingway and call on her to explain. She would draw it on her account, that way Dennis need never know. It brought back memories of other transactions she had made on her son's behalf, and she accepted that she had paid heavily for her deceit in many ways.

Now he had gone. She might never see him again, and knew in her heart she would rather have him back with all his troubles than lose him. He was her son.

Chapter Twenty-Two

Peggy found Beth at home when she arrived at the vicarage around eleven, a bright-eyed young mother going about her duties, preparing vegetables, the washing line full, a huge basket of apples just waiting to be peeled.

"Beth dear, I wonder if you could spare me a moment? It's rather important."

"Of course, Peggy – sit down and make yourself at home, I don't have to collect Freddie until twelve."

"Oh, it won't take that long – what I have to say," Peggy said drily.

Beth raised her eyebrows. Such a tone was unusual for Peggy.

"Is something wrong?"

"You could say that," she said, taking the coffee Peggy had poured out for her. "You've heard nothing from Jackie Hetherington, I suppose?"

Beth shook her head. "No."

"Well . . ." Peggy said, not quite sure of the way to begin. "It seems that she and my son Malcolm have eloped – if that's the right word." And she waited for Beth's reaction.

Beth stared at her, her mouth open.

"Jackie and Malcolm?" She hardly knew Malcolm at all, having met him only two or three times.

Peggy nodded. "I didn't know they even knew each other that well."

"Neither did I," Beth said, "but then I wouldn't. We never really met socially, and she was a little unusual, to say the least."

"Hmm," Peggy agreed.

"What do you mean – eloped?"

Thoughts were whirling through Beth's head. Surely, it wasn't possible – what about the husband? Where did he come in?

"When I got home last night, I found a note," Peggy said. "In it, Malcolm said he was leaving England to make a fresh start – in New Zealand."

"New Zealand!"

"And that Jackie was going with him."

"I don't believe it!" Beth gasped.

"It takes a bit of believing, although if you knew my son . . ." Peggy said grimly. Only now did the full realization of what they had done sink in.

Beth had a sudden pity for Peggy. What an awful shock it must have been for her.

"Tell me about it," she said, and Peggy related how she had arrived home the previous evening to find the note. She added nothing about her own personal letter.

"New Zealand! Good Lord!" Beth repeated, shocked. "What on earth did Dennis say?"

"Well, he doesn't know yet – he's out of town overnight, won't be back until later today."

The lie came easily.

"Well," Beth said at length, "I don't know your son, but to imagine Jackie doing such a thing – I know she was unhappy . . ."

"Was she?" Peggy asked quickly.

"Yes, there seems no harm in telling you now. She told me about it but asked me to say nothing."

"I see." Peggy sat tight-lipped.

"I said nothing, but then Maggie told me that she had also told her, and to keep quiet."

Peggy screwed up her small monkey face.

"I don't like the sound of that," she said harshly. "I had no idea. I thought her husband was away a lot . . ."

"Yes, I think he is," Beth said.

They sat quietly for some time, then Peggy sighed and made ready to go.

"I shouldn't have bothered you," she said. "You have

quite enough to do, but I thought you might have had some ideas, however vague, of their friendship."

"I can assure you I hadn't the slightest. I only saw Jackie once or twice outside rehearsals, and then only briefly."

"Well, it's an awful business – and I feel sorry for that husband of hers. I expect he's away and she has taken advantage of that to abscond." She sighed deeply. "Oh, Beth, don't people do dreadful things!"

The moment she said it, she was overtaken by guilt, remembering all those years ago and what she had done. That hadn't made sense, either. Well, it was all water under the bridge now, but it proved that people could and did do irrational things.

She kissed Beth swiftly.

"Thank you for listening to me – there's nothing anyone can do now. The die is cast, as they say."

Beth sat for a long time after she had gone, thinking how unpredictable people were with the things they did to each other. Never a week passed without something or other that didn't bear thinking about.

And Jackie – what had made her tick?

She was a mystery.

Beth didn't have to wait long for the answer to her question. The next day a car drew up at the vicarage, and a man got out and walked to the front door.

He was tall and fair, good-looking and a gentleman, if she had been asked to sum up.

"Mrs Pennington?" he asked. She nodded. "Beth Pennington?"

"Yes," she answered. "Can I help you?"

"I'm Tony Hetherington. May I come in?"

Beth's heart missed a beat. "Of course." She held out her hand, "How do you do?" and led the way into the sitting room.

He was so unexpectedly different from what she had imagined that she was lost for words. He sat down on the sofa and looked at her frankly.

"I expect you know that Jackie – my wife – has left me?" he began.

"Yes, I heard yesterday."

"She left me a note. In it she said she was going away with a man called Malcolm Mansfield – do you know him?"

"No, not really. I have met him once or twice, briefly. I wouldn't say I know him. I do know his parents though, his mother particularly."

"I see."

He seemed so dignified, totally unlike the man she had imagined.

"I came because I found your name in the telephone directory which she keeps in the hall."

"Let me get you something," Beth said, jumping up. "This can't be easy for you – how about coffee?"

"That would be nice," he said, relaxing against the back of the sofa. "I only got back from New York last night."

Poor man, Beth thought. He must be tired, and to arrive home to this!

"Thank you," he said gratefully when she returned. He stirred his coffee. "I suppose she told you I was a monster?" He looked up with an attempt at a smile.

Beth blushed. "Oh. Well, I mean – no –"

"It won't be the first time this has happened," he said, "although I have an idea it may be the last."

She waited for him to go on.

"I'm sure you realized that Jackie was an unusual person. Gifted – but unusual."

"Ye-es."

"I expect she told you I forbade her to join the local societies or to work?"

"Yes, she did."

"Not so." He smiled. "If anything I encouraged her."

"But why did she . . ."

"It's a long story, and by no means the first time this has happened. I was shocked the first time I found out, but after that – well, I got used to it. Every time I hope it will get better, but it never does. This time, I think I've reached breaking point."

"But I don't understand."

"Jackie has a personality disorder. A lack of security in childhood, many things, have gone towards making her the person she is. I feel she will never change – there's nothing more I can do."

"How sad," Beth said, beginning to see daylight.

"It was her wish to come here, lead a quiet life."

"Oh, but I thought it was you –"

He smiled.

"I expect she told you a lot of other things." He put down his coffee cup. "That I was Jewish, for instance?"

Beth nodded.

"Not that it matters one iota, but I'm not."

Beth didn't know what to say.

"Did she tell you we had a child – and it died?"

"Yes," Beth said miserably.

He shook his head. "Sadly, we had no children, although she would have liked one. I think that was half the trouble, thwarted motherhood. At any rate, it certainly helped to make matters worse. She often invented a child, a boy or a girl."

Beth bit her lip.

"Yes, it is sad," he said. "But if you have to live with it over the years, it becomes almost unbearable. I never know what I'm going to find when I come home, and that's why . . ."

She could see he was at the end of his tether.

"I've been on the point of chucking it all in – my job everything – in order that we could go away and be together, and for her to try psychiatric treatment which I'm sure would benefit her. But so far she's always refused."

He looked such a nice man, Beth thought. Was he telling the truth?

"This man – Mansfield – what sort of a man is he?"

What a difficult question, Beth thought, considering the rumours she had heard in the village.

"He is a divorced man, recently come back to the village where his parents live, and I think he met Jackie at the Ainswick Players event in June."

"Is he with the dramatic society?"

"No, he's not a member – he came to see the play."

"I expect she gave a wonderful performance," Tony said drily. "She always does."

"We all thought she should be doing it professionally."

"She did for a time in the States, but didn't have the staying power. She missed rehearsals, even the opening night once, and she caused trouble – I don't want to go into it now. You see, she craves attention, desperately wants to be loved, to get people's sympathy –"

"Wouldn't she find that as a professional actress?"

"It's not enough," he said. "She needs it in her personal life."

"Where did you meet her?" Beth asked. "She said she was in an orphanage – and –"

"Yes, that's true. She ran away and was lost and desperate, sixteen, alone in London. I did what I thought was the right thing and took her on as receptionist at the hotel I was running then. Very good she was at it too. But it soon began . . . tales that weren't true, trouble with the staff . . . oh, I can't go into it now – but, well, I protected her. I fell in love with her and wanted to look after her, I thought with a modicum of success at first, but things have gone from bad to worse."

He put his head in his hands.

"I'm sorry, Mrs Pennington, to go on like this, but I'm at my wit's end. She's done this before, gone off with someone, but she always – always comes back. This time, well, I don't know if I want her back."

Beth stuck her neck out.

"I was told that they've gone to New Zealand."

He showed no surprise.

"Once," he smiled, "It was South Africa – but she came back from there too."

Beth wondered if Malcolm knew what he was getting himself into.

"What will you do?" she asked.

He sat silent, thinking.

"I shall divorce her," he said. "After all, I'm wasting my life, too. It's like being a father and husband and a minder all in one, but I despair now. I'm making no headway."

"It can't help that you're away so much," Beth said in Jackie's defence.

"Yes, that's true. But I've had enough of the lies. You do reach a breaking point, you know."

Beth felt sorry for him. As Marcus had said, she had only heard one side of the problem when she heard Jackie's tale of woe.

"What can I do to help?"

At the moment there came a tap on the door, and Marcus walked in.

"I'm sorry, I didn't know –"

Tony stood up.

"Oh, come in, Marcus," Beth cried with a great sense of relief. "Darling, this is Tony Hetherington – Jackie's husband. Tony – my husband Marcus."

The two men shook hands.

"Marcus, I have to go and collect Freddie at twelve – may I leave you in safe hands, Tony, while I collect my son from school? I won't be long. Perhaps you'd stay and have some lunch?"

Without waiting for an answer, she fled from the room, leaving Marcus to pick up the pieces.

And there was no one better, she thought. He was just the person Tony Hetherington needed, whether he was religious or not.

As she drove she gave thanks for her marriage and her husband. She was one of the lucky ones. He was such a good minister. One of these days Marcus could be bishop or even archbishop. There was so much to look forward to.

As for Tony Hetherington – what a shock. The mental picture she'd had of him could not have been more wrong. Marcus had said she had only heard one side of the story – but which one was true? And how would she tell Peggy, but first she would see what Marcus had to say.

What was the old saying: fools rush in where angels fear to tread?

But she couldn't help thinking of Malcolm Mansfield. If what Tony had said was true, then he was in for a grim time.

Chapter Twenty-Three

On the misty day in October when Nick Blakeney went back on location to Norway, Dennis Mansfield went home to Hunter's Lodge.

He had waited until it was all over, put Clare's financial affairs into order, seen to the funeral, then made his way home.

Peggy was there when he returned. She saw him walk in as though nothing had happened, and then as he stood there and she looked at him, without words, she put her arms around him, and they stayed like that for several moments.

Clare's name was never mentioned.

After a while he asked her, "How's Malcolm? Have you seen much of him?"

She had rehearsed this so often.

"Dennis, Malcolm has gone – left Ainswick and gone abroad."

"What?" He stared at her.

"He's cleared off – gone to New Zealand to make a fresh start."

"Good God!" he said. "When did all this happen?"

"Three weeks ago."

"You should have told me."

"I didn't want to give you any more worries." She took a deep breath and waded in. "He has gone with Jackie Hetherington –"

"Who's she?"

"The young woman who was so good in *The Twelve Pound Look*. You remember, Dennis."

"Dear God, but she was married, wasn't she?"

"When did that ever matter?" Peggy said wearily. "She was unhappy with her husband apparently. I'll get you the note."

"Oh, he left us a note, did he?" Dennis said drily.

She handed it to him silently and he read it. She thought how much he had aged when he looked up from reading it.

"You know, Peggy, I've never understood what makes him tick – not even when he was a boy. What urges him to do the things he does. He had every chance in life: a good school, steady parents."

She was silent as he sat staring in front of him, the letter in his hand.

"What's happened about The Grange?"

"I gave it to the agents in Cheltenham."

"And the shop?"

"He only had a short lease and I've arranged for Cancer Research to take it over."

He was silent for a while.

"Peg, do you ever think about those boys – our grandsons?" She could have wept.

"Dennis, don't!"

He looked across at her. "You don't deserve this," he said.

I do, I do, she said silently.

Presently, he undid his collar and tie. "Peg, why don't we go away somewhere?"

"What?" They seldom took holidays.

"Take a holiday – you know, the sort of thing other people do."

Her face lit up, then sagged. "Oh, Dennis, we're committed to so many things in the village."

"Hang Ainswick!" he said. "They can do without us for a spell – they'll have to when we've gone. Give someone else a chance."

She brightened. "Yes, that would be nice."

"We'll think about it. A week or two – the Seychelles perhaps, – India – Italy – "

"Oh, Dennis, what a lovely idea!"

He needed to get away even if she didn't, she thought. Oh it was good to have him home.

Yes, Dennis thought, it would do them both good. What did they have to look forward to with Malcolm gone? Now, perhaps, they would never see their grandchildren – so it was up to them to make a future for each other. He'd tell Philip he was going away – give him an opportunity to take full responsibility for the practice. It would do him a world of good.

Philip, at that moment, was thinking about Miss Reynolds, or Angie as he had come to call her – though not in the office. There, she was still Miss Reynolds. Who would have thought she had such hidden depths? He had really enjoyed last evening – and there was no doubt how she felt about him. It made such a difference. In fact, it was obvious she was quite dotty about him. He wouldn't be surprised if he didn't ask her out again, make things a little more permanent. As long as she didn't get ideas – marriage, that sort of thing. He could do worse . . . Still, there was no hurry. Shop around, as they said. Play the field. Yes, there was plenty of time.

After all, he was a man of experience, you might say, and there was no doubt in his mind now that Lucy Gilbert had been a bit of a cold fish. That was the trouble with these well-to-do girls with money – they wanted to pull the strings. Well, not with him, they wouldn't. Once let a woman think she can be boss and all hell would be let loose!

In The Grange, Mrs Hemingway had been sitting in the window and had seen the girl's small sports car go by. She watched it enviously. Oh, to be young and able to get about. She let the lace curtain drop and with the aid of her stick made her way back to the fireplace again and the television screen.

Life had become so dull since Malcolm went away – so suddenly just like that – and the disappointment of losing the dear little cottage was almost more than she could bear. She had been in some doubt about it for a time, but when she knew she had lost it, had wanted it more than ever. Still, today she had seen the agent take two lots of people over the vacant apartment upstairs, and perhaps they would be nice and friendly like Malcolm had been. She sighed. She supposed it was all for the best. She was used to this place, and perhaps it wasn't such a good idea to move at her age.

In Chestnut Lane, in the Little Field development, Granny Dorrington was making tea. She boiled the kettle by plugging it into the point provided; none of this old business of the iron kettle on the blackleaded range. This one didn't take a minute, and she had even made a cake in the new electric oven. It had taken ages to get used to, but she hadn't told anyone about that. Just persevered, that was all you needed to do, and the warden was very nice and helpful.

She moved from the tiny kitchen into the sitting room which was ever so cosy. With the table in the middle of the room, and the four chairs round it, that left room for two armchairs and her mother's mahogany occasional table in the window where sat the flowers that Kylie had just brought her.

"'Ere you are then," she said, setting down the cake and plates, the tray of tea.

"Oh, you should have let me do that," Kylie cried, jumping up swiftly.

"You don't want to make no quick moves like that, my girl," Granny Dorrington said reprovingly. "Don't do the baby any good. Now, 'oo's for a nice piece of cake?"

They was a nice couple, she thought. He was quite good looking really, with that slicked down hair, although she couldn't for the life of her see what he wanted that pony tail at the back for. Made him look – well, like a young woman, and she was sure he was nothing like that. She gave him a sly glance. Lovely black leather trousers he had on, tight . . . She turned away. Oh, he was a man all right – well, hadn't young Kylie proved it? Nice wide shoulder, she always liked that in a man, and nice colouring too, that very fair hair with dark eyes, eyes that had a touch of devilment in them. What with Kylie's good looks, they'd make a grand pair, and the baby would be lovely. She couldn't wait, it was a long tme since they had had a baby in the family.

October, she thought, and winter coming on. Well, it wouldn't be so bad this winter. She quite looked forward to it. The other day she'd thought she had seen the General' two girls as she called them looking at the development. She would bet the old man was still alive; she'd know if he passed on. Those girls never changed, looked exactly the same, year in year out. My word, it must have been a blow for the old chap when he knew they were building right alongside him. Sometimes she thought she saw a glow through the trees, but it was always so dark she could never be sure. Her eyes weren't what they were.

One dusky evening Edith and Lydia went down to Little Field to see for themselves. Sixteen dwellings were finished and the foundations down for sixteen more.

There they sat, in a row, with tiny front lawns, each with a different shrub, even Lydia was impressed.

"Well," she said grudgingly, "they give them plenty for their money."

They peered through a kitchen window, making sure they were not seen.

"A beautiful little kitchen," Edith said. "So modern."

Round the back was a frosted window through which could be seen the outline of a small bath, a wash basin and a WC.

"A proper bathroom," Edith said.

"Still," Lydia said, "they're little boxes. You can't get away from it."

"All our privacy has gone," Edith mourned. "You can't sunbathe in the garden or have tea."

"Since when have you wanted to sunbathe?" Lydia asked scornfully. "You'll be telling me next you've bought a bikini."

Edith blushed at the unaccustomed word.

"I," Lydia said, "shall continue to have tea on the lawns as if they were not there."

The General took to sitting inside his room with the doors to the balcony open. "The butcher calls them sentry boxes," Edith said, trying to amuse him.

"Does he?" the General said grimly. "More like matchboxes."

For a moment the girls remembered the sound of their mother's light laugh as she poured the tea for them, the lacy parasols, the scent of roses, themselves in lacy pinafores, long, long ago.

"Sentry boxes," the General scowled. "Sentry boxes."

He dozed and dreamed he was back in El Alemein. It was late when he awoke and in the rapidly gathering dusk he saw that every light in the new homes was switched on. All the windows glowed orange or yellow and the sight somehow warmed the old man's heart.

He liked that – the fact that they all looked exactly alike with their little front doors, and as he watched it seemed to him for a moment as if they moved on little legs. Left right, left right, like a row a soldiers.

The next morning he was awake at six-thirty, and sat up in bed to look out into the darkness. Every window in every house was ablaze with light. Now that was something he liked to see. No lazy ones – all up and about. He heaved himself out of bed and got into his thick dressing gown. He opened the doors to the balcony and stood outside for a few moments, breathing deeply.

One, two, three . . . Yes, they were all up and about. Later in the morning he watched as sixteen washing lines swirled around in the breeze, and as he dozed it seemed once more that the little homes marched along in time to a brisk tempo. He could hear an army band playing "Blaze away!" and before he slept imagined that each door saluted him as it passed.

That night, at almost the identical time, the lights went on, and the windows glowed orange and yellow, and downstairs Edith remarked to Lydia how well the old man was looking.

"You don't think he's going to be ill?" Lydia said. "He looked a little flushed, I thought."

"He is almost ninety," Edith said.

Much later, the General waited. His large pocket watch said 11.15 and all the lights but one were out.

He gazed irritably into the darkness at number seven which still burned a light in the kitchen downstairs. Presently to his relief, it was extinguished, and the light came on upstairs. For a time it shone like a beacon, then went out.

The General looked below at the silhouette of the house

in the darkness. Midnight, and all was well. All tucked up for the night, and once again he imagined they began to march.

He drew his curtains and got into bed, pulling the bed-clothes around him. Already he could hear the strains of "Colonel Bogey", and the thump of heavy boots.

He closed his eyes, happy in the knowledge that his own private little army slept.